Abby smiled, where she was going, stepped into the hall. She collided with a granite wall of flesh and stumbled backward.

Something warm, strong, yet gentle secured her arm.

"Oh. I'm sorry, I wasn't watching where I was—" Words deserted her the instant her eyes landed on the sculptured face of the handsome man gazing down at her, still holding her arm.

He looked every bit as startled as she was. "Are you all right, miss?"

"I'm— I'm fine. Thank you." She straightened. Only mere inches from him, her eyes never drifted from his. "I'm sorry for staring, but you have very unusual eyes. They're quite beautiful."

Those same eyes twinkled. "Thank you." The stranger said it as if he meant it, but his closed-lips smile didn't stretch very far. "Could you please tell me where I might find Miss Abigail Bowen?"

"I'm Abby."

Surprise flounced across his face, and his attention drifted over her again, starting with her feet and ending at her hair.

"You're...Miss Bowen?"

Books by Debra Ullrick

Love Inspired Historical

The Unexpected Bride
The Unlikely Wife
Groom Wanted
The Unintended Groom

DEBRA ULLRICK

is an award-winning author who is happily married to her husband of thirty-eight years. For more than twenty-five years, she and her husband and their only daughter lived and worked on cattle ranches in the Colorado mountains. The last ranch Debra lived on was also where a famous movie star and her screenwriter husband chose to purchase property. She now lives in the flatlands, where she's dealing with cultural whiplash. Debra loves animals, classic cars, mud-bog racing and monster trucks. When she's not writing, she's reading, drawing Western art, feeding wild birds, or watching Jane Austen movies, *COPS,* or *Castle.*

Debra loves hearing from her readers. You can contact her through her website, www.debraullrick.com.

The Unintended Groom

DEBRA ULLRICK

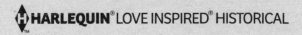

If you purchased this book without a cover you should be aware that this book is stolen property. It was reported as "unsold and destroyed" to the publisher, and neither the author nor the publisher has received any payment for this "stripped book."

Recycling programs for this product may not exist in your area.

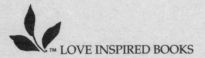

™ LOVE INSPIRED BOOKS

ISBN-13: 978-0-373-82970-5

THE UNINTENDED GROOM

Copyright © 2013 by Debra Ullrick

All rights reserved. Except for use in any review, the reproduction or utilization of this work in whole or in part in any form by any electronic, mechanical or other means, now known or hereafter invented, including xerography, photocopying and recording, or in any information storage or retrieval system, is forbidden without the written permission of the editorial office, Love Inspired Books, 233 Broadway, New York, NY 10279 U.S.A.

This is a work of fiction. Names, characters, places and incidents are either the product of the author's imagination or are used fictitiously, and any resemblance to actual persons, living or dead, business establishments, events or locales is entirely coincidental.

This edition published by arrangement with Love Inspired Books.

® and TM are trademarks of Love Inspired Books, used under license. Trademarks indicated with ® are registered in the United States Patent and Trademark Office, the Canadian Trade Marks Office and in other countries.

www.LoveInspiredBooks.com

Printed in U.S.A.

And we know that all things work together for good
to them that love God, to them who are the called
according to His purpose.

—*Romans* 8:28

To God be the glory. Without His help, and the help of my dear friend and author extraordinaire Staci Stallings—God blessed me abundantly by sending her into my life—my stories would never get written.

And to my husband and best friend, who throughout our thirty-eight years of marriage consistently told me whenever a problem arose that God would take care of it. Sweet hubby, you were right. God always did and still does. So thank you, darlin', for being my example of faith and trust in a loving Savior.

I love you so very much and always will. You're the other half of my heart and soul.

(MEGA HUGS AND KISSES)

Your forever devoted wife,

Deb

Chapter One

Hot Mineral Springs,
Colorado 1888

"What do you mean, I can't?" Abby Bowen fought to keep from slamming her hands on her hips and glaring down at the rotund man seated in front of her.

"I'm sorry, miss," the mayor and head chairman of Hot Mineral Springs, Mr. Prinker, said as his cheeks flushed.

"Why didn't you tell me this before I bought the place?" She clenched her teeth as hot anger boiled inside her. There was no excuse for this. None whatsoever.

"We didn't know what your intentions were for the building. We assumed you wanted to open a dress shop or a restaurant or even a luxurious mineral spa for women. We already have one for men, you know." He grabbed the lapels of his jacket and puffed out his chest like a zealous rooster who was full of himself. "Any one of those would have been allowed. However, we—" he glanced around the large rectangle table at each of the seven town committee members "—cannot allow a single woman to open a theater. Why, something of that nature would be quite scandalous and ruin our town's fine upstanding reputation. Not to say your own, young lady." He shook his forefinger at her.

Abby wanted to latch onto his meaty finger and shove it up his bulbous red nose. But that attitude would get her nowhere, much less please the Lord. She quelled her anger as she searched for another option. Why some townspeople thought women who ran a theater were of questionable repute, she didn't understand. In other towns, people did it all the time, and it was not considered a scandal.

"It's too bad that your name is not *Mr.* Bowen," Mr. Prinker said as if in deep thought. "For if it was, we might consider your proposal. However, as it stands, we will have to refuse the license required by our town to open such an establishment."

Such an establishment? What did that mean? Whatever it meant, she didn't care. She just wanted to make sure she understood him correctly. "Let me see if I get this straight. Are you saying if I was a *man,* I would be able to obtain this license?"

"In a manner of speaking, that's precisely what I'm saying. However—" he rubbed his double chin for the longest moment of her life "—there is one other alternative."

"And what, pray tell, is that?" Abby didn't even try to keep the sarcasm from her voice. She'd about had enough of these men and their preposterous accusations.

"If you were to take on a male business partner, a gentleman with an outstanding reputation, then we would consider allowing you to open your theater. Isn't that right, gentlemen?"

They all nodded their heads.

What?! Surely these buffoons weren't serious. Were

they? Abby gazed at each man to see if they indeed were. Their stoic faces confirmed her assessment. She shook her head at the utterly and completely outlandish idea. "So you're saying, *if* I obtain a *male*—" she emphasized the word male with abhorrence "—business partner, then you will allow me to open my theater? Correct?"

"Yes, ma'am. We feel it's the only proper way. I am certain, ma'am, that you will find there are many upstanding men in our community who would be more than willing to help you with your business adventure. Including any one of us here in this room." The mayor's horse teeth overtook his supercilious grin.

Oh, how she wanted to reach over and whip that arrogant smirk right off his thin lips. Humpft. As if she needed their help running a business. There wasn't one person in this room with whom she'd ever consider doing business with. They all looked shiftier and greedier than a gang of bank robbers.

"Excuse me a moment, gentlemen." She all but choked on that last word. These men were no gentlemen.

"Of course." Mr. Prinker's smile couldn't get any phonier than it was right now.

Abby stepped outside the room and slipped around the corner so she could be alone a few minutes. She paced up and down the sparkling-clean hallway, wringing her gloved hands. With each step she took on the polished hardwood floor, her button-up shoes echoed, her pink silk bustle gown swished and the pink plume on her hat danced.

She couldn't believe this whole ludicrous thing was even happening. After spending the last year and a half going to plays and even participating in a few, she knew what she wanted to do with her life. That desire had only escalated when her ex-fiancé, David Blakely, had broken their engagement—the very day she had told him she could never bear children. After that, every time she'd seen him with his wife, the woman he had married two weeks after he had ended their engagement almost one year ago, and their newborn son, the dagger of rejection plunged deeper into her heart. That's when she had plotted her escape from the Idaho Territory. Eventually, as she worked on her new life, the pain had gone away, and her focus turned completely to fulfilling her dream, a dream that was about to die before it even got started. All because of a room full of portentous, dishonest, stodgy old men.

And if she were honest with herself, her own stupidity, as well.

Why hadn't she listened to her brothers? Haydon, Michael and Jess had warned her about buying a building without seeing it first. But no, she had assured them the ad stated the mansion at the edge of town was previously owned by a prominent family, so therefore, it had to have been well taken care of. They weren't convinced. But she refused to let that stop her. Her stubborn exuberant way took charge as did her dream of life outside the confines of her family. Thus, she let them know she had prayed about the whole thing and was confident in her decision to go ahead with her plans.

The theater was third in her line of dreams, but it was all she had left to dream about. So using the money her father had left her, money he had intended for her and her siblings to use to fulfill their dreams, she'd gone ahead and purchased the place sight unseen. What a mistake that turned out to be.

The very day she arrived in Hot Mineral Springs, Colorado, she quickly discovered her brothers had been right. No maintenance had been done on the home since the owner had moved back east years ago. Because of the mansion's abandoned condition, there was no way for her to sell the place and get her money back so that she could move somewhere else. Someplace where she would be allowed to open up her business.

Abby stopped pacing. For a brief moment she closed her eyes and sighed. No, like it or not, she was stuck with the place.

She flicked her thumbnail with her teeth as she tried to come up with a plan, but nothing came to mind.

Oh, if only she could have opened her dinner theater back home in Paradise Haven, but she couldn't. They already had one, and the town wasn't big enough for two. Not only that, she had to move away.

She just had to.

Being at home constantly reminded her of the two things she wanted most out of life but could never have—children of her own and the love of her life, David. What she needed to do now was to expunge the past and its painful memories. She'd start now by forcing her mind to take a turn in another direction, to figure out a way to make her business adventure work. Operating a theater would not only keep her busy, but it would give her life meaning. Something she desperately needed.

With a new resolve, Abby determined it would be a hot day in a shed full of ice before she would allow anyone to throw away her opportunity for happiness and fulfillment. No one, not even these men, would steal those things from her. There had to be a way to fulfill her dream.

There just had to.

It was in the next moment Abby remembered that it

was God who had led her here. And it would be God who would solve the obstacles before her. She sent up a quick prayer for wisdom, and within seconds a plan formulated in her mind. It was a drastic one, but it just might work. Knowing it would be strictly for business purposes, she would place an advertisement for a business partner. A male one. She rolled her eyes at that one. But she'd do it. That would fix these pompous men's wagons fine enough.

Satisfied and feeling somewhat pleased with her scheme, she headed back into the boardroom. Abby put on her best acting face and eyed each man with a sweet smile. "Gentlemen, I've decided to do what you have asked. I will take on a *gentleman* business partner."

Their faces lit up and greed ravished their eager eyes.

"But—" she held up her hand "—it won't be with anyone here. Good day, sirs." With those words, she whirled on her heels and breezed out of the conference room, leaving each man with his mouth hanging wide open.

Now all she needed to do was make haste and find a gentleman who would be willing to become her partner. Was there such a man? One who would agree to the terms she'd already started formulating in her mind?

Outside, the light breeze brought with it the smell of sulfur from the hot mineral springs. She'd been here two months now and she still hadn't gotten used to the rotten-egg odor. To think that people actually bathed in that smelly water made her shudder. How revolting.

She'd been amazed to learn that Indians believed the waters to be sacred. That they relaxed in the natural hot mineral pools here, believing it healed their minds, bodies and souls.

To think that the mayor actually thought she would

want to open a women's spa utilizing that water. Did women actually bathe in that stinky stuff, too? She wrinkled her nose, then hiked a shoulder. If they indeed did, she might have to consider opening a spa. Something she would have to discuss with her business partner. Or would she? Could she do one on her own and the other with him? Whoever he was.

The very idea of having a partner, someone who would have a say in how things were run, was about as pleasant as the thought of a million spiders crawling all over her. Over the past two years, she planned exactly how she wanted to run her dinner theater. What it would be like. What meals would be served. What plays would be staged. What furniture and place settings she would use. All of it. Down to the very last detail. Would her new business partner, if she found one, try to change those plans? What was she thinking? She shook her head at her own silliness. Of course he wouldn't. She wouldn't let him.

Maybe the man would agree to split the business 60/40. That way she would have controlling interest of how things were run. Mr. Barker, her new stepfather back in Paradise Haven, whose business-savvy mind she'd questioned almost daily over the past year and a half all the way up until the day of her departure, had taught her that. But… She sighed. Where would she find such a man who would be willing to do that? She didn't know, but God did. Her lips curled upward with the knowledge that God was in control and that He would work it all out.

Abby gazed up at the clear, blue sky and sent up her prayer request. When she finished, she thanked God for the answer. After all, that's what living by faith was all about. Trusting Him for the answer before it ever came. Two scriptures popped into her mind. Hebrews 11:1 *Now faith is the substance of things hoped for, the evidence of things not seen.* And Philippians 4:6 *Be careful for nothing; but in every thing by prayer and supplication with thanksgiving let your requests be made known unto God.*

Confident she had done that very thing, her attention slid downward toward the tall mountains surrounding the eighty-five-hundred-feet-above-sea-level town. The high altitude had taken some time getting used to. At first, breathing the thin air had been difficult, and she had gotten a lot of headaches. Drinking more water seemed to help. Eventually, she had gotten used to the thinner air, and the headaches were gone. Because of that, she now loved living in these majestic mountains. Mountains unlike any she'd ever seen back home in Paradise Haven in the Idaho Territory.

Back there, the land was much different from here with its rolling hills, bunch grass, tall wheat and rich volcanic ash soil. Here there were large hay meadows, oodles and oodles of sagebrush and high mountains covered with aspen, blue spruce and ponderosa pine trees. Hidden in those breathtaking mountains were running brooks of crystal clear water, concealed waterfalls, wildflowers, caves, bears, mountain lions, bobcats, foxes, coyotes and lots of lots of deer and elk. Her favorite things in this remote mountain town were the hummingbirds, the tiny striped ground squirrels and the itty-bitty chipmunks. Each brightened her day with their cute antics.

The desire to stay in this beautiful town snuggled cozily into her. Only one way to make that happen, though. She'd better get to it. And now. Anxious to get home so she could word her advertisement carefully, and post it as soon as possible, she picked up her pace, sending up yet another prayer. "God, send me the right man. And make it quick."

Harrison Kingsley sat at his deceased father's massive mahogany desk and re-read Abigail Bowen's advertisement for the fifteenth time.

Wanted: Business Partner.

Prosperous business opportunity for the right gentleman. Guaranteed full return on investment within three months, including interest. If interested, please contact newspaper for more information.

At first he'd thought the ad had been some kind of prank, but his gut told him it wasn't. Years ago, he'd learned to follow his gut instincts and to trust in them, so three weeks ago he had contacted the paper. They informed him all correspondences would be made through them.

Within a week of responding to the advertisement, he'd received his first reply and was shocked to discover the advertisement had been written by a woman, a woman who had asked many questions about his life. Such as, how old he was, what he did for a living, where he was from, why he was interested in becoming a business partner and many more. Harrison answered each one honestly, and even asked some of his own. The hardest one to answer was, "Why are you willing to invest?"

Need. That's why. He glanced at the legal paper lying on his desk mere inches from his fingers. With a heavy sigh, he picked up his father's will and re-read the final stipulation, the very one he had memorized by now.

Notwithstanding anything contained herein, in order

*for my son, Harrison James Kingsley, to receive his full
inheritance as set forth above, he must first prove that
he is capable of operating my businesses. As proof of
such capability, Harrison must start his own business,
which business may be in any manner of industry or
trade but which (a) must be located in a community
other than Boston and specifically in a community in
which he is unknown to the other residents, and (b)
must show a profit of at least 1,000 dollars before his
twenty-fifth birthday. If he fails to satisfy the foregoing
requirements on or before his twenty-fifth birthday, all
my assets will be divided equally between the following charities...*

Anger bubbled up inside Harrison as it did every
time he read that section of his father's will. He tossed
the paper onto the desk, pinched his eyes shut and
pressed the bridge of his nose with his fingertips and
thumb. How could his father do this to him? Give him
so little time to accomplish this? Did his father really
hate him that much? Or was he still punishing him for
the death of his mother? Harrison didn't know. But what
he did know was that his father still controlled him,
even from the grave.

Harrison Kingsley, Sr. had controlled and manipu-
lated him since his birth. Every minute of Harrison's
day had been planned by his father, who ordered the
staff to see to it that his strict regimen was followed
to the letter. Not only had he been told what to wear,
where to go, when to go, who to see, but also whom he
was to marry.

It was there Harrison had drawn the line. On the day
of his twenty-first birthday, he eloped and married the
love of his life, Allison. When his father found out, he

was livid and stripped Harrison of any and all income. To this day, Harrison had no idea how his father had managed it, but no one would even consider hiring him for fear of his father's vengeance.

Harrison had even thought about moving out west in hopes of gaining employment there, but he'd had no money to support them along the way. The final determining factor came when his wife developed complications and was confined to her bed during the remainder of her pregnancy. No other choice remained but to once again succumb to his father's strict rule of thumb.

Soon after his sons were weaned from their mother's milk, Allison disappeared, leaving a note saying she no longer loved him. Harrison's heart had been ripped from him that day and his only consolation was his sons.

Days after his father's death, Harrison received a parcel that contained two letters. One from Allison, and one from a Mrs. Lan informing him that Allison had been killed in a buggy accident, and that the woman had been asked if anything ever happened to Allison, to send the letter to Harrison.

Allison's letter stated how she'd never stopped loving him, and that his father had forced her to leave by threatening to withdraw all financial support from them. When that hadn't worked, he'd threatened to send the boys to boarding school. Allison knew how Harrison despised the idea of sending his sons to boarding school and how powerless he was against his father. She loved him and the twins too much to let that happen, so she'd left. Harrison felt the pain of that decision even now. What kind of father did something like that to his son, anyway?

He'd always known his father resented him and

blamed him for his wife's death. But to go to those extremes? To strip him of the wife he loved and his innocent children of a mother's love? That was low, even for his father.

Determination rose up inside of Harrison like a geyser. His boys had suffered enough at the hands of their grandfather. He'd be hanged if he'd let them lose their inheritance, too. Therefore, he decided he would do whatever it took to make sure that didn't happen. His father thought he'd defeated him even in his death. Well, he'd show him.

His gaze slid to the will sitting in front of him.

His only hope in fulfilling the detestable stipulation his father had thrust on him in such short notice was the one line from Miss Bowen's advertisement, *"Guaranteed full return on investment within three months, including interest."*

He gaped at the envelope staring back at him, wondering if its contents would seal his fate or secure his future. Perhaps it was a good sign that this one had been mailed directly to him instead of going through the newspaper. He read the return address.

Miss Abigail Bowen

777 Grant Street

Hot Mineral Springs, Colorado.

Just where Hot Mineral Springs was in Colorado, he didn't know. Didn't matter. Going out west to see the rugged Rocky Mountains he'd heard so much about from his friends and their travels was something he'd always wanted to do. Now he just might get that chance.

He pressed his hand to his aching, nervous gut, and drew in a deep breath, blowing it out long and slow as he broke the seal off the envelope, and slipped the letter from its pouch.

Dear Mr. Kingsley,

From what you have said in your posts regarding the stipulation in your father's will, it sounds like this business arrangement would be as advantageous for you as it would be for me. Therefore, after much consideration, I have decided to offer you the first chance at this opportunity.

Please let me know what you decide as soon as possible so I can let the other gentlemen who responded to my advertisement know your decision. Thank you.

Sincerely,

Abigail Bowen

Harrison paused and gazed at nothing in particular in the large office decorated only with the finest of furnishings. This whole arrangement was almost too good to be true. Either that or it was just crazy enough to work.

The way he saw it, this was his only chance to get the inheritance he needed to secure his twins' future. And since no other prospect had presented itself, he had no other choice but to give Miss Bowen's dinner theater prospect, something she had mentioned in one of her previous letters, a try. What money he had saved from working for his father wouldn't go far if he didn't find a way to secure at least his position in his father's businesses, if not the outright inheritance.

It would also enable him to fulfill his lifelong goal to right the wrongs his father had done to the fine people in Boston, and to restore the Kingsley name to what it had once been.

The discovery of his father's true legacy still pained him greatly. It was after the death of his mother that his father had changed so drastically. He'd become a bitter, angry, vindictive man with no scruples when it came to business. Every time Harrison thought of the things his father had done, how he had cheated those poor people out of their businesses and their homes, his stomach churned with sorrow and disgust. Like now. The only way to take care of those matters would be to take Miss Bowen up on her offer, and then come back to take over the helm and set things right.

Rather than take the risk of his post to Miss Bowen getting lost in the mail and her taking on another partner, he decided to go a faster route. He would send a telegram and head out west immediately.

He quickly penned a short telegraph message and reached over and pulled the string, ringing for his butler.

Forsyth stepped into his office and stopped in front of the expansive desk, his posture stiff as a wooden plank, his black suit and white shirt pressed to perfection, his white gloves immaculate. "What may I do for you, sir?"

"Have Staimes pack my clothes. Tell him we'll be going out of town for a couple of months or so. Let Miss Elderberry know, too, so she can pack for her and the boys. I'll need you to take care of things here while I'm gone." Harrison handed his trusted butler, who never revealed or spoke of Harrison's affairs with anyone, a folded slip of paper. "Send this telegram out immediately and purchase tickets on the next train heading to Hot Mineral Springs, Colorado."

"Yes, Mr. Kingsley. Will that be all, sir?"

"Yes."

"Very well. I will take care of this immediately."

"I know you will. Thank you, Forsyth."

"You're quite welcome." With that, the aging man

who'd served his father well, and now him, turned and left the room.

The leather chair creaked as Harrison settled his back into its softness. His gaze dropped to the letter, her letter, still lying on his desk. A peace he hadn't felt in a long time settled inside him. He had a gut feeling this arrangement would indeed fulfill the nonsensical stipulations in his father's will along with everything else, too.

He could be back in Boston in three months with a new future for himself and his family, a future filled with hope that he himself had never known.

"Abby, this telegram is for you." Colette Denis walked into the room of Abby's three-story mansion, holding a slip of yellow paper. Abby was so grateful Colette and her two sisters had decided to come with her to Hot Mineral Springs. Since her mother's remarriage, the Denis sisters' maid services were no longer needed back in Paradise Haven. Mother refused to let them go, though, until Abby had come up with a plan to take them with her. She needed their services and the sisters had no family in Paradise Haven so they were more than happy to move with her and to work for her.

Abby dropped the washcloth she was using to wipe down the windowsills and bookshelves in her office into the bucket of soapy water. She dried her hands on the only dry spot left on her apron and took the telegram from Colette. "Thank you, Colette." She slid the paper into the pocket of her skirt. "Did you remember to stop by the mercantile and post my ad for a carpenter on their bulletin board?" Colette had a tendency to get distracted and forget what she was doing. Abby did, too, so she could relate to the girl who had a good heart but a somewhat scattered brain.

"*Oui.* Well, at least I tried to, anyway."

"What do you mean, you tried?" Abby's lips pursed into a frown, and she pushed back the wet strands of hair plastered on her cheeks.

"When I went to tack it onto the corkboard, I could not reach the only empty place. This nice man offered to help, so I gave it to him. But when he looked at the ad, he asked if he could keep it." Colette wrung her hands and her green eyes shaped like an almond shell drifted over to Abby, then cut to the floor.

"Is something wrong, Colette?"

Colette glanced at Abby, then back at the ground again. "I—I am so sorry, *mademoiselle,* but he is here."

"Who's here? The man who kept my post?"

"No, *mademoiselle.* Mr. Kingsley."

"Mr. Kingsley?" Abby frowned, then her eyes bounced open at the recognition of the name. "Mr. Kingsley is here? Now?"

"*Oui.* I am sorry." Remorse crackled through Colette's voice. "That telegram came several days back, but I forget to give it to you. When I went to wash my dress just now, I found it." Colette rattled on, intermingling French with English.

Abby heard nothing more as she looked down at her soaked apron and the simple blue dress she wore to do chores in. She caught Colette's gaze glossed over with unshed tears. Her heart went out to the poor girl who tried so hard, but always seemed to fall short. She looped arms with Colette and headed toward the door. "Don't you go crying now, you hear? I know you didn't mean to forget. Nothing in this life is worth fretting over. Everything will work out the way it's supposed to. God has a plan. Even in this." Abby encouraged her, sincerely hoping she could take some of her own advice. What was she going to do? He was here!

Well, she couldn't let that bother her. He was here, so she might as well go ahead and make the best of it. She just hoped and prayed he wasn't one of those snobbish businessmen like the city council members were, one who would surely look down his nose at her attire and might even judge her for it. Nothing in his letters indicated he was. But even if he was, she decided as they headed to the door, that was his problem, not hers.

Realizing she still had a hold of Colette's arm, Abby let it go, but her attention stayed riveted on the sixteen-year-old girl, looking for any sign that she felt better. The frown on the young girl's heart-shaped face disappeared, and Abby was glad to see it. "Are you all right now?"

A moment and Colette nodded.

"Good." Abby smiled, and without looking where she was going, she stepped into the hallway and turned right. Her body collided into a granite wall of flesh and stumbled backward.

Something warm, strong, yet gentle secured her arm.

"Oh. I'm sorry, I wasn't watching where I was—" Words escaped her the instant her eyes landed on the sculptured face of the handsome man gazing down at her, still holding her arm.

He looked every bit as startled as she was. "Are you all right, miss?"

"I'm—I'm fine. Thank you." She straightened. Only mere inches from him, her eyes never drifted from his. Something was different about his eyes. Abby looked at one, then the other. One was minutely wider, and the other looked like it hadn't quite awakened yet because the outer half of his eyelid rested against his eyelashes a little heavier than the other one did.

That wasn't what was different about them, though.

Abby placed her fingertip on her lip. It was something else. Then she spotted it. Her mouth formed into an O. Both eyes were grayish-blue except the right one. A third of the lower iris was hazel. The amber color started small at his pupil, but spread out, ending with the same grayish-blue as the rest of his eye. She had never seen anything like that before. "I'm sorry for staring, but you have very unusual eyes. They're quite beautiful."

Those same eyes, surrounded by long but straight medium brown eyelashes, twinkled. "Thank you." He said it like he meant it, but his closed-lipped smile didn't stretch very far. Far enough, though, to reveal a crescent-moon line on one side of his half-full lips and a quarter-crescent moon on the other. "Could you please tell me where I might find Miss Abigail Bowen?"

"Abigail? Oh. Oh. Yes. I'm Abby." She waved her hand at her momentary lapse into forgetfulness because no one ever called her Abigail. Except her mother, and that was only when Abby was in trouble.

Surprise flounced across his face, and his attention drifted over her again, starting with her feet and ending at her hair. "You're Miss Bowen?" One of his eyebrows peaked.

Hey. She knew she looked a mess, but the man didn't need to be so blatantly rude with his disapproving perusal of her. Abby pushed her shoulders back and stood as tall as her five-foot-six-inch frame would allow. "Yes, sir, I am."

Once again, his gaze roamed over her.

This time, she wouldn't let it steal her joy or her peace.

If he didn't approve of what he saw, again, that was his problem, not hers. But in all fairness, the man did have a good reason to be shocked. He probably wasn't expecting to see her looking like a scullery maid, especially since from his perspective, she should have been waiting to meet him for the first time. "Please forgive my appearance. Because of an oversight, I didn't get word of your arrival until a moment ago, so you caught me in the middle of cleaning."

"So I see." A chuckle vibrated through his low, brassy voice. "Well, Miss Bowen. I'm Harrison Kingsley." He reached for her hand.

Abby quickly tucked both her hands behind her back. "Trust me, Mr. Kingsley. You do *not* want to touch these hands. They've been in soapy water all morning and probably feel pricklier than pig bristles." And the rest of her, she was certain looked even worse. Oh, well, couldn't be helped. She had a lot to do. If his time was as valuable to him as hers was to her, rather than keep him waiting while she cleaned up, she decided to go ahead and get right down to business. "Colette, would you make some tea and bring it to the parlor?"

"Oui, mademoiselle." Colette curtsied.

"Thank you." Abby spoke to Colette's retreating back before she turned and faced Mr. Kingsley. What a fine specimen of a man he was. Like one of the heroes in the dime novels she often read. Only she hoped he wasn't as stuffy as some of the heroes in those books seemed to be.

She couldn't help but wonder, if instead of the dark blue three-piece suit Mr. Kingsley had on, what would he look like in a blue plaid shirt, denim blue jeans, Hyer boots and a black Stetson? No. Nix the cowboy hat. It would cover up that lovely head of medium brown hair. Abby liked the way he parted it—not on the side, not in the center, but in between the two, and straight in line with the inside of his right eyebrow.

She pried her attention from his broad-shouldered frame. "Shall we?" Abby swayed her upward palm toward the direction of the parlor. At his nod, she headed that way, tucking the loose strands of hair back into place as she went.

Having someone as handsome and fine-looking as Mr. Kingsley for a business partner was going to be a lot harder than she had anticipated. She'd always been a sucker for a handsome face. Probably due to all those romance novels she'd read. A handsome face didn't guarantee happiness, though, as she had discovered with David. The most important elements in any human being were their hearts and their souls.

While that was definitely true, a quick glance at the gorgeous man standing in front of her, and she knew because of the romantic nature in her, she would have to work very hard at keeping her focus on business, or she might very well risk opening up her heart. Having done that once before, she refused to do it again. Therefore, her hopeless romantic notions would have to stay locked deep inside her heart, tucked away safely, even from herself. No. Make that *especially* from herself.

Chapter Two

Harrison's footsteps thumped on the old hardwood floor that was in need of a good polishing, ricocheting off the walls of the large mansion as he followed Miss Bowen to the parlor. The place was almost barren. There wasn't much furniture and the walls were empty.

As they made their way toward the parlor, he marveled that the woman hadn't even offered to go and clean up first. The little beauty was an unpretentious woman, and he liked that. Back in Boston he was surrounded by ostentatious women. The type of women he would rather avoid.

His possible new business partner wasn't anything like them, or what he had expected. He'd expected a woman of sophistication. Pious and haughty like his ex-fiancée, Prudence Whitsburg. Not a veritable maid who smelled of cleaning soap and dust.

Yellow strands of hair had come loose from her bun. Some of them clung to her damp, yet slender neck. Black smudges brushed across her lightly freckled nose and above her delicately arched eyebrows. Yet none of that deterred her beauty from shining through. Her sapphire eyes smiled even when her lips didn't, and long medium brown eyelashes surrounded them. Her bottom lip was slightly fuller than the upper one, and when she smiled, straight white teeth sparkled back at him.

They reached the parlor door and stepped inside. Harrison held back his shock. The only pieces of furniture in the expansive room were a worn-out, faded, blue settee, a matching wing-back chair in the same shape as the settee, a scratched and marred coffee table and a small, round table with a blue globe oil lamp sitting on a white-and-blue doily.

His attention went to the massive fireplace. Several framed photographs lined the mantel, along with two oil lamps, one on each end. Other than that, the room was almost empty. Nothing hung on these walls, either. He didn't know if this was where she planned on opening her business or not. They hadn't gotten that far. But if it was, it was going to take a lot of money to fix this place up. More than he had right now. And that made him more nervous than he wanted to admit, even to himself.

"Mr. Kingsley, won't you be seated?" Miss Bowen's voice reverberated throughout the empty room and thankfully yanked his attention away from where his taxing thoughts were heading.

She motioned for him to sit. When he reached the chair, he noticed how clean it was. How clean the whole room was. Even the bare windows sparkled. He sat down and was amazed at how comfortable the aged chair actually was.

Miss Bowen sat across from him on the settee, facing him.

The young girl who she'd told to get tea entered the room. She set a tray with a teapot, two cups and saucers, and a plate of cookies with some sort of filling in the centers on the coffee table in front of them. She went right to work pouring the tea into the cups and serving it along with two cookies on the side.

"Thank you, Colette."

The girl turned.

"Don't leave just yet, Colette."

Colette faced them, nodded and waited.

Abby looked over at him and asked, "Mr. Kingsley, would you like to join us for dinner this evening?"

He saw no reason not to. "I would like that. Thank you."

She smiled and turned her attention back to her maid. "Would you tell Veronique we'll be having a guest join us for dinner this evening?"

"Oui, mademoiselle." With a quick curtsy, Colette left the room.

Miss Bowen faced him and sighed. "I still can't get used to her calling me *mademoiselle.* I finally gave up trying to get her not to. It sounds so formal. But it's much better than what she used to call me."

"Oh? What was that?"

"Miss Abigail. That just sounds so stuffy to me." She wrinkled her cute nose and shook her head. "And so gratingly formal and impersonal. Especially when she and her sisters are more like family to me than hired help."

Harrison understood exactly what she meant. They had that in common. He oftentimes asked Forsyth the same thing. After all, the man was more like a father to him than a butler. But Forsyth refused, and so Harrison had finally given up, as well. "You said that she and her sisters were like family to you. Do you have any family, Miss Bowen?"

After taking a sip of her tea, she placed the cup onto the saucer and rested it on her lap. "Yes. My father died a long time ago, but my mother recently remarried. I have three older brothers and an older sister, who are all married. Several nieces and nephews, too." She looked away. The moment was brief, but long enough for him to understand that something she'd said had bothered her. He'd seen it in her eyes. What it was, he didn't know. Nonetheless, whatever had caused that momentary look of sadness was none of his concern. He was here on business. Not to get involved in her personal life.

"What about you?" Abby asked him.

"There's just me and my two sons."

"Sons? Oh." She took a sip of tea, seeming to take in the news with excitement, worry or concern. He wasn't sure which. "How old are they?"

"Josiah and Graham will be four August twenty-ninth."

"Twins?"

"Yes."

"My brother Michael has twins, too. A boy and a girl." Affection softened the blue in her eyes before they glazed over with a faraway look mingled with pain, and the room grew quiet.

He wondered if she was thinking about her family and missing them. And if that would be a problem. Would she walk away from the business to go back to her home? Wherever home was for her. "Where are you from, Miss Bowen?" So much for not getting involved in her personal life.

She blinked, then looked at him as if she remembered he was in the room. "What? Oh. Sorry. Yes, you asked me where I'm from. Paradise Haven. In the Idaho Territory. And you?" She shook her head and waved her hand. "Never mind. I already know that. You're from Boston, Massachusetts. I don't know where my mind is." She steadied her teacup and wiggled in her seat, then sat up straighter.

Was she always this scatterbrained, or was it home she was missing? He doubted it was the latter because she hadn't looked exactly prepared for his arrival, either. Worry etched inside him, wondering what he had gotten himself into. Well, they hadn't agreed on anything or signed any papers yet. So he could still get out of this deal if he so chose, but his gut twisted, wondering what he'd do next if this plan failed.

"Mr. Kingsley." She paused and looked him in the eye. "Would you mind if I called you by your first name? All this formality isn't for me."

"Oh, by all means, please, call me Harrison. And may I call you Abigail?"

"No." She shook her head and frowned.

Taken back by her blunt answer, he moved backward.

"Please call me Abby. Like I said, Abigail sounds so stuffy." She wrinkled that petite nose of hers again, and he was certain those close-knit freckles had kissed each other when she did. "One thing you will discover about me, Harrison, is I am not a woman who believes in pomposity and strict formality when there is a real person on the inside just waiting to be met. When one is so reserved and refined, you never get to know the heart of that person, and what makes them who they really are. That's a real travesty as far as I'm concerned."

Harrison wanted to remind her that she had come across like that when she signed Abigail in her letters to him, but he didn't.

"After I sent my letter to you and had signed it Abigail, I wanted to snatch it back. I still have no idea why I did it. Anyway—" she waved her hand and shook her head again "—shall we get down to business? After all, that's why you're here." She smiled.

Harrison returned her smile with one of his own. He had a hard time keeping up with her bouncing from one subject to the next, but he found this down-to-earth woman to be quite an enigma. He was going to enjoy being her business partner. And that made him more nervous than a hunted fox. Better to plunge forward with business than to let his thoughts go down a road he didn't want to travel. "Do you have plans on how you want to run this business?"

"Of course I do." She drained her tea.

By the look on her face, he could tell that he'd offended her. "I was certain you did, but I thought I would ask." He sent her a smile, and that of-course-I-do look disappeared. "What building were you planning on using?"

"This one."

Just as he feared. His gaze slipped around the room and ended at her.

"I haven't purchased furnishings yet. After I hire a crew of carpenters to restore the place, then I will. Just so you know, because this will also be my home, I will be funding the total cost of remodeling the building. The kitchen is quite large so I won't need to do anything to it, but the rest of the place, well…" She sighed and raised a dainty shoulder. "As you can see, it needs a good cleaning, which we've already started, along with numerous repairs. I am certain that once all of that is completed, this place will make a fine dinner theater." The conviction of that shone in her blue eyes.

"I'm sure it will. Do you have a layout planned for the theater already?"

"Yes. I do. It's in my office. I'll run and get it. Be

right back." She pushed herself off the settee and fled the room.

Harrison blew out a long breath, grateful one of his fears had been put to rest and that he didn't have to come up with a large sum of money to fix up the place or for the theater. He only hoped the money he did have to fork over would be a small amount.

Abby's footsteps echoed outside the doorway, announcing her arrival. Harrison tugged on his sleeve cuffs and straightened the lapels on his jacket. He rose when she stepped inside the parlor, hands loaded with several rolled-up papers. Before he could even take one step toward relieving Abby of her burden, the woman had scurried over to him, sat down on the settee and unrolled them, pulling out and flattening the first one.

Harrison shook his head, marveling at the little bundle of energy. He lowered himself next to her, careful not to sit too close, but close enough to see the drawings.

"This is where the theater will be. The stage will go here…." She leaned over and pointed to the areas she referred to. "The chairs here. Sixty to start with, at least. Then as the business grows, more can be added. There will be chairs up in here in the balcony, as well. Maybe even a few dining tables and chairs, too. I haven't decided on that particular yet. Anyway—" she waved her hand as if remembering what she was doing "—here in the room next to the theater is where the dining tables and chairs will be. Guests will dine there before they head into the theater to watch the plays." She continued to explain the intricate floor plans to him.

Harrison was impressed. A lot of thought had gone into designing this place.

When she finished, she sat up straight and turned those smiling eyes up at him. Those eyes sparkled with the dream. This thing obviously meant a lot to her. One thing Harrison had discovered—if someone was willing to put the hard work it took to make a business come to fruition and put their whole heart and soul into it like she was, its chances of being a success were quite good. Somehow, after seeing her plans and witnessing how she lit up with the dream, that dream now mattered to him, too. And not just because of his inheritance and plans, either.

Abby rerolled the papers. Before things went any further, she needed to tell him something that had been pricking at her conscience from the very beginning of this whole thing. She sat up straight and turned her attention onto him. "Before we go any further, Harrison, I feel I must be honest with you about something. The only reason I'm taking on a partner is because the town committee will not grant me the license I need to open my dinner theater. The only way they will even consider it is if I take on a gentleman partner." She huffed.

"Can you believe it? I mean really. What difference does that make? I still can't believe they even suggested such a thing. As if I'm not capable of running my own business. I'm just as smart as any man. My stepfather, who is a brilliant business man, taught me…" She prattled on and on until she remembered she was talking to a potential business partner. "Sorry. As you can tell, I'm quite frustrated over this whole situation."

"I can see that," Harrison said with an amused chuckle. "Now, it is my turn to tell you something, Miss Bowen."

Her stomach tensed, wondering what he was about to say. Was he going to back out of this deal before it ever got started? "What's that?" She held her breath waiting for his answer.

"Once we get this business up and running and I get my investment back, plus interest as you stated in your ad—" his eyes twinkled along with his half grin "—then I plan on heading back to Boston to claim my inheritance and to run my father's businesses."

Abby's stomach relaxed. "Just as I had hoped."

He frowned.

"Oh." She waved her hand. "No offense to you personally. It's just that I was hoping things would turn out this way, and they have. Like I said, the only reason I took on a partner was because of the license. I really didn't want nor need one. So as soon as we, if you're interested, get this theater up and running, I will no longer need a partner. After all, the town didn't say how long I had to have one, now, did they?" She smiled.

"That plan may backfire on you, Abby."

"What do you mean?" She frowned.

"They could revoke your license."

"They can?" She hadn't thought of that. "Surely they wouldn't. Would they?"

"Yes, then can, and from what you've told me about them, I suspect they would, too. So here's what I propose."

Propose? She gulped.

"Even though I will be leaving, I am willing to remain your partner. A silent one, in name only, if you will. And I will only take a dollar a month from you."

"That's hardly a partnership."

"This would not be an equal-share partnership. The way I see it, you are helping me a vast amount more than I am you. I want to reciprocate by helping you, too, by remaining your partner in order for you to keep your license. You will be able to run the business the way you want without any interference from me. That way we both come out of this arrangement with exactly what we want—nothing more, nothing less."

"Do you think the town will object to you not being here?"

"I don't see how they can. You will still have a partner. I would even be willing to come back for let's say—" he rubbed his chin "—once a month for six months."

"You would do that?"

"Yes. I would. I am convinced that when they see the revenue your business will bring this town, and see what an amazing cultural place it will be, they will no longer care about such matters in time, anyway."

"You really think so?"

"I do. Or I wouldn't have said so."

Abby's insides danced with the fact that everything was going to work out the way she'd always hoped it would.

Harrison couldn't believe his good fortune. This was working out better than he had imagined. Only one question he needed to ask before he made this deal. "Do you have a dollar figure in mind of what you will need from me?"

"Yes. Five hundred dollars."

That was it? He thought he would have to put up thousands and live on an even stricter budget than he was right now over the next three months. Relief poured over him, but he didn't allow his face to show it. She didn't need to know about his dire financial situation, and five hundred was definitely doable.

Right then, he determined that even though he would get his money back and then some, he would help her as much as he could to make her business a success. Not that she needed his help or anything, but he wanted to make sure her endeavor came to fruition.

"So what do you think?" Abby asked. "Are you in?"

Harrison turned his attention onto her and smiled at the expectant look in her eyes. "Only one question first. I hate to ask, but I need to know how you can guarantee a profit so quickly."

"Oh, that." She waved her hand as if she were brushing away his comment. "The reason I can is because even if the business doesn't make a profit right away, the investor will. I am going to give them fifteen hundred dollars once we get the place up and running."

Harrison swallowed his shock. Not only would he get the amount his father's will stipulated, but his initial investment, as well. This was almost too good to be true. Maybe it was. Suspicion crawled over him. "Why would you do that?"

"Because. The investor or business partner, whichever you prefer, will be helping me to make my dream come true, so I want to make it worth their time. Your time. That is, if you're interested."

This woman wanted her dream. And she wanted it badly. He had a feeling she would do whatever it took to fulfill that dream, too, including giving the large sum she had guaranteed just for the trouble of helping her out. Before he'd left Boston, he'd had a background check done on her and knew she was good for the money. The woman came from wealth and her own bank account was hefty. The way he saw it, he had nothing to lose, and everything to gain. Not only would he get what he wanted, he would be helping her to get what she wanted. A mutual benefit arrangement. Those were the best kind of business deals. "I'm interested. Count me in."

She clutched her hands together with a smack and tucked them to her chest. Her smile lit up her whole face. "Excellent. Thank you!" She tossed her arms around him, gave him a firm hug and released him just as quickly. Her exuberance was contagious. He found himself wanting to hug her in return, but he didn't dare. "You won't regret this, Harrison, I promise."

He had a feeling that promise would hold true. Normally he would have had a contract drawn up, but that would only delay things. Knowing how much this meant to her, his gut told him she would hold to her end of the bargain, so he wouldn't bother with a contract this time.

They continued to talk about what needed to be done, the expenses, her plans, his thoughts and the whole general situation. An hour later, he looked at his watch. Three o'clock in the afternoon. "Well, I should go now." Harrison stood. "What time would you like me to come this evening?"

"Five-thirty. Dinner will be served at six."

"Very well." They walked side by side to the front door. There, he grabbed his fedora off the hat rack and held it in his hands, then shifted his focus onto her smiling face. "I will see you at five-thirty, then."

"Looking forward to it." They stood there for a moment looking at each other.

"Until this evening." With those words, he opened the door and stepped outside. Outside where the detestable smell of sulfur lingered in the air. But that vile stench didn't detract from his fine mood. For the first time in years, hope glimmered inside him. At the bottom of the steps, he stopped and looked up at the bright June sun. Forsyth would say God had arranged this whole thing because He loved Harrison so much. But Harrison didn't believe in a loving God. How could he? His life had clearly proven otherwise.

Chapter Three

Standing in front of the free-standing mirror, Abby perused her appearance. The sides of her hair were pulled back and held with pearl combs and a dark blue ribbon. Tiny curls framed her face, and the rest of her hair hung loosely down her back. Her white, tufted-cotton bustle gown with the dark blue lace and ribbons and midlength sleeves would be cool, but not too cool for a warm evening in the Colorado Rocky Mountains. But just in case it wasn't, she snatched up her knit shawl, then skipped downstairs to see if Veronique had everything ready.

The words to "Amazing Grace" sung by either Colette or Zoé, whose singing voices were very similar, floated through the massive room as she made her way into the formal dining room. "Hi, Zoé."

Zoé, the middle sister to Veronique and Colette, turned from placing a silver chafing dish on the mahogany serving table and smiled. "Good evening, Abby," she said in the same strong accent all of the sisters spoke with. Her soft gray eyes were the first thing a person noticed about Zoé. While the color was soft, because of the way her eyes were shaped, they appeared hard as if she were angry all the time, which she wasn't.

Abby looked at the long table set for two. Her mother's silver candelabra stood tall in the middle. Silver pedestal dishes set on each side piled high with fresh fruit and French pastries. Wedgewood bone china and crystal glasses sparkled like bright sunshine raining down on a clear mountain brook here in Colorado. Silverware…polished to perfection. "This looks great, Zoé."

The eighteen-year-old girl's face lit up. "You think so?"

"Yes. I sure do."

"Zoé," Veronique hollered from the other side of the swinging door.

Wisps of chestnut-blond hair swayed when Zoé yanked her attention in that direction. "I will be right there." She curtsied and scurried into the kitchen.

Abby followed. Fresh bread, beef and pine aromas from the wood stove met her nostrils.

Veronique stood in front of the massive cook stove, wearing the same blue-and-white uniform as Zoé, stirring something in one of the copper pans sitting on the stove with a wire whisk. Without looking, Veronique told Zoé to grab the pastry-wrapped cinnamon apples out of the oven.

Colette sat at the table, slicing and peeling carrots. She, too, wore a matching uniform.

Abby wasn't too keen putting on fancy dinners, but she had better get used to them for when she opened her dinner theater. "Something sure smells good, Veronique." Abby raised the lid on one of the pans, leaned over and breathed deeply. "Umm. What is that?" She pointed to the dish.

"It is *filet de boeuf charlemagne,*" Veronique explained without taking her eyes off the pan she was stirring.

"Trans-la-tion...?" Abby drew out the word and let her sentence hang, waiting for Veronique to interpret what she'd said into English.

"Beef tenderloin Charlemagne."

"Huh?" Abby frowned.

"Simply put, it is beef fillet steaks with mushrooms. What I am making now is a *béarnaise* sauce. I hope you like it."

"I'm sure I will. I haven't eaten anything of yours yet that wasn't absolutely delicious."

Veronique flashed a quick smile Abby's way before putting her attention back onto the saucepan.

Abby glanced up at the kitchen clock. Five-twenty. "Well, I'll get out of your way. Mr. Kingsley will be arriving in a few minutes."

Veronique nodded as she placed the copper lid on the pan she'd been stirring. She removed it from the heat, tossed a pot holder onto the breadboard counter then set the pan down.

Abby had just turned to leave when she noticed a tray of strawberry and apple tarts. With a quick glance back at Veronique, like a little kid sneaking an early dessert, she snatched a strawberry tart off the plate and tossed it into her mouth.

Through the dining room and into the main room of the mansion she went, munching happily on the delicious treat.

A knock came at the door. Abby chewed fast and swallowed. Colette, Zoé and Veronique were busy, so she hollered, "I'll get it." Her heels tapped along the floor as she made her way to the front door. She swung it open and blinked. There stood Harrison holding a small boy in each arm.

"I'm sorry, Abby, that this notice is so late, but a few minutes ago, the boys' nanny and my valet came down sick. Must've been something they ate this afternoon because my sons aren't sick. The food they ate wasn't the same as what Miss Elderberry and Staimes ate. I don't know anyone in town, and I won't leave my boys with a perfect stranger. So, I'm here to let you know that I won't be able to make it to dinner this evening. I'm sorry." Remorse wrinkled his handsome face.

Abby glanced at the two boys. A fresh ache filled her heart, but she refused to let it get her down or to dwell on what could never be. Instead, she sent the boys and their father her most inviting smile and quickly swung the French doors open. "Don't be silly. There's no need for you not to stay. Besides, there's more than enough food. I'll just have Zoé set two more places and find something for the boys to sit on. It'll be just fine." Now she just had to convince herself of that by reminding herself that God had a plan, as vexing as that could be sometimes. She leaned toward the boys, eyeing each one with a smile. "And who might you boys be?"

Neither of them said a word; they just tucked their tiny shoulders closer into their father's chest and eyed her warily.

"This one here—" Harrison nodded toward the child on his right "—is Graham. And this one—" he nodded at the child on his left "—is Josiah."

"Hello, Josiah and Graham. Welcome to my home. Won't you come in?" she said to the twins who resembled their father in much, much younger versions. They even had Harrison's light brown hair and grayish-blue eyes. Except neither of their eyes had a portion of hazel coloring like their father's did.

"Can you say hello to the nice lady?" Instead of saying hello, they buried their faces into their father's shoulder.

"It's okay," she mouthed, and waved him in with her hand. She moved out of the way, and Harrison stepped inside. "Are you sure about this, Miss Bowen? We really hate to impose."

She wasn't sure of anything, but she'd make herself be. "It's Abby, and of course I'm sure or I wouldn't have said so. Listen, why don't you take the boys into the parlor, and I'll inform Veronique there will be extra guests this evening? I'll be right back." Abby whirled around and headed toward the kitchen. Those adorable boys in their skirts and knee socks resurrected the pain shoved deep down in Abby's heart and soul. The one she rarely allowed to surface into her actual consciousness lest it rob her of her happiness completely. "Lord, help me get through this evening."

Harrison lowered himself onto the settee in the parlor, and settled a son on each leg. When Staimes and Miss Elderberry came up sick at the last minute, Harrison's own stomach had taken ill. Not from food sickness, but with worry. He feared upsetting Miss Bowen by ruining her dinner plans, but he didn't. Women of his society back home in Boston wouldn't have been so gracious. They would have shunned him for days, and some indefinitely over something like this.

He would have hated it if Abby would have shut the door in his face. And even though it couldn't be helped, he wouldn't have blamed her. After all, a lot of hard work and hours of preparation went into making a meal, not to mention the food that would have gone to waste if he hadn't been able to come.

Relief skimmed over him the instant Abby had smiled and opened her doors to him and the twins, and his stomach stopped hurting. He no longer had to worry about how she would be with the children.

Harrison's lips curled, knowing he wouldn't have to miss dinner with the twins. He and his sons almost always ate breakfast and dinner together, unlike most of his friends who sent their children away to boarding school or left them with a nanny twenty-four hours a day. That wasn't for him or his boys. No, he never wanted his children to feel like he had growing up— unwanted and unloved.

Just then, Abby breezed into the room, holding a medium-size box with toys sticking out of the top. "I found these in the attic. I was going to send them to my nephews, but I'm sure Josiah and Graham would enjoy playing with them." She set the box on the coffee table in front of his sons.

Their eyes widened, but at first they did not move. Finally, he slid them both to the floor and nudged them in that direction. They slipped from his protection, and with their heads together, they gazed into the box.

"Go ahead. You can play with them." They looked up at her, then at him as if seeking his approval. He nodded.

Each one quickly snatched a toy, and together, they headed over and sat down on the floor near the fireplace. They had each selected a section of train, and when Harrison brought the box over to them, they began removing the rest of the toys from the container.

Knowing they were occupied and having fun, Harrison came back and placed his attention on Abby. "Thank you for that. And thank you for understanding about the ruined dinner plans. I really hated to do that to you."

Abby waved him away. "It's nothing. Really. And you didn't ruin a thing."

"By the way, I meant to tell you, you look very nice this evening."

"You mean compared to earlier?" An amused smirk curled her lips.

"Oh. I see how that sounded. My apologies. I didn't mean it that way. I just meant you look very nice." She did, too. Dressed in a striking white dress that showed off her trim figure, and with her shining hair hanging freely down her back, she looked stunning. Even her hands looked nice. Her long graceful fingers weren't red like they had been earlier.

"I had it first, Siah!"

Harrison's attention darted toward his boys.

"No. I did!" Josiah yanked it from his brother's hands.

"Boys. That's enough." He stood and headed toward them, but he was too late.

Josiah snatched the toy in question, raised it and whacked Graham, hitting him squarely in the head. The wail that ensued could surely be heard in Boston.

Harrison picked up his screeching son and held him close, patting his back and speaking soothing words to him.

Abby was at his side in an instant, worry etched on her face. She dropped to her knees and started talking to Josiah. Harrison couldn't hear what she was saying because Graham's cries still filled his ears.

Minutes passed before Graham's tears finally let up. Harrison leaned him back to check the top of his head. A small amount of blood streamed through his hair.

"Abby, do you have a washcloth I can use?" Oh, how he hated having to ask, hated having to bother her with this. She was going to think he was far more trouble than he was worth.

She stood, holding a tear-soaked Josiah in her arms. "I sure do. I'll be right back. If it's okay with your father, would you like to go with me, Josiah?"

He wiped his eyes and slowly nodded, then looked over at Harrison. Remorse and trepidation filled his son's eyes. "You may go with her. But before you do, you need to say you're sorry to your brother. It is never okay to hit someone else. Do you understand that?"

Josiah nodded. "Saw-ree, Gam."

Graham wouldn't look at him. Instead, he buried his face into Harrison's collar.

"Graham, what do you say to your brother?" Harrison asked.

The boy did nothing.

"No. Come on. It's time to make up. Give your brother a hug." He put him on the floor.

Abby lowered Josiah, as well.

Graham shook his head.

"Very well, then, Graham. You will not be allowed to play with Miss Abby's toys any longer."

Graham turned wide eyes up at him, then rushed to his brother and hugged him long and hard. Pretty soon they were giggling. His sons sat down on the floor again next to the toys.

"That didn't take long." He turned to Abby, who was smiling up at him.

"You sure handled that nicely."

Her words made him feel proud. His biggest fear was failing as a father. "Thank you."

They smiled at each other.

"I'll run and get that washcloth now."

"Thank you."

Harrison watched his sons as Abby exited. He sighed. Great first impression they were making.

Abby entered the room a few minutes later holding a bowl and a clean cloth. While Harrison and Abby cleaned his small wound, Graham squirmed and fretted, acting as though they were torturing him or something. When it was all over, he settled back onto the floor and started playing as if nothing had happened.

"*Mademoiselle,* dinner is ready."

The woman standing only a few yards from him was tall with chestnut-blond hair and grayish-green eyes, who spoke with a French accent very much like Colette had earlier.

"Harrison, this is Zoé, Colette's sister. Oh. I forgot to introduce you to Colette earlier. I was, um, a bit disheveled." Abby's soothing laughter reminded him of the musical sound of a sparrow songbird back home in Boston. "Anyway, Zoé, this is Mr. Harrison Kingsley."

"It is a pleasure to meet you, sir." She curtsied.

"Nice to meet you, too," he said. Even though he wasn't used to people in his society introducing him to their help, he liked it. He liked the informality a lot. Back home it sure wouldn't be acceptable. But, then again, he wasn't back home. He was here. A quick glance at Abby, and he was glad he was, too.

"Shall we head into the dining room?" Abby asked.

His heart plummeted to his perfectly shined shoes. Abby had no idea what she was getting herself into when she'd invited his boys to dinner. He should have warned her before accepting her generous offer.

Abby's arm rested on top of Harrison's. "It'll be okay.

I have several nephews and nieces. I know how they can be."

Harrison let out a long breath of relief. It was nice not having to worry about someone wanting to whisk his rambunctious sons off to another room. Or even worse, a boardinghouse, like Prudence had wanted to send them to once they were married. Over his dead body would he have ever allowed her or anyone else to send his boys away.

Good thing this whole arrangement with Abby was strictly business because with her kind heart and gentle way with his boys, he could easily fall for her. And he was never going to let that happen again. He'd been duped once before by a pretty face and a sweet disposition toward his children. Prudence had always acted like she loved children. Loved his sons. Even though he hadn't loved Prudence, something she was very much aware of, it was because of her love for his sons that he had asked her to marry him. He hoped love would eventually follow. However, he soon discovered that her fondness toward them had been nothing but a ruse to marry a man who could keep her in the style she was accustomed to.

He'd never forget the day when Prudence had roughly handled his boys and said intolerable and cruel things to them. Of course, she didn't know Harrison had been nearby. Thankfully, he had been. He had immediately put an end to her abuse as well as their relationship, and sent her away for good that very day.

Thus, Harrison needed to remind himself often that Abby was a business partner and nothing else. One look at her smiling blue eyes and sweet face, though, and he knew keeping it strictly business was going to be a challenge.

* * *

The early morning sunrise peeked through the curtain in Abby's sparsely furnished bedroom. Snuggled under the red-and-white quilt Mother had sent along with her, Abby rubbed the sleep from her eyes.

Her thoughts drifted to the calamitous dinner from the night before.

Poor Harrison had been so mortified.

Not her; she laughed the whole time—inwardly of course.

The near-four-year-olds' antics had more than tickled her, even when they'd tossed glazed carrots at one another and a piece had landed in her hair. And even when they'd dumped mashed potatoes and gravy onto the floor, or when they'd spilled their milk all over the white linen tablecloth.

The whole thing had been hilarious to her, but not to Harrison, who had profusely apologized, repeatedly. She had assured him none of it had bothered her, that nothing in this world was worth getting fidgety over, and that they were just things that could be washed.

Other than those few incidences, everything had gone quite well. Dinner conversation flowed freely until the boys had fallen asleep with the sides of their faces resting in their dessert.

She and Harrison cleaned them up before he left with the promise of arriving early the next morning.

Speaking of arriving early, Abby tossed her quilt off and went to the window and pulled the curtain back. Dark clouds drifted toward the direction of town bringing with them a Rocky Mountain rainstorm. Didn't matter. She wouldn't let anything stop her from today's mission.

While she donned her peach satin bustle gown and

plumed hat, she couldn't help but think about Harrison's boys again. The longing to have her own children chopped away at her heart. Why did she think moving away from her beloved nieces and nephews would solve her problem? At the time, it sure made sense. Of course, back then she didn't know that the town committee wouldn't let her start her business without a male partner.

And back then, she didn't know that the man God had placed in her life would have two adorable little boys who would capture her heart with a single look, either.

Abby closed her eyes and sighed.

What was she going to do?

Ever since Doctor Berg, who she'd only gone to see because she had missed several of her monthly cycles in a row, had told her she had womb death, her life had never been the same. The drying up of her womb, something most women started in their forties, meant she would never bear children. Hearing that diagnosis had crushed any hopes she had of being a mother. That dreadful day she had fled from his office and cried until her heart felt numb with grief. Grief for the children she would never carry. That same day, when she told her fiancé, David, about it, he immediately broke off their engagement, telling her how important it was to not just him, but any man to have offspring of his own. Watching him strolling around town with another woman on his arm and later, holding his baby, had been much too painful for her to endure.

Same thing with her siblings. While she was extremely delighted for her brothers and sisters, seeing them happily married with children reminded her daily of what she herself would never experience—a loving husband and a house filled with children.

It was because of all that she decided to open a dinner theater far away from Paradise Haven. She loved how when she was on stage acting, or sitting in the audience watching, she was transported into another world.

A world of happily ever afters.

A world she could participate in, instead of standing on the sidelines and being an observer only.

Of course, none of it was reality, but still, it helped take her mind off the pain of her reality.

Thinking about reality, she needed to hustle her body downstairs. Harrison would be there any minute to pick her up.

At the bottom of the winding staircase, Abby saw Veronique heading toward the front door.

Harrison must already be here.

"Good morning, *Monsieur* Kingsley. Won't you come in?" Veronique stepped aside to let him in. "May I take your *chapeau*, sir?" He handed his fedora to Veronique, who hung it on the hat rack.

"Thank you. Veronique, isn't it?"

"Yes, sir."

His gaze shifted from Veronique and onto Abby as she strolled toward him.

Veronique slipped away.

The closer Abby got to him, the more she realized no one should be allowed to be that handsome. It wasn't fair to women who were trying to not notice that fact. Women, like herself, who had to disengage her emotions in order to guard her heart where the male species was concerned. Still, she couldn't help admire how nice he looked.

Dressed in a finely tailored, dark gray suit with a

light gray waistcoat, white satin shirt and a dark gray neckerchief, he made an intimidating presence. Just what was needed when going up against the committee board.

"Good morning," she said with a bright and chipper pitch to her voice.

"Good morning to you. You look very nice."

"So do you."

"Thank you, ma'am. Well, are you ready for this?"

"Am I ever." She couldn't wait to see the mayor's face or the committee members' faces, whichever of them would be there this morning, when she walked in with Harrison.

Abby started to wrap her shawl around her shoulders, but Harrison finished the task for her. She grabbed an umbrella, and Harrison offered her his arm. She looped her arm through his, and as they headed out the door, he snatched his hat off the hook and set it on that lovely head of hair of his.

Cool morning air greeted them as they stepped outside.

Abby's attention went to the sky. Judging by the black ominous clouds, she knew it would be only a matter of minutes before a downpour of rain came gushing down on them. "We'd better hurry."

Harrison followed her gaze. "You're right."

Down the steps they scampered. Abby paused at the buggy sitting in front of her house. "You didn't need to do that. It's only a short walk to the town hall."

"I know. And yes, I did. Can't have a fine lady such as yourself walking now, can I?"

"I do it all the time." She shrugged.

"Well, not today." His half smile showed up. He extended his hand, palm up.

Abby laid her hand in his and immediately noticed how liquid warmth spread up her arm and throughout her chest. She'd never experienced anything like that before, and she had no clue what it meant, either. But it was a very nice feeling just the same.

"Abby?"

Abby blinked, then looked at him. "Yes?" He gave a light tug on her hand. "Oh. Forgive me." She raised her skirt above her shoes and stepped up into the buggy, then tucked her skirt inside.

Harrison went around to the other side and sat next to her. His wide shoulders came close to touching hers. He picked up the lines and clicked them. The buggy lurched forward, yanking her backward a tad.

"How are your valet and nanny feeling this morning?" she asked.

"Much better." His gaze trailed to her hat. "You're not hiding the carrot my son tossed at you under that hat, are you?"

Abby laughed. "No."

"I don't know how my nanny does it. The boys can sure be rambunctious."

"Don't I know it. If you think your boys are rowdy, you should see my nephews. Your sweet sons are mild compared to them."

His brow spiked.

"Well, maybe not."

They both laughed.

Harrison stopped the buggy in front of the town hall just as a bolt of lightning pierced the sky and the thunder boomed immediately afterward. Abby screeched.

"We'd better get inside."

Yes, they'd better do just that. Hurry and get inside so she could get her license. A thought flicked through her brain that if for some reason she didn't get it, there would be even more thunderous rumbling going on and it wouldn't be from the storm, either. Especially after doing what they'd asked, obtaining a gentleman business partner, how could they possibly say no now?

She looked into Harrison's eyes as he helped her down. Make that a very handsome business partner. *Careful, Abby. Don't get too close to him. You'll only end up hurt if you do.*

Harrison forced himself to look away from Abby's piercing blue eyes. She was a beautiful lady who didn't flaunt her beauty.

A rare thing in this world. Or at least the world he came from, anyway.

Another snap of lightning zigzagged through the sky. It was only a matter of seconds before the rain came. Cupping Abby's elbow, Harrison led her up the steps and inside the extravagant building.

They walked up to a steely-looking lady seated behind an oak desk. "May I help you, sir?" No warmth or friendliness came through her voice.

"I'm here to see the mayor."

"And you are…?"

"Mr. Harrison Kingsley and this is—" he looked at Abby "—Miss Abigail Bowen."

"Yes. I know. We've met. How are you today, Abby?"

"Very well, and you, Miss Elsa?"

"Well, my shoulders are giving me fits again and my leg is acting up because of the weather, but that's to be expected. I ain't as young as I once was."

Harrison couldn't believe this was the same lady who came across so stern. Perhaps it was because of the pain she was in. He waited patiently while the ladies chattered on.

"We're here to get my business license," Abby finally finished.

"Business license?" The woman tilted her head, looking confused. "You don't need a license to run a business."

Harrison looked over at Abby, and Abby looked at him, wide-eyed. His frown started at his forehead and dropped all the way down to his heart. "What's going on here?"

She genuinely looked surprised. "I have no clue. All I know is I was told I had to have a license, and that they wouldn't give me one unless I took on a business partner. A male business partner." She looked as confused as he now felt.

"Well, we'll get to the bottom of this." He turned his focus onto Miss Elsa.

Miss Elsa's face turned the color of sheep's wool. "Abby, please don't tell the mayor I said anything. I can't afford to lose my job."

"Don't you worry about that, Miss Elsa. We won't say anything, will we, Harrison?" Abby's eyes pleaded with him for Miss Elsa's sake.

He didn't want to cost the elderly woman her job, but something fishy was going on here, and he was going to find out exactly what it was. He'd just have to figure out a way of doing it without saying anything. "We won't say anything. Will you please tell the mayor we're here?"

The color returned to the lady's face. "Yes, sir." She rose, paused and looked at him. "Thank you."

He gave her a quick nod.

The woman limped slowly toward the end of the hall.

Seeing her handicap, Harrison embedded it into his brain not to say anything about what the woman had said to them. He didn't want to cost anyone their job. Especially someone who could barely walk.

Miss Elsa returned. "The mayor will see you now."

"Thank you, Miss Elsa," Abby said with a smile.

Harrison and Abby followed Miss Elsa down the long hall. Portraits hung on either sides of the wall. "Who are these men?"

"That one's the mayor." She pointed to the largest portrait. "The others are the town committee members."

"I see." That painting of the mayor told Harrison a lot about the person he was about to encounter. He was full of himself. Harrison knew exactly how to handle someone like him. After all, he'd had a lot of practice at that endeavor.

Miss Elsa knocked on the door.

"Come in."

The woman opened the door and moved out of the way. "Get us something to drink," the short rotund man sitting behind the massive desk demanded of Miss Elsa without so much as a please anywhere in sight. No wonder the woman had looked so miserable when they'd first walked in. Anyone who had to work with someone like him, someone with no manners, would be miserable. He knew that firsthand working for his father. From what Miss Elsa said, she had no choice. She needed the job. Well, when they got their business up and running, he'd talk to Abby about hiring the older woman to help ease her misery.

The portly mayor didn't even stand when they entered the room. Harrison mentally shook his head. This was going to be an interesting meeting. But he loved a good challenge.

"Miss Bowen, good to see you again." The way he said it spoke volumes. He hadn't meant a single word of his greeting. This arrogant snob was phonier than fool's gold. His eyes ran up and down Harrison, a look meant to size him up and to intimidate him. Harrison wasn't the least bit fazed. He'd come across his type before.

"Mr. Prinker, may I introduce Mr. Harrison Kingsley? My new business partner." Abby's gaze stayed on Harrison, though he caught the smug look she gave the mayor just the same.

Mr. Prinker's thin lips separated, and his bushy brows rose toward the ceiling.

Harrison grinned inside and extended his hand. "Mr. Prinker."

The mayor just stared at the hand as if it were something that would devour him. He was right; Harrison just might cause the man some bodily harm if things were as he surmised they might be. Moreover, he knew he had the upper hand the moment the mayor showed the slightest sign of weakness. One always had to assess their opponent before going into battle. His father had taught him the art of combat well.

Mr. Prinker quickly masked his surprise, and his face turned stern. "There's been a change in plans, Miss Bowen. I was going to send a message to you this afternoon. We've decided not to grant you a license, after all." He sent Harrison a sly grin. The challenge was on.

Chapter Four

Abby's ire rose. Something that happened a lot since coming to this town. How dare this man try to stop her dream from coming true? Especially after dragging Harrison and his boys halfway across the country. "What do you mean you've changed your mind?" Her anger came through her voice loud and clear and she didn't care one whit that it did.

"Before you answer that…" Harrison glanced down at her, and she immediately caught his silent message to calm down. She'd try, but it wasn't going to be easy.

Harrison stared down at Mr. Prinker. His tall stature, broad shoulders and glare made for quite an intimidating figure. "You need to explain yourself, why you have changed your mind and why Miss Bowen even had to obtain a license in the first place."

Mayor Prinker's eyelids lowered toward his meaty hands, then his gaze came back up to Harrison. Gone was the haughtiness, replaced with uncertainty.

Abby hid her grin of satisfaction, knowing the man had met his match.

"The committee and I decided with Hot Mineral Springs growing as rapidly as it is, in order to make sure no unsavory businesses soil our upstanding town or bring trouble to our quiet community, we voted to implement the business license law. We feel a dinner theater will bring too much riffraff here."

"What?" Abby slammed her hands on her hips. "Just what kind of an establishment do you think I will be running?"

The mayor turned his eyes on her, then at Harrison, whose one eyebrow spiked and whose other eye narrowed menacingly at him. Swaying and tugging on his tie, the rotund man loosened it. Sweat drops formed on his balding forehead. He pulled a monogrammed handkerchief from his pocket and blotted his forehead with it.

"Explain yourself, sir." The authority in Harrison's voice snagged Abby's attention. He crossed his arms, and the glare he sent the mayor was even more pronounced. "Before you do, you need to apologize to Miss Bowen for insulting her with your misguided insinuation. Anyone with class can tell just by looking at her that she is a fine, upstanding person. I am not sure I can say the same for you, however."

"Now just you wait a minute." Mayor Prinker shot upward, his chair scraped across the wood floor. He slammed his palms flat on his desk and leaned toward Harrison. "I'll not sit here and listen to you insult my reputation."

Harrison's brow hiked again. "And yet isn't that exactly what you're doing to Miss Bowen?"

The mayor blinked and closed his eyes for a brief moment, then plopped his bulky form back onto the black leather chair. "I see what you're saying." He looked up at Abby. "Please accept my sincere apology, Miss Bowen." He folded his hands together and lowered them onto the desktop in front of him. "However sorry I am, I still cannot issue you a license." The apology was sincere, not only in his voice, but his eyes, and Abby actually felt sorry for him.

"Mr. Prinker." She stepped forward. "I thank you for your apology, and I understand your concern. However, I assure you that my—" her attention swung to Harrison "—our establishment will only bring culture and even more refinement to your...to our lovely community."

His eyes slatted as if he didn't believe her.

Abby restrained herself from allowing her frustration to show. None of that would get him to trust her or get the license she needed. "I can assure you our theater will host only the finest of plays. Are you familiar with Jane Austen's work, Mr. Prinker?"

"Yes, I am."

"Well, then you know what wonderful works of art her novels are."

"I sure do." His chest puffed out.

"That there is nothing questionable in them to perform. Correct?"

The mayor nodded, and Abby noticed the slight curl of Harrison's lips.

"No alcoholic beverages will be allowed in our establishment, only the finest teas and beverages will be served. Our guests will dine in high fashion. They will savor six-course French cuisine meals prepared by my cook, Veronique, who hails from France." At that, the man all but drooled. Abby wanted to roll her eyes but didn't because she herself was on a roll. "They will then be escorted to the theater where they will sit in exquisite, plush-velvet chairs and watch plays put on by reputable people only." She gave that a minute to sink in before she proceeded.

"A theater such as the one we intend to create, like the one back home in Paradise Haven, did not bring in riffraff, nor did it cause the town or anyone else any trouble. On the contrary, actually. When word got around, society's very elite traveled from miles away to watch the productions. Those very people stayed in the town's hotels and increased the revenue of every establishment there."

Greed shrouded his eyes.

She refused to tell him that people who didn't have much came, as well. From the little bit she'd been around the mayor, he might deem them as riffraff or undesirables, which they weren't, of course. "I assure you, Mayor Prinker, just as the theater in Paradise Haven did not tolerate anyone who caused trouble, we will do the same."

The mayor sat back in his chair and raked his fingers across his double chin.

Abby looked over at Harrison. His smile of approval meant a lot to her.

Mayor Prinker rose and walked around his rich mahogany desk and stood within feet of her. "I need to discuss this new information with the other board members. I shall call a quick meeting in the boardroom. You and Mr. Kingsley can either wait here in my office, or you may come back later this afternoon."

"We'll wait here." Harrison spoke before she had a chance to.

"Very well. I shall be back in a few minutes. Have a seat and I will send Miss Elsa in with some tea."

"That won't be necessary. But thank you." No matter how thirsty she was at the moment, Abby didn't want the poor older woman to have to walk any more than she had to with her bad leg.

"Very well." With those words he stepped out of his office and disappeared from their sight.

Abby and Harrison sat down in chairs not nearly as nice as the mayor's.

"You handled that very well, Abigail."

She felt so good about things, she didn't even mind that Harrison had called her Abigail instead of Abby. "Thank you. So did you." She nibbled at her lip a moment. "Do you think they'll agree to give us the license now?"

"Judging by the greed in Mayor Prinker's eyes, I'd say that's a pretty good indicator that we'll get the license."

No sooner had the words come out of his mouth than Mayor Prinker came rushing through door, huffing and puffing. That had to be the shortest meeting in history.

"Miss Bowen, Mr. Kingsley." He breathlessly said their names as he scurried around to the other side of his desk and plopped down in his chair. He pressed his hand against his chest and drew in several streams of air. "I—I t-talked to the other members..." He panted out the words, then reached for his cup. Between breaths, he took several sips of his beverage. When his breathing neared normal, he spoke again, "We have decided to issue you a license, after all."

Abby wanted to jump up and down and hoop and holler, but in order to maintain a professional persona, she restrained herself.

"But—"

Uh-oh, here it comes. She should have known there would be a but in there somewhere. There always was with him.

He held up his hand, looking only at Abby. "Anytime either I or the committee members feel your establishment is harming our community, or it doesn't conform to the high standards we have set for our town, we will shut you down. And, the stipulation of maintaining a male business partner remains the same, or we will shut you down. Is that understood?" This time the mayor looked at Harrison.

"I foresee no problem with that," Harrison answered with a confidence she didn't feel.

Abby yanked her gaze in his direction, wishing she had the same assurance as he did as she had no intentions of maintaining a business partner, and he had no intentions of staying here. Unless…hmm. Unless he eventually became the silent business partner they had discussed the day before. She didn't know why that wouldn't work. After all, nothing was said about him having to remain here in town.

The whole thing was a huge risk. One she was willing to take. Convinced once the mayor and his cronies saw how much money the business brought to their town and just how classy the place was, she had a feeling they wouldn't care if her business partner lived here or elsewhere. Doubt niggled at her, but she paid it no mind. Nothing would douse her joy. Nothing.

Pride was the only way to describe how Harrison felt. The way his new business partner handled things just now amazed him. There was more to Abigail Bowen than a pretty face. It was a good thing he was indeed heading straight home. He'd been fooled once too often by a pretty face. He needed to be extremely careful just who he let into his heart. Not only for his sake, but his sons', as well.

He cupped Abby's elbow and led her outside the town hall building. Unlike when they'd first arrived for their meeting, nary a rain cloud could be seen, only miles of pale blue sky. Humidity and fresh air with a hint of sulphur filled his nostrils. Wagon ruts raked through the street reminding him of his sons' drawings.

At the edge of the boardwalk, Abby stopped. She closed her eyes and turned her face upward. The sun covered her youthful skin with its bright glow. She drew in several long breaths. What a lovely vision she was. Harrison watched her with fascination. She was a woman of means, yet there was something outdoorsy about her and completely refreshing from the women he had been raised around.

Her eyes, the same blueness as the sky, slowly opened. Beauty bathed her in all its glory. Only one other woman was as comely as she, his dear departed wife. He pinched his eyes shut to blot out the painful memories that routinely followed thoughts of his sweet Allison.

"Are you all right, Harrison?" Abby's hand settled on top of his arm.

His gaze drifted toward it. The gesture, meant to comfort him, sizzled his arm with her feminine awareness. A feeling he knew all too well. When he'd first met his wife, the same thing had happened to him back then, and he'd married her. Stunned at the correlation and its impact on him, he abruptly stepped to the side, allowing Abby's arm to separate from his. "I'm fine."

One look at her face and he knew he hadn't fooled her, her disbelieving frown told him as much. "Why don't we go and celebrate?" he asked to keep her from questioning him a second time. "Pie and coffee. My treat." He pulled his attention from her and settled it on the town before them. "Who here makes the best pies?"

Her sigh was audible as she pointed to a sign hanging

several doors down from the hall. "Lucy's Diner. Her pies are exquisite. Almost as good as my mother's. Her pie crust is so flaky and light, it barely holds together."

"Sounds like my kind of pie. Shall we?" He offered her the crook of his arm. Big mistake that turned out to be. That same heat sizzled up his arm again, only this time he refused to let his mind dwell on it or its implications. Instead, he reminded himself that he was here for the sole purpose of securing his inheritance for not only his sons' sake, but for the sake of the unfortunate people back in Boston who his father had greatly wronged. A quick glance at Abby and he needed to add one more reason to the mix. After meeting Abby and seeing just how much she wanted this business to succeed, he wanted to do everything in his power to make her dream come to fruition, as well.

They strolled down the boardwalk, their footsteps echoing underneath them. When they reached the steps that separated one building from the other, Harrison glanced down at the muddy ground, then at her delicate gown, and contemplated what to do. If she was his wife, he would swing her into his arms and carry her across, but she wasn't. And yet, how could he do nothing and allow a lady to soil her garment. "If you will permit me, I would like to carry you across the mud."

Abby blinked as if he'd gone daft or something. "Thank you. But no. I can walk. I was raised on a farm. I'm used to mud. A lot of it." With those words, she hiked her skirt and tiptoed through the thick mire to the other side.

Harrison stared at her back. No Bostonian lady would have ever done that. In fact, they would have insisted Harrison call for a servant to carry them across or that he lay his coat down for them to walk on. Abby was nothing like those ladies. She was more like Allison in that way, too. Realizing what he was doing, he reprimanded himself for comparing Abby to his deceased wife.

They arrived at Lucy's Diner. Harrison opened the door for Abby. Apples and cinnamon filled the air.

Abby headed to a table by the window, and he followed, holding her chair out and waiting for her to be seated before he took the chair across from her. His gaze slid around the room at the informal, homey establishment. The sparkling-clean place was small but not cluttered. It was also void of patrons, which had him wondering why since according to Abby, it served the best pie in town.

"How fortunate we are that we missed the morning breakfast rush." Abby answered his unspoken question.

A petite, slender woman in a bright yellow dress with a stained apron over it bustled toward them. "Abby! It's so nice to see you again. Couldn't stay away, huh? You come back for some more of my strawberry-rhubarb pie? I made a fresh batch this morning. There's three pieces left. So if you want one, you'd better grab a slice before the next rush of customers comes barreling in. You want coffee with that pie, or tea? Oh, I'm sorry. I didn't even ask. Maybe you don't want strawberry-rhubarb today. I have two pecan pies coming out of the oven in a few minutes. You want a slice of that instead?" As if she finally realized Abby wasn't alone, the woman stopped her rapid-fire talking and her brown-eyed gaze fell to him.

"Oh, dear me. Forgive me, sir. Don't know where my manners are. Hello. I'm Lucy Cornwall. Owner of this here place." She grabbed his hand with her sticky one and pumped it vigorously with a grip as strong as any man's. A grasp that certainly didn't match her petite size.

"Lucy, this is Mr. Kingsley. My new business partner. We're here to celebrate."

"Oh." Her eyes lit up. "What you celebrating? Oh, wait." She shook her head. "You said he's your new business partner. This must mean that ornery old mayor and his little cronies gave you your license, then. Good. Cuz, if he didn't, I was fixin' to march down there and give that man a good tongue lashing, and let him know he'd get no more pie from me. That'd serve him right. Won't have to now. Okay, what'll you have?" She pulled a piece of paper and a nub of a pencil out of her apron pocket, chewed on the wood like a beaver gnawing on a log until more lead exposed itself, then she placed the dull point on the paper. Her friendly smile landed on him first, then Abby. "Now I'm ready."

The woman reminded him of a hurricane, long-winded and unpredictable. He glanced at Abby. She winked at him and smiled before turning her attention to Lucy. "I'll take the strawberry-rhubarb pie and tea."

Lucy scribbled it down and turned to him.

Harrison couldn't believe she needed to write their orders down. After all, the place was empty and it wasn't like she had a ton of orders. Didn't matter what she did or didn't do, it wasn't his place to decide how she did things. "I'll have the same. Only make mine coffee instead of tea."

"Yes, sir. I'll be right back with your orders." She whirled around and within seconds her tiny form disappeared behind a swinging door.

He shook his head.

"You get used to her."

"You do?"

Abby laughed. "Yes. You do. I promise. She's really a very sweet woman. One who would give you her last bread crumb. Lucy gives more food away than she has paying customers. I have no idea how she even stays in business. But she does. And people love her."

He settled his elbows on the arms of his chair and clasped his hands. "You come here often, then?"

Heat filled Abby's cheeks. "Yes. Once you taste Lucy's pie, you'll understand why. But don't tell Veronique."

"Your secret's safe with me." His lips curled upward.

The swinging door leading to and from the kitchen squeaked, and out came Lucy advancing toward their table like a locomotive trying to make its destination on time. How the woman moved so fast holding a tray loaded with two filled cups, a cream pitcher, a sugar bowl and two large slices of pie, Harrison didn't know. Not one drop had spilled, either.

"Here you go." She set their orders in front of them, chattering like a wound-up parrot as she did.

Harrison had a hard time keeping up with her and finally gave up—thankful Abby occupied the woman. Well, thankful wasn't quite the word. He wanted to visit with Abby without distractions, to talk about business so they could get the theater up and running as soon as possible. The sooner the better so he could get back home. In the next breath, the mayor's stipulations ran through his mind.

As soon as Lucy left to tend to the three customers that had just walked in, Harrison turned his focus onto Abby, who had just forked a bite of pie and settled it into her mouth. He waited until she swallowed, then asked, "What did you think about the mayor's stipulations?"

Abby took a drink of her tea and dabbed the corners of her mouth with her napkin. "What stipulations?"

"About maintaining a male business partner."

"Oh. That." She placed her napkin on her lap. "You and I already discussed that, remember?"

"I do. But what if he doesn't approve of my being a long-distance partner? Then what will you do?"

"I'm not sure. But what I am sure of is, God will take care of it. He's taken care of everything else up to this point, and He will finish what He started." Her smile swelled with confidence. She continued to eat her pie, sighing contentedly with each bite.

Harrison wondered how she could be so certain God would take care of it. God had never done anything for him. Course, it had been years since he had asked Him to, and God hadn't answered his prayer back then. Since then, he wanted nothing to do with God or church. In his experience, most people who prayed or went to church did it solely for show and for social reasons.

Every Sunday he and his father sat in the front row of the largest church in the city, listening to the minister go on and on about money and how much he needed for this project and that project. Father gave the greedy man what he needed. In front of the whole congregation filled with only society's elite—poor folks weren't allowed there—his father made a huge display of his donation.

Then all the way home and all day long, Harrison had to endure his father's complaints about the money he'd just donated and about how God never did anything for him, and how everything he owned he worked hard for. It ended with the same warning that God couldn't be depended on for anything. If He could be, then he wouldn't have to give his money and his wife wouldn't have died. That was the one thing Harrison and his father agreed on. Just why Abby thought she could depend on Him, Harrison had no idea, but in his curiosity, he wanted to find out. "What makes you so sure God will take care of this?"

"Because He always has." She took another bite of her pie, and a patch of red juice clung to her lower lip.

Without thinking, Harrison picked up his napkin, reached across the table and brushed her lip with it.

She stopped chewing, and stared at him.

Harrison yanked his hand back. "Forgive me. I'm so used to wiping my sons' mouths that I didn't stop to think about what I was doing. It's an automatic response, I suppose."

She relaxed her fixed stare, finished chewing and swallowed. "Trust me. I understand." Her eyes dimmed, and her gaze suddenly fell to his untouched pie. "Aren't you going to eat your pie?"

Confused about the sadness in her eyes and the abrupt change of subject, it took him a second before he realized what she had asked. His attention drizzled to his full plate, then over to her empty one. "Why? You want it?"

She licked her lips, a gesture that lit a spark inside him. He yanked his focus onto his plate and suddenly became very interested in his pie, devouring it within minutes.

"I guess that means yes." Her smiling eyes danced with amusement.

He couldn't help but smile, too. He sat back in his chair and patted his flat stomach. Something so uncharacteristic of him to do, but Abby brought out the playful side of him, just like his Allison had. *Stop comparing her with Allison.* He cleared his throat. "Sure was."

They finished their drinks, talking about the weather,

the mountains and nothing else of consequence, and then they headed back to her place.

He pulled his buggy in front of her mansion and stopped. He jumped out and went around the side of the buggy to help her down. Their hands connected, and the spark flew into him again. This was going to be a long three months.

Abby ignored the heat that ran up her arm when Harrison's hand clutched hers. Soon as her feet touched the ground, the man yanked his hand from hers and stepped back. His abrupt action shocked her, but she shrugged it off. No time to worry about what had just happened; she had a business to build. And nothing, not even the charming, handsome Harrison Kingsley would stop her. She hoped. "Would you like to come inside?"

His brows pulled together.

"To discuss business. The sooner we get started, the sooner I—we—can open."

He removed his pocket fob watch and flipped the gold H K engraved cover open. After a quick glance at it, with a click he snapped the lid shut and nestled it back into his pocket. "I told my boys I'd take them to lunch today. It's still early. So yes, we can do that."

"Wonderful."

Up the mansion stairs they went.

Zoé met them at the door and took Abby's wrap and Harrison's *chapeau*. They made their way to the parlor.

Before sitting down next to him on the settee, she retrieved her writing tablet containing all her notes, along with a fountain pen. "Would you care for something to drink?"

"No, thank you. But if you do, please go ahead."

"I don't care for anything, either." She smiled at him

and shifted her knees his direction, careful to not touch his. "First of all, we need to hire a carpenter. I had Colette put up an advertisement on the bulletin board, but someone took it from her. If we don't hear from whoever that was today, I thought we could put up another ad and ask around town to see if anyone knew of someone who could get the job done in the next couple of months." How strange it felt to keep saying *we*. It had always been *I* up until today. In an even stranger way, it sounded nice.

She never thought she would admit something like this to herself, but truth be told, she liked having a partner. Oh, not just any ol' partner, of course, but one particular strong-figure-of-a-man sitting next to her. Close enough in fact that she could detect the scent of lemon spice and something entirely masculine.

Something about the man awakened her senses to a new height and made her want to… *No. No romantic thoughts allowed, Abigail.* That's what she called herself when she needed a good talking to. She shook all thoughts of romance from her head and reminded herself that no man wanted a woman who couldn't bear children. Besides, Harrison would be leaving soon. And she'd do well to remember that, too.

"You all right, Abby?"

Her gaze darted to his. She waved her hand. "Oh. Yes. Yes. I'm fine. Now, where were we?"

"We were discussing—" Harrison stopped talking; his attention was toward the door of the parlor.

Abby shifted in the settee to see what he was looking at.

"Forgive me for intruding, *mademoiselle*. But there is a gentleman here to see you," Zoé said.

"Thank you, Zoé. Send him in, please."

"Very well." Zoé left.

Abby twisted back in her chair. "I wonder who that could be. Hopefully the mayor didn't change his mind again." Abby tugged on her lip with her fingertips.

"In here, if you would, please, sir."

Abby turned in time to see Zoé make a motioning gesture with her hand.

In stepped a man she'd never seen before.

She and Harrison stood at the same time.

"Miss Abby. This is Mr. Fletcher Martin." Zoé presented him to her.

The man strode over to Abby. He towered over her by at least a foot. "Ma'am." He extended his hand.

Abby accepted the gesture. Rough calluses met her hand when she did. With a sweep of her hand toward Harrison, Abby introduced him. "This is Mr. Kingsley. Harrison Kingsley."

"Pleasure to meet you, Mr. Kingsley," Mr. Martin said.

Two large, very masculine hands met in between them.

From the corner of her eye, Abby noticed Zoé standing by the door with her hands clasped in front of her, looking around uncomfortably. "Thank you, Zoé. You can go now." She sent her a smile, one filled with appreciation.

Zoé relaxed and smiled. She turned and left the room with a scurry in her step.

Abby shifted her focus back to the stranger. "What can I do for you, Mr. Martin?"

He removed a slip of paper very similar to the one she'd given Colette to post on the bulletin board from his shirt pocket and unfolded it. "I've come about your advertisement."

"Please, won't you sit down?" She motioned to the empty chair across from her, and then sat down. Harrison did also.

Mr. Martin lowered his tall, broad-shouldered frame into the chair across from them. Dark brown eyes trailed to her. Fletcher Martin was an extremely handsome man, but not as handsome as Harrison. He had many more edges to him, and most of them looked quite rugged.

She stopped in midthought. Why was she comparing him to Harrison? Ridiculous. That's what it was. Just plain ridiculous.

Drawing on her business persona to get her mind where it needed to be, she slogged forward. "Mr. Kingsley and I are looking for someone to not only repair this place—" her arms made a wide arc of the room "—but also someone to build a theater stage and props."

"I can do that."

Her insides danced with the prospect of having found a carpenter so soon.

"What kind of experience do you have, Mr. Martin?" Harrison asked.

Now why hadn't she thought to ask him that?

Mr. Martin looked at Abby, then at Harrison.

"Mr. Kingsley and I are business partners."

"Oh." He gave a quick nod. "I see." He reached inside his pocket again, pulled out another slip of paper and unfolded it. "Here's a list of references." He stood and handed the list to Harrison.

Something about that bugged her. She was in charge here, not Harrison. Of course, Mr. Martin didn't know that. At that moment, she realized she'd better get used to it. They were partners, after all.

Harrison studied the paper as she sat with her hands in her lap patiently waiting while he did.

Finally, Harrison nodded. "That's quite an impressive list, Mr. Fletcher."

"Thank you, sir."

"Do you mind if we keep this? We'd like to check your work before we consider hiring you."

How sweet of him to include her.

In a million years, she never thought she would like someone taking over the charge of her business affairs, but something about the way Harrison did it was so attractive and so alluring and so like the heroes in her romance novels.

Stop thinking like that. She reset her gaze on the carpenter across the way, determined to keep her notions—romantic and otherwise—under wraps.

"Not at all." Mr. Martin stood. "If you would like to see some of my work, you can head over to the town hall. My crew and I built that building. We made most of the furniture in it, too."

"Oh. You make furniture?" Abby's interest and excitement piqued.

"Yes. We do." His attention gravitated from Harrison to her.

"What kind do you make? Do you have any pieces for sale?"

"Yes. I have a storehouse outside of town full of furniture."

Her eyes widened in hope and surprise. "You do?"

"Yes, ma'am. When things are slow, especially during the winter months here, we build furniture. Not to boast or anything, ma'am, but some of our items have shipped as far east as New York, even."

"Wonderful. I'd love to come see what you have. I

need to fill this place with furniture. What you can't supply me with, I can have shipped from catalogs." She stopped and gazed over at Harrison. "That is, if it's all right with you."

He hadn't left her out, and she wasn't going to leave him out, either. Besides, she knew it hurt a man's pride to have to take orders from a woman or to not look like he was in charge, so she'd let him think he was. But she knew the truth. And that was all that mattered.

Chapter Five

Dressed in a simple cotton dress, Abby grabbed the blue wrap that matched it and waited by the front door for Harrison. Before he'd left the night before, they had agreed to go to the furniture place together. They'd also agreed if they liked Mr. Martin's work, they would hire him and his employees.

Harrison pulled his buggy in front of her house.

Abby swung the door open, scurried down the steps and met him just as he stepped out of the carriage. "Good morning." Her cheery attitude chirped through her voice.

"My, you're quite chipper this morning."

"I have reason to be. I can hardly wait to see what furniture Mr. Martin has in his storeroom. I'm so tired of looking at those sparsely filled rooms. I hope, hope, hope he has what we need."

Harrison helped her into the buggy and hurried over to the driver's side. With a flick of the reins, the black mare clomped forward. Harrison glanced over at her then back at the road. "I don't want to put a damper on your good spirits or anything, but I wouldn't count on him having enough chairs to fill the theater or enough tables and chairs for the dining area."

"Huh? Oh. I didn't mean that. I meant for the parlors, the seating area and the foyer. He won't carry what I have in mind for the dining area and theater, anyway."

"What do you have in mind?"

"I want royal blue, plush-velvet chairs for the theater and shield-back style Chippendale chairs with gold, padded seats and matching Chippendale tables for the dining area."

"Chippendale is extremely pricey furniture," he stated.

"Yes, I know."

"Do you also know how expensive they will be to ship out here?"

"Of course I do. You know, I may have been raised on a farm, Mr. Kingsley, but I'm no country bumpkin, and I understand business. My father was a successful New York City businessman. My brothers are successful businessmen. My stepfather owns several successful businesses, half of Paradise Haven, actually. And my mother, my brother Michael, and my brother Haydon all have Chippendale furniture in their homes. So I am very much aware of how much things cost." She hadn't meant it to sound so huffy, but his insinuations bothered her. Besides, she didn't know anyone of his means who would be concerned about the cost of things. Then again, maybe his wealth was tied up in his father's will. That would explain it.

"I didn't mean to insult you. I just wanted to make sure you knew how expensive it would be."

"I can assure you, I do. I've been planning this for a very long time now. I have several furniture catalogs, and I've checked on the prices of everything, including the cost of shipping the items I want. I would be foolish not to. The Bible makes it clear when it says, 'Consider the cost.' Well, I've done that for all of it. And I have more than enough funds to cover everything. My father saw to that before he passed away."

She narrowed her eyes. "Listen, if you're worried about me asking you for more money, I already told you that all you need to invest is five hundred dollars. The rest is at my expense. And I will keep my end of the agreement that within three months' time, you will get your original investment back, plus the profit I promised you. Even if there is no profit from the business, you will obtain one at my expense." She knew she sounded defensive, but after being judged by the town committee and now having Harrison questioning her business instincts, too, well, enough was enough. How doltish did they all think she was, anyway?

His hand settled on her arm. "Abby, I meant no offense. I didn't bring up the subject because I was concerned about having to invest more money. I was only watching out for your interests."

Her gaze slid to his bluish-gray eyes and the amber color settled at the bottom third of his right eye. Gorgeous was the only way to describe those orbs of his.

She knew she should look away. But she saw no harm in admiring his good looks and stunning eyes. After all, she knew there would never be anything more between them than a business relationship. Even still, that didn't mean she was dead. She admired a handsome man just as much as the next woman did. Only difference was, she had to be careful not to give him or any other gentleman the wrong idea, as she could never marry.

The reminder that she could never bear children came as it always did when she thought about marriage, but she refused to entertain it. Instead, she shifted her mind back onto business. "Thank you, Harrison. I appreciate your concern. It is my turn to apologize. I fear I have overreacted. My only excuse is, after what the town committee put me through, treating me like I, a mere woman, had no business running an establishment, well, I guess I'm a little sensitive about the whole thing."

"That's understandable. But I want you to know from what little I've witnessed, you have a great mind for business and for detail."

His words embraced her with sweetness and confidence. Knowing he had faith in her meant a lot.

He drove the buggy down the main road through Hot Mineral Springs. A quarter of a mile out of town, a large building with a sign *Martin's Furniture* came into view. Bubbles of excitement popped throughout her stomach as this was one more step in making her dream become a reality.

Harrison came around to her side of the buggy and helped her down. Cupping her elbow, he led her inside the building.

They stepped inside and Abby stopped. Her hands flew to her cheeks, and her mouth fell open. "Oh, my! I've never seen so much furniture in one place before!" Rows and rows of bedroom furniture, settees and sofas of various colors, kitchen tables, dining room chairs, dressers and much more lined the walls and filled the whole interior. There was furniture everywhere. And not just any furniture, either, but beautifully crafted pieces.

Her inspection ended at Mr. Martin, standing in the back of the store. As soon as he spotted them, he said something to one of the three men standing with him, then headed their way gazing at them with a smile on his face. "Nice to see you again, Miss Bowen."

Harrison noticed Mr. Martin's gaze lingered on Abby longer than necessary. He also noticed the attraction in the man's eyes. Not that he could blame him. Abby was an extremely beautiful woman. A man would have to be dead not to notice.

Mr. Martin extended his hand toward Harrison. "It's good to see you again, too." His smile was genuine, and he shook his hand as if he were a long-lost friend.

So far, everyone here in this small town treated Harrison the same as they did everyone else. Something Harrison found refreshing.

Back home, his father had been known as a ruthless businessman. While he hadn't done anything illegal, some of his business dealings were definitely unscrupulous. By association, Harrison had been thought to be like him, and, therefore, a lot of people treated him with the same disdain they had his father. Except for those who wanted something from him or his deceased wife. Allison had loved him for who he was, the real him. The others? Well, he was either resented or used— neither of which set very well with him.

He shook hands with Mr. Martin and offered him a friendly smile, then looked around the room. "When you said you had a storehouse full of furniture, I expected to see a few pieces. Not this." He eyes took in the room as he spoke the last words. He studied the intricately carved dresser closest to him. "I've never seen such fine craftsmanship anywhere. What are you doing here? You need to move back east. You could make a fortune back there."

"Thank you for the compliment. But I have no plans to live anywhere else. I'm happy where I am."

Harrison could understand that. Hot Mineral Springs was a beautiful place filled with friendly people, except for the mayor and his cronies. Then again, if Harrison was being honest, he didn't blame them. All they were trying to do was protect their town and keep it safe and clean from undesirables.

Would they consider him an undesirable if they knew about his father and how he managed his affairs?

Harrison did what he always did when that thought came around. He reminded himself he was nothing like his father, and he would prove it when he got back home by righting as many wrongs as he could, and by earning the good folks of Boston's respect. "Well, if you ever change your mind, you let me know. I'd be glad to help you get set up and would even be interested in investing in your company. You could even move your operation into one of the Kingsley buildings."

"That's right nice of you. But like I said, I'm happy here." He smiled. "Now, what can I help you folks with?"

With a look, Harrison turned that question over to Abby.

Her already bright blue eyes sparkled even more. "Well, let's see." She ticked the items off her long, mental list.

That began a trek around and through the workshop as Mr. Martin showed her piece after piece. After she purchased what seemed like over half of the storehouse, she turned to Harrison and asked, "May I speak to you privately for a moment?"

He nodded. "If you will excuse us…"

"Of course." Mr. Martin grabbed his list and went

to the back of the store where the other three men were working.

Abby led him out of earshot of the others and gazed up at him. "If this furniture is any indication of the type of work he does, I think we should hire him. What do you think?"

Harrison knew how hard it was for her to include him in her plans. She'd never wanted a business partner and resented the fact that she'd been forced to get one. From what he'd witnessed, she didn't need one. Still, he was pleased to be included in the decisions. "I agree. But before we do—"

"—we need to do a walk-through and show him exactly what needs to be done and find out how much he will charge to do the job." She finished his sentence.

"You read my mind." He smiled at her. "Do you want me to ask him, or do you want to do that?"

"You can ask him."

"Very well." They strolled back to where Fletcher was. "Mr. Martin, when would be a good time for you to come to the mansion again? We would like to show you everything that needs to be done and get an estimate from you as soon as possible."

"If you two are free now, I can follow you over there."

Harrison glanced down at Abby. Anticipation sparkled through her eyes, and she gave a quick nod.

"Yes. That'll be fine. We'll meet you there."

They turned to leave, but Abby stopped. "When's the soonest you can deliver my furniture?"

"My men can deliver it this afternoon if you'd like."

"That would be wonderful." She clasped her hands together. "Thank you, Mr. Martin. I shall finally have real furniture. What great joy!"

The carpenter's face registered the enthusiasm of her words, much to Harrison's displeasure.

"Please, call me Fletcher."

Her smile resembled summer sunshine. "And you may call me Abby."

For some odd reason, Harrison didn't like the informality between them. But Abby wasn't one much for formality. Besides, he had no claims on her.

"We'll see you back at the mansion." Harrison normally cupped her elbow, but this time, he looped her arm through his and led her outside. Did he do it on purpose? If so, what for? To give Fletcher the idea they were an item so he wouldn't pursue her. That wasn't fair to Abby. After all, he would be leaving, and she would be here. She deserved to find a nice man. He discreetly moved his hand to her elbow. If she noticed the change, she didn't say anything. Much to his relief.

On their way back to her place, her excitement bubbled over and so did her words. "I'm so happy. I never expected to find everything I needed right here in town. Can you believe it? I mean, really, who would have thought such a thing? Well, with the exception of the theater furniture, that is. Oh, I wish Fletcher had time to make our chairs for us. Did you see the quality of his work?" Her gaze darted to his, but she didn't wait for his answer. Instead, she went on and on about Fletcher, the furniture, his talent and more.

All the accolades about Fletcher almost made Harrison jealous. Almost. But that was just plain ludicrous, and he knew it.

The three arrived at the mansion at the same time and headed inside.

They showed Fletcher through the house. In each room, he jotted down notes. Lots of them. While Harrison was no carpenter, he did know a bit about buildings. And this one needed a lot more repairs than even he originally thought. He wondered if Abby knew just how many repairs were needed. She said she'd counted the cost, but judging by the smile on her face, he had a feeling she didn't know just how much money this place was going to take to fix it up.

Somehow, he needed to warn her before they got the estimate. In the meantime, he could only hope he was wrong.

In the massive theater room, Abby told him about the stage and props she would need built, and Fletcher continued to jot down notes. His list grew, and so had Harrison's dread. What if she didn't have enough money to cover all the expenses this place needed? Would she still pay him as promised? While that was important to him, it was equally important that she succeed at making her dream come true. And once again he was determined to do whatever it took to help that dream become a reality.

When they finished the lengthy inside and outside tour, she ordered tea and cookies for them. Abby sat next to Harrison on the settee, and Fletcher sat in the chair across from them. She asked the man a million questions, ending with, "How soon can you get those figures to us?"

"Tomorrow morning."

"Will that work for you, Harrison?"

"Yes. That'll be fine."

Fletcher stood. "Well, I need to get going. Thank you for the tea and cookies. I'll bring my estimate by tomorrow morning. Around nine, if that's acceptable."

Abby looked up at Harrison. He nodded.

"See you at nine." Fletcher headed toward the parlor door.

Harrison started to follow him.

"You're not leaving now, too, are you?"

He stopped. "I was. Why? Did you need something?"

"Well, we still have business to discuss." She glanced at Fletcher, then back at him.

"Very well."

"I'll walk Fletcher out, and I'll be right back." Her warm, grateful smile made him glad he'd stayed.

What was it about her that had him wanting to please her?

Abby couldn't wait until she finished seeing Fletcher to the door so she could get back to Harrison. Back inside the parlor, Harrison stood at the window with his back to her. How regal he looked, a fine figure of a man to be sure. But she'd already established that earlier and many times in between. "Well, that was a productive morning, I think." She breezed over to where he stood.

Harrison turned toward her, and if she wasn't mistaken, unease dotted that gorgeous face of his.

She wondered what had him so concerned. She peered out the window in time to see Fletcher swing his tall frame onto his saddle and ride out of sight; nothing out of the ordinary there.

Should she ask him what the matter was or wait until he hopefully volunteered the information? The latter won. "That man sure does exquisite work. I can't wait to get my new furniture and get rid of this old stuff." The sway of her arm and her eyes took in the whole of the parlor, and she wrinkled her nose in disgust. The furniture had definitely seen better days.

"That he does." The furrow between his brows was still there.

"Is something the matter, Harrison?"

Troubled eyes shifted to hers.

Something was definitely wrong. Her stomach pinched with worry. "Please, tell me what's bothering you?"

He stared at her for a moment as if contemplating what to do.

She laid her hand on his arm. "Whatever it is, you can tell me," she assured him, then braced herself for whatever it was.

"This is very awkward, Abigail."

Abigail? Uh-oh. That wasn't good.

"I don't want to offend you or anything, but I need to ask you something."

"All right." She nodded.

"You said you had counted the cost and that you had plenty of money. That your father had seen to it." He swallowed, looked away then returned his focus to her. Each moment he didn't speak caused her stomach to pinch harder.

"And…"

"There's no easy way to say this, so I'll just come right out and say it."

Again she nodded, again she braced herself.

"Do you realize just how many repairs are needed on this place? And just how much money it's going to cost to fix those repairs?"

She tilted her head and frowned. "What do you mean?"

"Several of the windows and doors need replacing. The fireplaces are in need of repair, not to mention needing to be cleaned thoroughly. Plus, there are a few weakened and cracked walls that need fixing."

"Weakened and cracked walls?"

"Yes. I'm just hoping they're not from a foundation problem."

"Foundation problem?" She knew she was mimicking him, but she didn't understand what he was talking about. She hadn't seen any cracks in the walls or anything wrong with the building's structure. Of course, she was no carpenter, either.

"Part of the kitchen floor needs to be replaced, as well."

"It does? Why?"

"Because, when I stepped in front of the water pump, the floor caved some. It will only get worse, and you can't have someone falling through that and breaking a leg or getting hurt."

How come she'd never noticed any of those things before? Especially the kitchen floor. Her gaze brushed over Harrison's stout physique, then over her petite frame. Did the weight difference have anything to do with the floor giving? She made a mental note to ask Veronique if she had noticed the weakened floor. She wondered just how many more things she had missed. What if the repairs were numerous? More than she'd estimated? While she had plenty of money, she also knew she would need a vast amount to get everything set up and to run things for a time. She rolled her lip under with her top teeth. Might her dream crash at her feet before it ever got a chance to be realized?

"I can see I've upset you, Abby. I'm sorry. I shouldn't have said anything. Fletcher did a thorough inspection of the place. I'm confident that he noticed those things, and that he knows what he's doing, so why don't we just wait to see what he says and how much his bid is?"

She gazed up at him and nodded.

"Now, what did you want to discuss with me?"

"Excuse me?"

"You asked me to stay, to discuss business."

"Oh. Oh. Right. I wanted to show you the chairs and tables I'm going to order. I have the catalogs here." She strolled over to the coffee table, and he followed.

They sat down on the settee, and she turned the catalog to the earmarked page.

Harrison scooted closer to her. Leaning over, he peered down at it.

His nearness and aftershave swirled through her senses, making it hard to concentrate on anything but him. Being a dreamer and a romantic most of her life, she had to forcefully turn her mind off his masculinity and on to the task at hand. "These are the chairs I had in mind for the theater." She pointed to a picture of them. "And these are the ones I had in mind for the dining room."

"Very nice. You have exquisite taste, Abby."

She turned her face toward him, and his was close enough to where she could see that half-moon color again. Something she found extremely attractive and very appealing. But before she started daydreaming again, she quickly thanked him, flipped to the next earmarked page, and pointed to the next item on her list. "This table is the one I've chosen for the dining room." As an afterthought she added, "That is if that's all right with you."

"It's very nice." His gaze alighted on hers. "You know, Abby, while I appreciate you running everything by me, you don't have to. Again, I know that you only have me here because of the town committee's stipulation. You already know what you want. You should just order it. After all, you'll be the one to have to look at it when I'm gone."

Gone. That one word drove through her, leaving its painful mark. Truth was, she rather liked having a partner, someone to run her ideas by. And not just any partner, either; she liked having *Harrison* as a partner.

After all, the man was easy to get along with and had a special way of easing her loneliness.

As he said, though, he would be leaving, best not to get too used to having him around. She closed the book and sat up straight. "You're right. I do have to look at it when you're gone. And I was forced to take on a partner. But I don't mind running things by you. Truth be known, I rather enjoy it. But if you don't care to know or to see what I'm doing, then…" She hiked a shoulder and left the sentence dangling for him to pick up.

"I do care. I want this place to succeed. For your sake as well as mine. I just don't want you to feel like you *have* to share everything with me is all."

"Oh, but I truly do want to. After all, two heads are better than one, right? Besides, I really am enjoying working with you."

"I'm glad you feel that way. I'm enjoying working with you, too." He smiled at her.

Her lips smiled back at him, as did her heart. Mixed emotions, both turbulent and sweet, scattered and rolled across her brain like fast-moving storm clouds.

If only she could have children.

And if only he wasn't leaving when this business deal ended.

And if only her heart didn't skip with happiness every time she was around him.

But… She sighed. The "if onlys" would always be there. So it was best if she saved her emotional fantasies of having this man around for the rest of her life for her daydreams because that's all any of it would ever be.

A fancy.

A dream.

And nothing more.

Chapter Six

"Mademoiselle." Veronique entered the study. "There is a gentleman here to see Mr. Kingsley. He says it is rather urgent."

Abby glanced up at Harrison.

"Excuse me." Harrison turned and exited the room.

Abby didn't know whether to follow him or not, so she opted to stay in the parlor and wait for him.

Minutes ticked by, the noise of a loud ruckus came from outside the room. She pushed herself off the chair and stepped out of the parlor. Her attention immediately flew to the sound of giggling boys near the front door, and to Harrison who was chasing one of his sons, and to a very distraught, yet distinguished gentleman running after the other.

An overturned potted plant lay sprawled across the floor. Harrison's sons dodged the men, giggling as they did, and kicked at the dirt, sending the mess flying across the floor.

Seeing that the disgruntled men needed help, Abby took pity on them, and bustled their way.

"Josiah! Graham! That's enough!" Harrison's loud

voice, filled with anger and frustration, echoed off the walls in the large, near-empty room.

His twins stopped and turned wide eyes up at their father. Tears pooled in their gray-blue orbs, and loud wails followed.

Abby's heart broke seeing their little faces like that. How her arms ached to comfort them, but it wasn't her place to get involved like that; they weren't her children. But oh, how she wanted to.

Harrison dropped to his knee, giving no attention to the fact that he had just settled his expensive, tailor-made suit right smack in the middle of the moist plant soil. He pulled the boys into his arms and held them. When they stopped sobbing, he leaned back and peered into their faces. He brushed the moisture from their cheeks with the handkerchief he removed from his pocket, then returned it. "I'm sorry I yelled at you. But you mustn't run in the house. We need to find Miss Abby and ask her for a broom so you can clean up the mess you made."

The boys' blinking eyes widened. Their little gazes took in the mess on the floor. "But we don't know how to cwean the mess."

This time Abby stepped in. "I'll go and get a broom and a dustpan."

All three pair of eyes swung in her direction. Make that four counting the gentleman in the perfectly pressed suit.

Harrison rose, clasped his sons' hands, and held one at each side. "I'm sorry about the plant. I'll have my valet, Staimes, here—" he glanced over to the distinguished gentleman standing feet away from him, then back at her "—find another one and replace it."

Abby brushed her hand in a dismissing wave. "No,

no. That won't be necessary. It's just a plant. No harm done." She smiled down at the boys. "I'll be right back with the broom, and then if your father doesn't mind, I'll show you how to clean up the mess. All right?" Her gaze slid to his.

He nodded and mouthed, "Thank you."

With a quick brisk to her walk, she made her way into the kitchen, grabbed a broom and a dustpan from the closet and hurried back to them.

After she finished patiently showing Josiah and Graham how to clean up the mess, she eyed each child. "You did a lovely job, boys."

Their faces beamed, and little chests puffed out.

"You sure did," Harrison added. "I'm proud of you two." He glanced over at his valet standing by the door, stiff as a statue. "Staimes, can you handle the boys for a few minutes?"

The valet's brows yanked upward, then dropped into a V. He glanced down at them, then back up at Harrison. Fear and desperation blinked through the man's eyes.

"It's only for a few minutes. You'll do fine."

Staimes didn't look convinced, but he gave a curt nod and stepped forward.

Harrison handed the children over to him, making sure the man had a hold of their hands before letting go. "Boys, do not let go of Staimes's hands. If you do, Daddy will have to discipline you. Do you understand?"

They lowered their eyes and nodded.

"Very well, then. I'll be right back." He looked at Abby. "I need to speak with you, if you will."

"Is everything all right?"

He led her to the far end of the main room, opposite of where the children were, and stopped. "I'm sorry, but I have to leave. Miss Elderberry, the boys' nanny, quit, and I have no one to watch my sons. I'm going to have to find a replacement nanny as soon as possible."

Abby struggled with what to do. She wanted to offer to let the children come with him, but being around them on a daily basis would be too hard. Knowing just how hard it would be for her, after much contemplation, she decided to instead offer to help him find a nanny. "If you'd like, I could help you." Then as an afterthought, she added, "Until you find one, I'll see if Zoé would mind watching them for you. She's very good with children."

"So was Miss Elderberry. But Staimes said she couldn't handle these two any longer, that they were just too rambunctious for her."

"How long was she with you?"

"Two months."

"Two months!"

"Yes. She stayed longer than the last nanny. Miss Rothman lasted only two weeks."

"Two weeks?" There she was parroting him again.

"Yes. Mrs. Fairchild, the one before Miss Rothman, stayed the longest, which was four months." He ran his hand over and under his chin. "I don't know what to do. I've tried every form of discipline, but they have so much energy. If they aren't fighting, they're destroying things." His focus shifted to where the plant had spilled.

"Don't you worry about that plant. As for the boys, do they get out much? I mean, do they have a place to burn off all that energy? And are they fed a lot of sweets?"

"No. None of the nannies took them out very often because they were just too much of a handful for them. As for the sweets, I don't know about them other than the desserts they had after dinner." His brows furrowed.

"Come to think of it, Staimes did say that Miss Elderberry mentioned how bribing them with sweets hadn't worked, so…" He let his sentence hang.

"I could always tell when my nephews and nieces were given too much sugar. They'd talked a mile a minute and couldn't stand still for a minute. My brothers finally gave the boys chores to do, and their wives cut down the amount of sugar they consumed and started planning more activities for them during the day."

"What kind of activities?"

"Well, in the summer, they took them fishing and on long hikes where they explored some of the hidden caves on the ranch and studied different species of animals and rocks. Stuff like that. A lot of times, they just went for a long walk through the woods. In the winter, they'd play games or have treasure hunts in the house. A lot of times they were outside building snowmen, or going for sleigh rides."

"Weren't they worried about them getting sick being out in the cold so long?"

"No. In fact, I think children that play outside are healthier than ones who stay indoors all the time. We, my siblings and I, were always outside doing something. Whether it be chores or riding horses or playing in the dirt and snow. We went on a lot of picnics, too. A lot of times, Mother would sit on the bank while we played in the stream. Honestly, most of the time we worked. There was so much to do on the ranch that we all had assigned chores. I was so glad when they hired more hands to help. I hated cleaning the chicken coop."

"Somehow I can't picture you cleaning chicken coops."

"Oh, but I did. And much worse, too." She wrinkled

her nose at the memory of mucking the pig barn and horse corrals.

"I don't live on a ranch and never have, so I'll have to see what else I can come up with for them to do. But first, I need to find a nanny. And right away, before they get into any more trouble."

As if on cue, a loud crash sounded at the opposite end of the room.

"Oh, no," Harrison groaned and quickly made haste toward his boys.

Abby followed.

Pooled in the middle of the floor was a shattered drinking glass amid a puddle of milk.

"I'm sorry, Mr. Kingsley. It was my fault. I dropped the glass." Staimes's words came out rushed.

Harrison's eyebrows spiked. "You're responsible for this mess?"

"Yes, sir. The maid brought the boys some milk and cookies. I was trembling so bad that they slipped out of my hand." The blushing look on the poor man's face was so comical that Abby couldn't help herself. She covered her mouth with her hand and tittered.

Harrison and Staimes gawked at her. That, too, was comical, and she wanted to laugh even harder, but she quickly suppressed it so as to not stun the men even further. But on the inside, she was roaring.

Lunch had been a complete and utter disaster. Harrison wanted to find the nearest rock and crawl under it. Once again, Graham and Josiah had made a mess of things. He shouldn't have let Abby talk him into staying for the noon meal. Instead, he should have been out searching for another nanny.

Did they even have nannies in Hot Mineral Springs?

Before he decided to stay and help Abby arrange the furniture that would be delivered within the hour, Harrison had tried to talk Staimes into taking the boys for the afternoon, but his valet surprised him by threatening to quit. Harrison knew he wouldn't, but he also knew that's how frightened Staimes was of watching the children. The man wasn't much on taking on young wards. Besides, Staimes wasn't just his valet, but his only true friend.

He had to admit he'd been relieved when Abby had asked Zoé to watch them for a few hours. The woman was only too happy to, which gave Harrison some peace. Still, he wondered what they were doing right now and if they were minding the woman.

"Don't worry." Abby's hand settled on his arm. "Zoé loves children, and like I said, she's very good with them."

"How did you know what I was thinking?"

"It wasn't hard to figure out. You kept going to the window and looking outside."

"For all you know, I could have been watching for Fletcher."

"True, but you haven't stopped pacing since Zoé took them. And I seriously doubt that you have reason to be nervous about my furniture."

He smiled down at her. "You got me there."

"Would you feel better if I went and checked on them?"

"Would you?" He sent her his most hopeful look, and Abby grinned in return.

"I'll be right back." She scuttled out of the room.

As soon as she disappeared, he realized that he should've gone and checked on them himself instead of letting Abby do it. He hated to admit it, but as much as he loved his sons, sometimes they were even too rambunctious for him, and spending too much time around them made him nervous. What kind of father was he that his own sons made him edgy?

Minutes later, Abby returned.

Harrison turned anxious eyes on her and met her at the doorway. "Well?" His breathing halted while he waited for her answer.

"They're fine. They're having the time of their lives."

He released an audible sigh.

Abby giggled. A sound he enjoyed.

"What are they doing?"

"Playing in the mud."

"They're what?" His voice came out louder than he'd meant it to.

"Relax. Zoé found some old clothes up in the attic. They're wearing them and having a grand time playing out by the water pump. Don't worry. She'll clean them up before she brings them inside."

Relax? How could he? A Kingsley never played in the mud or dirt. Father would never stand for that. It was too low of a thing to do. But then again, his father wasn't here. And unlike him, his boys would enjoy their childhood, and do the things he'd never been allowed to do. Like play in the mud—something he had to go and see for himself. "Would you show me where they are?"

That brought out one second of uncertainty in her soft face. "Sure."

Side by side they stood at the back door. His heart smiled, hearing his children's laughter and seeing them having so much fun. In between bouts of adding another layer to what he assumed was a mud castle, a rather lopsided one at that, he watched his sons toss mud in the air and follow it with their eyes until it landed. The urge to join them was strong. But his deeply embedded upbringing prevented him from doing so. Besides, the furniture would be delivered any minute now.

He stepped back out of the doorway and looked at Abby.

Her smile was infectious, and so were the laughing blue eyes she turned up at him. "I told you they were having fun."

"That you did. That you did." He chuckled, and she joined him.

Together they headed back to the front part of the house.

Harrison hadn't felt this carefree or this good ever, and he had Abby to thank for that.

Abby. She was one special woman. A woman he could easily attach himself to if he wasn't careful. Careful, he would be. In the meantime, however, he was no fool. He would enjoy every precious moment of the time he had with her before he had to head back to Boston and leave her behind. That thought caused a hitch in his chest. And that was not good. Not good at all.

The instant Abby saw Fletcher's wagons pull up in front of her house, her heart skipped, and she felt like a child at Christmastime. She always loved Christmas, watching her nieces and nephews opening their gifts and searching for hidden treasures that she and her siblings would hide all over her mother's house.

Abby rushed to the door and flung it open.

"You aren't anxious or anything, are you?" Humor brushed through Harrison's voice as he came and stood behind her.

She glanced back at him. "No. No. Not at all. Why do you ask?" She sent him a playful smirk.

"No reason." He sent her one back before he removed his jacket and hung it up. When he rolled up his shirt sleeves, she noticed the rock-solid muscle that had been hidden underneath them. She wondered what it would be like to be held and to be protected by those arms.

Stop it, she silently reprimanded herself. *You've been reading too many romance novels.* Harrison wasn't some knight riding up on his white steed to sweep her away and to defend her against the forces of evil. Then Mr. Prinker and the committee members faces popped into her mind. On second thought, maybe he was. She muffled a giggle.

"Miss Abigail Bowen, if you will let me by, I will go and help them. That way you'll get your furniture much faster."

"Oh, indeed, I shall let you by, Mr. Harrison Kingsley," she said with a dramatic flare and using her imitation of a British accent. Abby stepped out of his way and let him by.

He met Fletcher just as he hopped down from the wagon he'd ridden in on.

Seeing Harrison and Fletcher side by side, she noticed they both had wide shoulders and trim waists. Fletcher's physique, however, was lankier than Harrison's.

Both had powerful arms. Very powerful arms, if the bulge in their muscles when they hoisted the dresser out of the wagon was any indication.

Both were very handsome. Harrison especially, whose grayish-blue eyes had that unique hazel half-moon, and whose hair resembled the color of pecans. Yum. She loved pecans.

Fletcher's eyes, on the other hand, were the color of molasses, and his hair, a ginger-blond.

Both were tall, Fletcher a bit taller than Harrison, too tall for her taste. She preferred Harrison's height.

With one on each end of the dresser, Harrison and Fletcher turned and headed toward her, ending her comparisons.

Movement behind them yanked her attention to it. A little girl, clutching her doll, followed them closely behind.

"Where do you want this, Abby?"

"Oh." She blinked and stepped out of their way. "Um. Uh. Follow me." She glanced back at the pretty little girl with the ebony hair and whose brown eyes were like her father's, and smiled.

"That's my daughter, Julie," Fletcher answered her unvoiced question.

One of Julie's shoulders rose, her eyelids lowered and her thumb went to her mouth.

"Hello, Julie. I'm Abby. It's nice to meet you."

The girl never looked up.

"Can you say hello to Miss Abby?"

Ebony curls swung with the shake of her head.

Fletcher shrugged his apology to Abby, then the two men moved forward.

Abby rushed ahead of them and on up the steps, glancing back down at the lovely child who continued to follow her father like a puppy.

Upstairs in her bedroom, they placed the dresser where she wanted it, and then headed back downstairs. Before the little girl could follow them outside, Abby called her. "Julie. Would you like some cookies and milk?"

Julie's eyes widened. She looked over at her father.

"Yes, you may."

"There are two little boys outside who I'm sure would like some, too. Shall we go see?"

The child gave a quick nod.

She quickly instructed Fletcher and Harrison where she wanted the pieces to go before extending her hand out to Julie.

Julie nestled her small hand into Abby's, both warming and saddening Abby's heart with the gesture. But Abby refused to feel sorry for herself and instead wanted to do her best to ease the shy girl's discomfort. As they headed to the kitchen, she wondered where Julie's mother was. Without asking the child directly, she decided to inquire in a roundabout way. "That's a beautiful doll you have there. What's her name?"

No response.

Well, that didn't work. She'd try something else. "Does she look like your mama?"

Julie hiked a shoulder.

That didn't work, either. Abby wasn't about to give up, though. "Does your mama have pretty brown hair like your dolly does?"

Julie's only response, another hiked shoulder.

Not knowing what else to say to get the little girl to open up to her, Abby decided to drop the subject. She refused to ask the girl outright and risk upsetting her.

A few steps from the kitchen, Abby barely heard the little girl when she finally spoke, "My mama left us."

"What do you mean she left you?"

"She took sick and left us. Mama lives with Jesus now." Sorrow covered her face and warbled through her tiny voice.

Abby stopped and squatted until she was eye level with the child. "Oh, honey. I'm sorry your mama is gone. Do you remember her at all?"

Her curls bounced as she nodded her head. "She was pretty. Like you. Only her hair looked like mine. Papa says I look like her." Her eyes brightened and her tiny lips curled upward.

"Was she as sweet as you?"

"Uh-huh." Her head nodded slowly. "She used to make me cookies and give me milk."

"She did? Well, let's see if we have some cookies like your mama used to make, shall we?"

"Uh-huh," she said with a passel of exuberance.

Abby stood. Through the dining room window, she caught a glimpse of Harrison's boys, still playing and having a grand old time, something they needed desperately. Not wanting to interrupt that, and knowing Zoé would feed them when they were finished playing, she decided not to bother them.

Together, hand in hand, she and Julie walked into the kitchen. Cinnamon and apple, along with yeasty bread, floated in the air.

Bent over the open oven door, Veronique drew out a pan of cookies, turned around and screeched when she saw them. The pan of cookies nearly flew from her hand. "You gave me such a fright, *mademoiselle*."

Abby giggled. "I'm sorry, Veronique. I didn't mean to." She turned her attention on to Julie. "Julie, this is Miss Veronique Denis. Veronique, this is Miss Julie Martin."

"'Tis a pleasure to meet you." Veronique curtsied, and Julie tried to mimic her but it came out rather awkward.

"Nice to meet you, too, Miss Dee—" she paused, frowning "—Miss Dee-niece." She smiled, rather pleased with herself that she'd pronounced Veronique's last name correctly.

"Should we see if Miss Denis's cookies are anything like your mama's?"

Julie nodded, sending her curls bouncing yet again. "What kind do we have today?"

"Oatmeal. With apple chunks and walnuts," Veronique replied.

Julie tugged on Abby's skirt and cupped her hand. Abby leaned down and the girl spoke in her ear, "She talks funny."

Abby whispered back into her ear loud enough so that Veronique could hear. "She sure does talk funny. That's because she's from France." Abby winked at Veronique, who tried to look upset but failed.

"Where's France?" Julie asked.

"It's way across the ocean. A long ways away from here."

"Oh," was all Julie said.

Abby grabbed two glasses and two plates from off the shelf and set them on the table while Veronique retrieved the milk from the cellar. After the glasses were filled with milk, she settled Julie on the sturdiest one of the kitchen chairs, and sat down to join her. "Veronique, would you like to join us?"

"No, thank you, *mademoiselle*. I have to finish the bread." She smiled at Abby and Julie and turned back to the wad of dough on the breadboard counter.

Julie slid from her chair and turned two chairs sideways. She climbed back on her chair and looked over at each one. "Bobby and Billy need cookies and milk, too."

Abby didn't mean to but she stared at the little girl. "Are Bobby and Billy your imaginary friends?"

Julie frowned. "No. You said two boys might like to join us. When I didn't see them, I thought you invited my brothers, Bobby and Billy."

Before she could stop them, Abby's eyes went wide. "You have brothers?"

She shook her head and the sadness was back. "Not anymore. They live with Jesus now, too."

Abby couldn't believe her ears. This little girl and her father had lost so much. She was surrounded by people who had endured more heartache than anyone should ever have to.

Abby's thoughts went to Harrison's sons. "Were your brothers twins?"

Julie's curls wiggled as she shook her head. "Bobby was ten and Billy was eight. I'm four." She held up four small fingers.

Same age as Harrison's sons.

"Bobby and Billy went fishin' when they weren't 'pose to. Papa said they fell in the pond and drownaded." Julie tilted her head. "What is drownaded?" Julie looked at Abby with expectant eyes.

Abby peered over at Veronique. Veronique turned the palms of her hands upward, pinched her lips and shook her head. With a look of empathy, she turned back to kneading her bread dough.

How on earth was Abby going to answer that one?

"Julie, are you being a good girl for Miss Abby?" Much to Abby's relief, Fletcher chose that moment to step inside the kitchen. Harrison was right behind him.

Harrison looked at the table and then at the empty chairs. "Where's Graham and Josiah?"

"Who's Jos—Jos. Who's Sigha and Grrahm?" Julie asked.

"My sons."

Julie looked over at Abby.

"They're the two boys I told you about, Julie. But they were having so much fun playing in the mud, I didn't have the heart to bother them," she said more for Harrison's sake than Julie's.

Julie wrinkled her nose. "I don't like mud." She looked over at the empty chairs and shook her tiny finger. "Billy. Bobby. Don't you go playin' in the mud, or you won't get any cookies."

"Billy? Bobby?" Fletcher's voice caught, his face paled. His gaze swung to Abby's, then back to his daughter.

Abby didn't know what to say or do. All she knew was she suddenly felt very uncomfortable. This was a conversation between father and daughter, not her, or anyone else. She sent Harrison a silent look to get her out of this situation.

"Abby, do you have time to show me how you want the parlor furniture situated?"

She pressed her palms on the table and rose quickly. "I'll be happy to." Abby glanced at Veronique, who worked her dough faster and harder than necessary. She tossed the huge lump into a bowl and covered it with the decorative, empty flour sack they'd washed and now used for a towel. With a quick glance at Abby, she rushed from the room.

Her focus slid to Julie, who seemed completely oblivious to the awkward atmosphere in the room. Julie took a drink of her milk and a bite of her cookie, swinging her legs crossed at the ankle as if all was right in the world.

Abby then turned her attention onto Fletcher. As if he understood her discomfort, he walked to the table and sat in the chair she'd just vacated. "Hurry up and finish your milk and cookies, sweetheart, so Papa can finish unloading the rest of the furniture."

That was the last words she heard as she and Harrison left the kitchen together. More upset than she'd been in a long time, she wondered how much more her heart could take, and why God was allowing so many children to cross her path. And not just any children, either, but motherless ones. Didn't He know how hard this was on her? And didn't He care? At that moment, the urge to scream at God, to kick something, to punch something, bombarded her until she thought her heart would burst from the overflow of pain attacking it. She brushed at a tear that had slipped out. *Why, God, why?*

"Are you all right, Abby?" Harrison asked from beside her.

She stiffened, remembering that she wasn't alone. She drew in a long breath and forced a smile onto her face before looking up at him. "I'm fine."

Harrison narrowed his eyes. "Sure you are. Care to talk about it?"

"Nothing to talk about," she answered with a fake lilt to her voice.

"If you say so."

She hadn't fooled him, but neither did she want to talk about it. David had made it perfectly clear that a woman who couldn't bear children wasn't a desirable woman, much less a human being.

While she knew that she and Harrison would never be anything more than business acquaintances, she didn't want him to know she was one of those undesirable women. It would change everything, and she rather liked that he treated her with respect. As if she were really someone. Since he would be leaving in a few months' time, he need never know the truth about her. She would enjoy the fantasy she had created in her mind just a little longer.

Chapter Seven

The way things had gone the day before, Harrison couldn't wait to get to Abby's house to see if she really was all right. All afternoon she had been quiet, subdued even. Every time he had inquired about it, she plastered on that same phony smile and acted as if everything was fine. Well, she hadn't fooled him. Not one little bit.

Unlike Boston, the June mornings here were nippy. One would think because of the high altitude and being that much closer to the sun that it would be warm, but that was not the case. Not that he'd experienced so far in the few days he'd been here.

He made his way down the winding, steep incline toward town. A chipmunk darted out in front of him, followed in hot pursuit by another. Birds sang in the pine and aspen trees that surrounded the road like tall pillars. Gnats swarmed the air just several yards ahead in front of him. All of this he found enchanting. This place was nothing like Boston.

The day before, he had rented a furnished, fourteen-room house up in the trees on the side of the mountain from a sweet elderly lady who was thrilled to know someone would be living in it, even if it was only for three months.

He'd been fortunate to hear from Lucy at her diner that Mrs. Morrison was looking to rent her place. Lucy had also informed him that the woman had taken a smaller house in town because with her age, it was just too hard in the winter to travel the half mile up the trees. Didn't seem that far to him. But then again, he wasn't an old woman living alone, either.

"Siah. That mine." Graham's voice shattered Harrison's thoughts. He yanked his gaze down at his sons sitting next to him in the buggy and at the carved Indian in question.

"Na-uh. It mine." Josiah yanked the wooden toy from Graham's hand.

"Josiah, give that back to Graham. You have the cowboy. You can't have them both. You boys need to learn to share."

"But I want Indian. Gam can have cowboy."

"Which one did you bring? The cowboy or the Indian?" he asked, not understanding why when they each had a cowboy and an Indian that they didn't bring both of them so they wouldn't fight.

Josiah dropped his head. "The Indian."

"Well, if that's what you brought, then you need to give Graham back his cowboy."

Josiah pursed his lips and his brows puckered.

"Now, Josiah."

The cowboy smacked against the palm of Graham's hand when Josiah grudgingly handed it over to him. He crossed his arms and protruded his lips in a pout. For a brief moment, Harrison closed his eyes and let out a sigh of frustration.

Both the cowboy and the Indian had been carved to

straddle the wooden carved horses they'd brought with them. Did the difference between the Indian headdress and the cowboy hat matter that much to his boys? A toy was a toy as far as Harrison was concerned. Then again, he'd never had to share any of his. What little he'd had as a child, anyway.

Harrison swatted a horse fly that had plagued them persistently on their journey down the mountain to Abby's house.

He hated having to bring his sons to work. Over the past eight months or so, he'd had to do just that a few times because his nannies had resigned. Make that more like making a hasty retreat with only a moment's notice. All he could do now was hope that someone would answer the ad he and Staimes had placed on the bulletin boards all around town late yesterday afternoon. And answer it soon.

"Whoa." He brought the horse to a stop in front of Abby's mansion.

Josiah leaped off his seat and took a giant step.

Harrison grabbed a handful of the back of his shirt. "Where do you think you're going, young man? Sit down."

Indecision tumbled across Josiah's face.

"Now." Harrison used his sternest voice, and it worked. "You will be spending time with Miss Denis this morning. I want you to mind what she says. If I hear any report that either of you have misbehaved, you will be disciplined. Do you boys understand?"

They both nodded.

"Very well. Now, wait there until I come around and get you."

Harrison helped them down. Grasping their hands in his, the three of them walked up the steps to the front door. He raised the lion-head door knocker and tapped it thrice.

Seconds later, the door swung open. "Good morning." Abby's voice was bright and cheery and her smile appeared genuine, unlike the day before. Relieved to see her doing better, his own lips curled upward.

Her gaze went down to his boys. "How are Josiah and Graham doing this morning?" She squatted down and studied the toys in their hands. "What do we have here? A cowboy and an Indian? Oh, and horses, too. What are their names?"

"My horsey's name is Little Eagle and this is Big Feather." Josiah held up his wooden Indian. "Daddy helped name 'em." His son smiled up at him.

"My horsey is Bucky. And my cowboy—" he held up the cowboy for her to see "—is named Daddy." Graham tucked the cowboy to his chest, but his eyes were fixed on Harrison. "I name it Daddy 'cause I love my daddy."

Harrison's heart melted and swelled with love for his sons. There wasn't anything he wouldn't do for either one of them.

"Well, I think your father and you two boys did a fine job of naming them." She turned those smiling eyes of hers up at him, and theirs locked for a brief but meaningful moment. "Now, shall we go inside? Miss Denis has lots of fun activities planned for you this morning. Are you ready to have some fun?"

Their eyes brightened, and they both nodded.

"Very well, then. Shall we?" She rose and offered each of them a hand. Graham and Josiah slipped their hands into hers, and they preceded him inside. How well the twins looked with her. As if they were a family. That thought stopped him cold. They weren't a family. And never would be. She had her life here, and he had his back in Boston. Love, and especially marriage, were not on his agenda here.

The night before while lying in bed, as she had so many times in the past, Abby struggled with her feelings of unfairness about how she could never bear a child of her own. She confessed her anger and asked God's forgiveness for it and for her poor attitude concerning the whole thing. Josiah, Graham and Julie were all delightful children, and even though they were a painful reminder of what she could never have, right now they needed her, of that she was certain. So, putting her own feelings aside, she would be there for them as much as possible.

Making sure the boys were settled in with Zoé instead of going to the parlor as was their usual routine, Abby led Harrison to her office. The day before, before the furniture was delivered, Colette had cleaned it from top to bottom.

When she and Harrison stepped inside, she stopped and gazed up at him, wondering what he thought of the furnished room they would be sharing for three months. "Well, what do you think? It looks quite lovely with the new furniture, does it not?"

She followed his perusal of the room. The dark-stained oak desk with the three squares of a lighter shade of oak in the front and on each side outlined with a gold, leafy vine design looked regal in the bright, airy room. The three floor-to-ceiling, matching cabinets behind it and the matching bookshelf alongside the massive desk added to its appeal.

The sculptured oak chair with the black, padded-leather seat and arm rests behind the desk reminded her of Queen Anne furniture, as did the two chairs situated in front and off to the side of the desk. Only they were padded with a burgundy and gold material that resembled hundreds of miniature checker game boards.

A blue, gold and burgundy Victorian rug, one of the few perfectly salvageable pieces that had been left behind, the two new carved burgundy bench settees, cream-colored sofa, two end tables and the coffee table that matched the desk filled the other side of the office.

Knowing he'd finished viewing the whole room, she looked up at him with eager anticipation.

"Very nice, Abby. I fear, however, that it makes my office back home look quite shabby. I must say, you have excellent, excellent taste in decor."

Abby beamed under his praise. "How very kind of you to say so. Thank you." She clasped her hands together. "Well, would you like some coffee or tea while we wait for Fletcher to arrive with our bid?"

"No, thank you. But if you do, please do not let me stop you."

"I'm fine. I thought while we were waiting that we could start putting together our order for the things we will need for the business."

"Very well."

Abby grabbed everything she needed and motioned for Harrison to sit on the sofa. They went over everything they needed and had the list almost completed when Colette entered the room. "Excuse me, *mademoiselle,* but Mr. Martin is here to see you."

"Thank you, Colette. Send him in."

"*Oui,* Miss Abby."

Abby smiled at how formal Colette, Veronique and Zoé were in the presence of others. Even though she'd told them they didn't have to be, and that they were family, she had to admit, it made her feel as if they respected her—something she found quite nice.

Fletcher stepped into the room. "Morning." Was it just her or did she detect apprehension in his voice and on his face?

Harrison stood and the two men shook hands.

"I wonder if I might have a word with you before we begin," Fletcher asked Harrison.

That surprised Abby. What could the two men possibly have to talk about that didn't include her? Well, whatever it was, it was none of her business. Or was it? Did it have something to do with the Royal Grand Theater, the name she'd finally decided on? Whatever it was, if they wanted her to know, they'd tell her. No sense in getting fidgety over something that may or may not have anything to do with her or the business.

Harrison glanced down at her with a question on his face, too. Best not to read anything into that, either. "Excuse me, Abby. We'll be right back."

Abby rose. "No, you gentlemen stay here. I'll run and get us something to drink. It's warming up outside rather fast. Would either of you care for some cool tea?"

They both liked that idea, so she scurried out of the room, retrieved the tea from the cool cellar and headed back to the office. Two feet away from the door, she overheard, "I don't know how to break the news to her."

What news? She stood outside the door, waiting and listening to see if they would say more, but their voices were too low, so she stepped into the office and set the beverage tray on the coffee table. "Here you go, gentlemen." She handed each of them a glass. "Would either of you like sugar or lemon in your drink?" Both declined. After adding lemon and sugar to hers, she sat down beside Harrison. "Shall we get down to business? Do you have your bid ready?"

Fletcher and Harrison exchanged a look, a rather disturbing one at that.

"Something's not right. What's going on? What's wrong?" Her stomach twisted into knots while waiting for them to answer.

"I want you to know—"

"Allow me." Harrison cut Fletcher off.

Fletcher nodded.

"Remember when we talked about the repairs and the cost?"

She swallowed, wondering just how much they were going to be. While she had plenty of money, she still had a lot to buy, and she didn't want to spend it all on this place. After all, she needed money to live on until the business took off. "Yes."

"There is no easy way to say this, I'm afraid. The repair costs are massive."

She tilted her head, furrowing her forehead. "I don't… I didn't see that much that needed fixing."

"To the untrained eye, there isn't. I mean no offense by that. But unless you were a carpenter, you wouldn't notice certain things."

"Like what?"

"Here, let me show you." Harrison handed her Fletcher's itemized bid.

Abby's eyes trailed down the long list of repairs. With each one her eyes grew. By the time she got to the bottom figure, her eyes had all but popped out of her head. The amount was ten times the amount she'd calculated they would be, but that wasn't what bothered her. She stood, walked over to the window and draped her arms around her waist.

Behind her, she heard Fletcher say he'd be back later. Without saying goodbye to him, she stared out the window.

Concerned for Abby, Harrison stepped up alongside her. "Are you all right?"

She gazed up at him. "I'm fine."

His eyes narrowed.

"All right. I admit it was quite a shock."

"I know it's an exorbitant amount. One you probably weren't expecting. Perhaps I can help." How, he didn't know. Until he received his inheritance, his funds were limited, and he couldn't even take out a loan at his bank.

"It's not about the money, it's about the time. All those repairs are going to take much longer than I expected. It's just disappointing is all. But—" she turned her beautiful face upward toward him "—God will take care of it. He always does. As far as I can tell, Fletcher's figures are reasonable considering all that needs fixed around here. I think we should hire him. What do you think?"

The woman amazed him. She'd just had a huge blow and yet here she was as bubbly as ever saying God would take care of it. Well, he hoped for her sake that her God did. "I think you're right."

"Wonderful." She clasped her hands together. "Then let's not delay another minute. Let's go find him and see when he can get started. The sooner he does, the better. What should we have him start on first?" Not waiting for his answer, she continued. "The upstairs can wait. We need to have him work on getting the foundation fixed first. Then... Oh, why don't we wait and see what he says? Then afterward, if you don't have plans, would you and the boys like to have lunch with me?" He had never met a woman that could talk as fast as she could. Her excitement was contagious.

"Mademoiselle," he imitated the three French sisters, "lead the way."

Abby laughed, a sound as pleasing and soothing as a fine musical instrument.

Without thinking it through, he reached for her hand and looped it through his arm. The connection sent a warmness flowing through him. He gazed down at her, wondering if she felt it, too.

Their eyes met and locked.

Since his coming here, this was the first time he had a strong urge to pull her into his arms and kiss her. He wondered what it would be like to love this woman who was beautiful both inside and out. What it would be like to… She blinked, breaking the connection, along with his trail of thoughts. Good thing. He couldn't entertain what it was like to be married to her. Nothing good could come from that kind of surmising.

"Did anyone ever tell you that you have very unique eyes?"

It was his turn to blink. Where had that come from? And is that why she was staring at him? That it had nothing to do with the connection he'd felt? Why that idea disappointed him, he had no idea, but it did, nevertheless. Brushing it aside, he answered, "Yes. I've been told that before. Has anyone ever told you that you do?" *Watch it buddy, you're flirting with trouble.*

She tilted her head, and her perfectly shaped brows curled into an S. "Mine aren't unique."

"Oh, but they are. They're always smiling."

"Huh? What do you mean?"

"Even when you aren't smiling, you're eyes appear to be. They're very beautiful, you know?" *And so are you.* But that last part he didn't voice out loud. Best to keep that to himself, as it was too personal of a thing to say to a single woman, and could very easily be misconstrued as more than the simple compliment it was meant to be. "Shall we go?" He changed the subject.

Harrison arrived at Abby's minutes earlier than what had been discussed the day before. Zoé met him at the door, and after leaving his sons with her, he made his way into the parlor. He stepped into the room, and his heart jumped to his throat. There Abby was, standing precariously on a rickety ladder, leaning over the fireplace mantel at an angle, holding a huge picture.

"Abby, what are you doing? You're going to hurt yourself," he said, rushing toward her.

Abby jerked her head in his direction, and when she did, her body yanked with it. The ladder flew out from under her and the picture went crashing to the ground along with the ladder. Her arms shot out but not before her head whacked against the corner of the mantel. Harrison caught her right before she landed on the hearth. With her still in his arms, he asked, "What on earth were you doing up there on that thing?" His blood pounded hard into his ears.

"What do you mean, what was I doing? What did it look like I was doing? I was hanging a picture." Her blond hair covered one side of her face.

"That's a good way to get yourself hurt."

"I was doing just fine until you came in and scared me half to death," she puffed.

She had a point there. It was his fault she'd fallen. Still, one look at the rotten ladder and he knew it was only a matter of time before that thing collapsed.

Abby yanked her head with a quick jerk to the side

and winced. She reached up and brushed the hair away from her face. Her fingertips patted at her forehead. When she pulled them back, they were coated with blood.

"You're bleeding."

"It appears that way, yes."

"Let me see that."

"No need. I'll be fine." She tried to get up, but he sat on the hearth and settled her onto his lap.

"Mr. Kingsley, this is highly improper." She arranged her purple day dress by tugging its skirt to where it hung farther over her ankles.

"Hang propriety. Right now I'm concerned about that knot on your head and the blood dripping down your forehead." He pulled out his handkerchief and pressed it over the wound, making her wince away from it.

"You're ruining your monogrammed handkerchief. And, *I* care about my reputation even if you do not."

"What? Who said I didn't care about your reputation?"

She glanced at the way he held her nestled on his lap, then at the parlor door, then back at him again with one raised pointy eyebrow.

She was right. The way he was holding her could easily be misconstrued. "I see your point." He laid her hand over the handkerchief, quickly shifted her off his lap and stood.

He helped her up and led her over to the couch. "Sit."

Her small hand perched at her waist. "Sit? Excuse me? Do I look like a dog to you?"

"A dog? You? Well, if you are, you're a very cute one." He laughed, but she didn't join him. Realizing how that must've sounded, his laughter died in his throat. "I didn't mean to imply that you were a dog. I only meant…" Good-night, how did he get himself into these messes, anyway? "I mean you'd make a cute dog. Not that I think you look like one or anything. I just meant…" He clamped his mouth shut, deciding he'd better hush up before he buried himself even further into the hole he'd already dug for himself.

Her nostrils expanded, her lips twitched. "Gotcha!" Laughter bubbled out of her. "You should have seen the look on your face when you thought I was upset with you. I knew what you meant, but it was fun watching you try to talk your way out of it."

"Ha-ha. Very funny. I'm not amused." His lips compressed into a thin line, and he crossed his arms over his chest.

"Oh, don't be so stuffy. Lighten up," she said, giving a quick flip of her hand. "I'm just teasing you."

He continued to scowl at her.

"Look, I was only—"

"Gotcha!" He smiled and uncrossed his arms.

Her mouth fell open. Then as if she finally caught on, her lips curled in that cute way that made her eyes smile, too. "You got me a good one, and I deserved it, too."

When they stopped laughing, Harrison's eyes caught sight of the blood-soaked cloth.

"We'd better take care of that." He pointed to her forehead.

"Oh, right. I was having so much fun, I forgot about it."

He was, too. Fun was something he didn't experience much. It felt nice. Something he could get used to.

Abby enjoyed the easy camaraderie with Harrison. Who knew under that business suit lay a man with a sense of humor? An extremely attractive man at that.

He leaned over and removed the cloth from her forehead. Fingers light and gentle brushed the hair from around the wound. She peered up at him, his eyes intently glued to her forehead.

Her attention dropped to his chin, a firm, chiseled, neatly shaven one. A combination of bay rum, cinnamon, nutmeg, cloves and orange, a very enthralling aftershave fragrance on a very intoxicating man, floated around him.

Her eyes slid upward to his bottom lip, soft and not too full, but not thin, either. Her vision climbed to his upper lip. What would it feel like to be kissed by those perfectly shaped lips, and to feel the passion of the man behind that masculine mouth and tender heart?

Daydreams of what it would be like acted out in her mind like a romantic scene from a play, and she allowed them to.

Harrison wrapped his arms around her, pulling her close, their hearts beat to the tune of a single drum. Her knees weakened as he dipped his head until his lips were but only a breath away from her own. His gorgeous eyes connected with hers, seeking permission to kiss her.

"May I?"

Abby's eyes darted open. "May you what?" She blinked.

"May I have permission to doctor your wound?"

To doctor my... Uh. Oh. Jolted back to reality, she relaxed, relieved that Harrison hadn't been privy to her romantic thoughts, because if he had, he would hightail it back to Boston quicker than a jackrabbit fleeing a fox. "Have you done much doctoring?"

His mouth and brow quirked sideways. "I have two sons. What do you think?"

Abby chuckled. "I think that I'm in very good hands. How bad is it, anyway?" Growing up on a ranch, she'd encountered many a cut and bruise. Some a whole lot worse than this one, and she had survived. Other than a throbbing headache, a bit of dizziness and a slightly blood-soaked handkerchief, how bad could this one be?

"It's not bad." The man had impeccable timing. As if he could read her thoughts. Now that was a frightening thought. Especially with all the daydreams she had conjured up about him. "Just a little cut that doesn't need stitches or anything. But still, it does need to be cleaned and bandaged to keep infection out."

"I'll go and fetch my medicine bag." She started to rise, but his hand gently pressed down on her shoulder, forcing her in the gentlest of ways to be seated.

Their eyes met as they seemed to do so many times.

"Oh, forgive me. I didn't mean to interrupt anything."

Abby's gaze flew to the door.

Fletcher turned to leave.

"Don't go, Fletcher. You didn't interrupt anything."

Fletcher's eyes drifted to Harrison's hand still lingering on her shoulder.

She slouched her shoulder until Harrison's hand slipped away. "Oh. Yes. Well. You see. I hit my head on the mantel. I was just going to head to the kitchen to get my medicine bag, but Harrison stopped me. He insisted I stay put and that he go get it." She rushed out the words and glanced up at Harrison, who was looking at her as if to say, "Why are you explaining yourself to Fletcher?" Just why was she? Nothing was going on here. She had no reason to feel guilty. Well, all right, in a way she did because of her daydreams about the man. But no one knew about them except for her and God.

Flattening her hands on the sofa, she pushed herself up.

Pain pounded into her skull.

Stars twinkled in front of her.

Light pressure on her arm steered her back into a sitting position.

"Abby. Are you all right? You don't look very well."

"I'll run and fetch the doctor." That was Fletcher's voice she heard.

"No. No, that won't be necessary." The stars faded and light slowly replaced them. Harrison's face came into view first. Seeing his concern, she reassured him. "I'm fine. I just rose too quickly, is all."

"Fletcher. Go ahead and fetch a doctor for Miss Bowen."

Before Abby had a chance to stop him, Fletcher was gone. "Really. I'm fine." As if to prove it, she rose. Big mistake that turned out to be. The twinkling stars returned, then disappeared into the blackness that overtook her.

Chapter Eight

"Abby, Can you hear me?"

Abby turned her head toward the sound of Harrison's voice and slowly blinked her eyes open. "Harrison? What happened?"

"You fainted."

"I—I did?"

"Yes. Doctor Wilson is here to see you." Harrison moved from her view, and a handsome young man with blue-black hair and a thick matching mustache replaced him.

"I'm Doctor Wilson." He pulled a chair over in front of the sofa she lay on and sat down. "From what Mr. Kingsley here tells me, you hit your head pretty hard on that mantel. Is that correct?"

"Yes."

"Well, while you were out, I took a look at your cut. Harrison is right, it doesn't need stitches. I've already cleaned it and bandaged it. It appears you have a mild concussion. Therefore, I want you to rest today and to do nothing, especially anything strenuous."

Rest? Oh, no. There would be no resting for her. She had work to do. She shifted her legs off the settee and pushed herself into a sitting position. Her head throbbed and the blinking stars tried to return, but she drew in a long breath, forcing them into a hasty retreat. "Excuse me, Doctor, but I don't have time to rest. I have a business to tend to."

"*I* will tend to business. *You* will take care of yourself." Harrison's formidable tone had Abby's attention flouncing in his direction.

Excuse me? Who do you think you are ordering me about like that? You might be my business partner but you have no right to tell me what to do and to take over like that. She wanted to say the words out loud, but there was no way she would embarrass him in front of others, so she kept the thoughts to herself.

"Please, Abby?" He must have noticed the aggravation on her face. Noting his concern, her heart softened. He wasn't trying to be bossy; he was only troubled about her welfare.

Her frustration evaporated. "I'll try. But—" she held up her hand "—I'm not promising anything."

After leaving a few final instructions, the doctor left.

"Where's Fletcher?" she asked.

"He and his men are working on stabilizing the foundation."

"Oh. I see."

"As there is no immediate business to tend to right now, and as much as I hate to leave you, Abby, I must. I'll only be gone a short time, though. I have a couple of pressing errands to run, and then I'll be right back. In the meantime, however, I will leave strict instructions for no one to bother you if something does arise. I'll let them know where they can find me."

Reluctantly, she nodded.

He turned to go.

"Oh, before you leave." She sat up, wobbling with the effort. "I was wondering if you and the boys would like to come to church with me on Sunday. Then afterward, I thought we could have a picnic down by the river here in my backyard. Maybe the boys could do some fishing."

Harrison didn't answer right away. Had she been too forward? Did he read more into the invitation than what was there? "I thought I would invite Fletcher and Julie, too."

Still no answer.

"I'd love it if Staimes joined us. Colette, Veronique and Zoé will be there, too."

"I'm sure my valet would like that. And I'm sure the boys would enjoy it, too. Especially the fishing. Yes. Very well. We'll come." He sounded so formal about it all, but Abby decided not to dwell on that.

In fact, it was quite easy to push it out of her throbbing thoughts. "Wonderful. It's settled, then. You know where the church is, right? We drove by it on our way out to Fletcher's."

Harrison nodded as he spun his hat slowly in his hands. "I know where it is, but I'm afraid I won't be able to make it for services, so I'll just meet you here afterward."

"Oh. Okay." She wondered why he wouldn't make it to church but didn't ask. It was none of her business.

"Well, I'd better go. I hate to leave you, but this one pressing matter cannot be delayed. Promise me you'll rest like the doctor said to, all right?"

"I won't make promises I can't or don't plan on keeping. But I promise I will try my best. Fair enough?"

He sighed, gave a short nod and left.

Abby tossed a couple of decorative pillows onto the

settee and lowered herself onto its firm, yet soft, surface. She closed her eyes and tried to rest, but after forty minutes of shifting and trying to sleep, she gave up. Despite the fact her head still hurt, she decided to go see how Fletcher was coming along with the foundation. The sounds of work had been reverberating through the house most of the morning, so she knew they were, in fact, working hard.

Dry summer heat clothed her the second she stepped out the front door of her house. Rotten egg odor from the hot mineral springs hung in the air. She discovered she was getting used to the sulphur smell that was sometimes stronger than other times, so it didn't bother her nearly as badly as it used to.

One day, she'd take the time to go soak in the natural cave pool on her property to see what all the hoopla was over about bathing in the stinky water. Sure didn't make sense to her to bathe in something that directly afterward required a bath in order to remove the odorous water from a person's skin. What sense did that make?

She took a moment to stare at the magnificent mountain view across from her front door. One she never tired of. Hundreds of trees dotted it and the light blue sky outlining it made for a breathtaking backdrop.

Seconds later, she headed down the steps and rounded the corner. Knee-high weeds brushed against her skirt as she strolled through the perimeter of her yard. Unattended rose bushes created a fence barricade for the sorely neglected flower garden.

Potentilla and forsythia bushes smattered the yard. Along with white-and-yellow daisies, blue columbines, bluebells and another bright pink flower she couldn't identify. The tiered rock fountain was in need of a good scrubbing. She made a mental note to ask Fletcher if he knew of someone she could hire to rejuvenate the gardens. She would do it herself, but there was too much to do to get ready for the grand opening.

She went in search of Fletcher and found him and his men busy stacking rocks and bricks. Strong muscles flexed as Fletcher loaded his arms. Impressed with how much weight the man could carry, she watched him as he took them over to the pile with little effort. Before he caught her staring at him, she strolled over to him. "How are things coming along?"

Fletcher glanced over at her and smiled. He settled his burden, raised his hat and ran his sleeve over the sweat on his forehead. "It's a little too early to tell. But so far everything's going along pretty well."

"That's good to hear. Hey, I was wondering something. You wouldn't happen to know anyone around here with great gardening skills, would you? I need someone to turn this yard into the glorious garden I'm sure it once was."

Fletcher hooked his thumbs in his front pocket and looked around. "At one time, this place and this garden was the nicest one around these here parts." He rocked on the heels of his cowboy boots. "Sure was a shame to ride by and see it so run-down. But I'll tell you who can have it restored to its former glory in no time, and that would be Mr. Samuel Hilliard. He loves working in gardens. Matter of fact, he used to work for the folks that owned this place."

"Who does he work for now?"

"No one. Not much use for a gardener around here. He does odd jobs for folks around town just so he can stay living here. In fact, if I remember rightly, I heard he just finished a job and was looking for work. So he might be available."

Abby clasped her hands together against her chest. "Wonderful. How can I get a hold of him?"

"I can take you there during lunch if you'd like."

"Oh, yes. Yes. I would like that very much. Thank you." They stood there for a moment, neither saying a word. Finally, Abby spoke. "Would you and your men like something cold to drink?"

"That would be very nice. Thank you. I'm sure my men could stand a break. Lugging rocks and bricks is hard work."

With those arms, it shouldn't be too hard for him, but she wouldn't voice that. Hogwash rules of propriety prevented a woman from expressing those kinds of compliments. "Very well, I'll be right back."

"Wait. Harrison said you were supposed to be resting. Why don't you let me go and get it?"

"Nonsense. I can handle it."

"That's what Harrison said you'd say."

"Harrison said you'd say what?"

Abby whirled toward the sound of Harrison's voice and instantly regretted the fast shift. Her head swam in protest, but she would not let either of these men see her pain or the dizziness that was already lifting.

"That she could handle it," Fletcher answered with something between a grin and a grimace.

Harrison turned those stunning eyes of his on her. "You're supposed to be resting."

"I tried, but I couldn't sit still." Why was she answering to him about this, anyway?

Who was she kidding? She knew why she was. As much as she didn't want to, she liked having a man take charge and watch over her. She just better make sure she didn't get used to it was all. No harm in enjoying it while it lasted, though.

"That, I can believe. What were you doing that you weren't supposed to be doing?"

"I was just going to get these men something to drink, is all. I mean, really. That's not strenuous, and I'm more than capable of carrying a pitcher of fresh lemonade and four glasses. It's only a slight concussion, and the doctor said it only appeared that I had one. He wasn't even certain. Besides, if I didn't feel like I could do it, I wouldn't." That wasn't quite an accurate statement as she wasn't one to take things lying down. "I need something to keep me busy or I'll go mad. I thank you for your concern, but I'm going to go now and get those beverages."

Harrison caught up with her. "No. You won't. You go and sit down in the shade, and I'll go and get it."

A fleeting glance at the rickety bench that looked in worse shape than the ladder she'd fallen off earlier, and she wanted to laugh. Not used to taking orders, one glance at him, however, and she changed her mind. Yet again. The man had a way of affecting her like that. "Oh, all right. But don't think I'm always going to give in this easily." She shot him a serious, albeit teasing, smile.

"Trust me, I don't." He sent her a teasing smile of his own. "I'll be back." With that, he ducked into the house.

Abby headed over to the shade, but not the spot Harrison had indicated. Without a doubt, if he saw just how poor of shape that bench was in, he would have never asked her to sit there. Of course, there was no way he could tell that from a distance.

Underneath the large cottonwood tree, she found a grassy spot and sat down, fanning her skirt out around her.

Fletcher headed toward her.

She gazed up at him, but the sun shining directly behind him made it difficult to see his face, so she cupped her hand to shield her eyes. "Harrison is getting your drinks."

Fletcher moved until the sunlight no longer blinded her. She lowered her hand and settled it onto her lap.

"He didn't need to do that. My men and I would be just fine filling our canteens down at the river. The water's nice and cold there."

"I haven't tried the water from there yet. I was afraid it would taste like sulphur."

"It doesn't. The springs and the river aren't anywhere close to each other."

"Whew. That's good to know. I'll have to give it a try sometime. Oh, by the way, I'm having a picnic Sunday after church down by the river. Would you and Julie like to come? Harrison and his sons and Veronique and Zoé and Colette will be there, too. Oh, and Staimes, Harrison's valet."

Fletcher hooked his thumbs in his pocket again and for a time looked everywhere but at her. Moments passed and he finally turned his focus back onto her. "We'll come."

Was that disappointment she heard in his voice? "If you don't want to…"

"It isn't that. It's just…" He rubbed his finger over his bottom lip. "Thank you. We would love to come."

Although his tone wasn't completely convincing, it pleased her they would be there. "Wonderful. I'm glad you'll be joining us." That brought a smile to his face.

Abby loved doing things for people and this was just one small way she could do something special for those who were helping to make her dream become a reality. To make sure everyone enjoyed the day off, she'd hire Lucy, from Lucy's Diner, to supply the food. Abby loved big, outdoor get-togethers, something her family back in Paradise Haven did often.

Plus, she couldn't wait to spend more time with Harrison and his adorable sons. She knew she was opening herself up for more heartache by subjecting herself to being around the children, but she also knew children were a blessing, so therefore, she would enjoy them while she could. Before long, they would be gone. With the exception of Julie, perhaps. But even then, Fletcher would be gone, too, once the job was finished and so would Julie. She just hoped they didn't take her heart with them and leave her to pick up the pieces again.

Having never made lemonade before or anything else for that matter, Harrison was extremely grateful when Veronique insisted she prepare the drinks. Not only had she prepared the beverages, but she'd also added some delicious-looking French butter cookies to the tray, as well.

On his way to give Fletcher and his men their lemonade and cookies, something his servants would have done back home, Harrison searched for Abby. He spotted her sitting under a large tree with her purple dress fanned out around her, looking very regal. She was the type of woman who could fit in anywhere. There were times she appeared every whit the high-society lady, and other times a person wouldn't be able to differentiate her from the household staff. Either way, the lady was a breath-stealing vision of loveliness. One he could drink his fill of every day.

After he gave the men their drinks, he made his way over to Abby and handed her the already filled glass of lemonade with a slice of lemon hooked on the side of the glass.

"Thank you." She smiled up at him.

Good-night the woman was beautiful.

He held the tray in front of her. "Veronique sent along cookies, as well. French butter, she called them."

"Oh, how thoughtful of her." Abby peered at them like a small child would. She snatched two of them off the plate and took a rather large bite out of one.

Harrison marveled at how down to earth and genuine Abby was. The women in Boston would devour a woman like her. Good thing she didn't live there. He'd hate to see just exactly what the women there would do to her. They would probably strip her of her loveliness and her playfulness. Then again, maybe not. Abby was a woman who could hold her own.

He set the tray on the ground, lowered himself onto the hard, lumpy ground opposite of Abby and took a long pull of his drink. Sweet mingled with tart saturated his taste buds.

"Mercy. You must have been thirsty."

He looked at his nearly drained glass and chuckled. "I confess. I was. And *you* must have been hungry." Both of the cookies she'd taken were devoured in less than a minute.

"I must confess. I was." Her eyes twinkled as she imitated his response to her.

"Touché," he said, raising his glass to hers. They clinked them together before he drained the rest of his beverage.

Abby took several slow sips, and when she finished, she placed it on the tray and looked over at him. All of a sudden her blue eyes sparkled. "Oh. Guess what?" He had no time to take a guess as she hurried on. "I talked to Fletcher, and he knows a gentleman who does gardening. In fact, it's the same man who had taken care of this place for the previous owners."

Harrison scanned the weed infested, unkept yard that was definitely in need of much tending to.

"I said, 'had.'"

"Yes. I heard you. That's wonderful news. I'll find out where the man lives and take you there tomorrow. Today you need to rest."

"That's very sweet of you, but Fletcher offered to take me during his lunch break today." Her emphasizing the word "today" didn't get past Harrison. "I would love it if you would come with us."

The idea of her riding alone or spending time with Fletcher gnawed at Harrison's insides. "Are you sure you're up to it today? You're supposed to be resting."

"I won't lie, I do have a slight headache, but that's all it is, a slight one."

He thought about it for a couple of moments, debating on whether or not they should wait until tomorrow.

"Nothing's going to stop me from going, Harrison."

"I figured as much. I'll let Fletcher know."

Noontime arrived quickly.

Fletcher rode his horse alongside Abby's side of Harrison's buggy. All the way to the gardener's house, Harrison watched Fletcher from the corner of his eye. The man rarely took his eyes off Abby, and the two of them conversed as if they'd known each other forever, instead of only a few days.

This time there was no denying it; Harrison was jealous. He wanted Abby to himself. And yet seeing the futility of that, he stopped watching their interaction. Who was he to deny her a chance at happiness?

Ten minutes later, they arrived at a small, picturesque

log cabin nestled near the side of the mountain. An array of purple, pink, blue, yellow, orange and red flowers, manicured shrubbery and blooming rose bushes that were all perfectly uniformed and organized surrounded the place, and not a weed in sight. The outside of the log house had been well taken care of, with no missing chinking or defects of any kind.

"Isn't his place lovely?" Abby sighed loud and long.

"It is quite impressive. The man does superb work." Harrison tied off the lines, hopped out of the open-top buggy and headed to Abby's side to help her down, but was too late. Fletcher was already there assisting her, and Harrison thought his hand lingered on hers longer than necessary.

Abby perused the area, her lips tilted upward higher and higher with each turn she took. Awe and delight emanated from her. "Shall we go see if he's home?" She eyed both men with expectant eyes.

Up the path and onto the steps they went.

Strong stairs.

Sturdy railings.

Not one protruding nail.

Neat and swept clean, too.

Far as Harrison was concerned, the man was hired. But that decision wasn't up to him. It was Abby's to make.

Abby stopped feet away from the door. "Did you make those lovely rockers, Fletcher? They look like your handiwork."

"Yes, ma'am. I did. I gave them to Samuel for his fifty-fifth birthday."

"Oh. When was that?"

"In March of this year."

The door opened without squeaking, Harrison noted.

A man no taller than Abby stepped into the light. "Fletcher, how good to see you." They shook hands, and the man's eyes shifted from Abby and to Harrison. "And who are these fine folks?"

"Mr. Hilliard, this is Miss Abby Bowen."

"Pleased to meet you, ma'am." The slightly balding man gave a nod in her direction, then turned his focus over to Harrison.

"This is Mr. Harrison Kingsley."

Harrison stepped forward and shook the man's hand. Firm. Solid. Not a wimpy grip. The man was strong, that was for sure, and likely more than able to handle the job. "Pleasure to meet you, Mr. Hilliard."

"Samuel." He glanced at Abby and Harrison. "Mr. Hilliard makes me feel old."

"Very well, then. Samuel it is," Harrison agreed.

"To what do I owe this pleasure?" Samuel turned his question toward Fletcher.

"Miss Bowen bought the Glenworth place, and she's looking for a gardener. I thought you might be interested."

"Interested?" he all but bellowed. "How soon can I start? Today? How about right now?"

Abby's laughter and joy hovered through the air. "I have but one question for you first. Who did your yard?" At her teasing, knowing question, Harrison smiled.

Samuel puffed out his barrel chest, tugged on his red suspenders and ran his thumbs up and down the length of them. "Why, I did, ma'am."

"I knew that." Abby chuckled. "I was just teasing you." She turned questioning eyes up at Harrison, seeking his approval. That gesture pleased him immensely. A slight nod and the matter was settled.

"Samuel, Mr. Harrison and I would love it if you would come to work for us."

"Excellent! I'll run and get my horse." He bolted toward the steps and was halfway to the corral when Abby hollered, "Wait! We haven't even discussed your pay yet."

Samuel stopped and whirled toward them. "Who cares about that? I'm just thrilled to be able to restore the place to its former glory. It's bothered me for years to see it so neglected. But I'll have it looking great in no time." With that, he jogged his way to the corral, where a dark palomino horse stood in the shade of a perfectly erected lean-to, swishing her tail. Samuel swung open the gate, and the mare nickered and walked right up to him.

"Thank you so much, Fletcher."

Harrison turned to find Abby gazing up at Fletcher with gratitude. In that moment, Harrison wished he was the one who had found Samuel and not Fletcher. He wanted to be the one to put that smile on her face. *Good-night, Harrison. Stop this nonsense. You're leaving, remember?* Yes, he was, and was it ever going to be a challenge and take every bit of willpower he possessed to walk away from her when he did. She was a delight to be around. Her bubbly, upbeat, yet feisty personality was the type of woman he liked—immensely. But, alas, his businesses and his home were in Boston. Hers was here. And he didn't think anything would take her away from her dream. Not even him.

Neither could he give up his lifelong dream of righting the wrongs his father had done to the good people of Boston. Not one of them deserved the evil his father had done to them. The sooner he rectified things with them, the better he'd feel.

Soft pressure applied to his forearm cleared his mind of his daunting thoughts. He glanced down at Abby's hand, then at her face.

"I asked if you were ready to go."

Fletcher stood at the bottom of the steps, and Samuel sat atop his horse, waiting. "My apologies. For a moment there, my mind took a turn in another direction."

"Well, turn it back in the right direction, then. We're ready to leave." Mischief sparkled through her eyes as she said it low enough that only he had heard her.

"Very well, Miss *Abigail*. As you wish." Cupping her elbow, he led her down the stairs and handed her into the buggy.

They headed toward her place, bouncing and jostling along the bumpy road as they did. Halfway down from Samuel's place, Harrison pulled his horse to a stop.

Abby peered up at him with confused eyes. "What's wrong? Why did we stop?"

Harrison pressed his finger against his lips, signaling for her to be quiet, and pointed into the trees.

Abby followed the point of his finger. She squinted, looking hard through the trees.

He cupped her chin and turned it toward the direction of a deer and her fawn. Abby's eyes widened, and her mouth formed the word *oh*. They sat there for a few minutes, watching, until the deer yanked her head up, sniffed the air and darted off deep into the woods, her fawn leaping and hopping behind her.

"Oh, my, that was beautiful. Thank you."

"You're welcome," he said, thrilled that he was the one responsible for the pleasure and serenity that shone on her pretty face and striking eyes. Better him than Fletcher. Not one normally prone to thoughts like that, he mentally shook his head, and gave a click flick of the reins. Abby was getting under his skin and that wasn't good.

Chapter Nine

Three days later, Abby sat at the end of the long pew closest to the front door of the white clapboard church, wondering what was so important that Harrison couldn't come today. Nothing should take precedence over God. Nothing. But, she wasn't Harrison's judge. Whatever he did or didn't do was between him and God, not him, God and her.

After singing *Amazing Grace* and two other hymns, the congregation sat down. Reverend Andrew Wells stepped up to the podium. At forty-three, no wrinkles lined the minister's face, but he looked more like sixty or better due to his snow-white hair.

He gazed out at the congregation. Sun-darkened skin made his lime-green eyes and bright white teeth appear even brighter. Reverend Wells was a fine-looking man with a beautiful wife and five well-behaved children. All five had dark brown hair with red highlights like their mother, and their father's green eyes. "If you have your Bibles with you, I'd like you to open up to the book of first John four, verse eighteen." As it always did, his slow Southern speech reminded her of her sisters-in-law, Selina and Rainee, who were both from the South.

For the umpteenth time since leaving home, Abby wondered how they were doing. How everyone was doing. Especially her nieces and nephews. Had they grown since she'd last seen them? How she missed them and longed to see them, and yet a part of her was glad she wasn't there to see them. It was the same battle that always went around and around in her mind with no real lasting solution.

Children, whether it be her nephews and nieces or other people's children, were a constant reminder of what she couldn't have. Being around little ones always brought a fresh bout of raw pain no matter how hard she tried not to let it.

Light tapping on her arm stopped her train of thought. There stood Julie, looking at her with those innocent, big, brown eyes. Here stood a motherless girl who needed a woman's attention.

No matter where Abby went, there was no getting away from children. But oh, how she loved them. What she didn't love was the pain of being around them and the constant reminder. It wasn't their fault. She refused to be rude. *God, please take away this pain and let me enjoy this little girl, but help me not to fall in love with her so I don't get hurt.* "Hello, Julie," she whispered. "Would you like to sit with me?"

Julie turned and bent her head way back to gaze up at her father standing behind her. "Papa, can we sit with Miss Abby?" She whispered the question so low, Abby barely heard it.

Fletcher leaned over, and Julie repeated the question into her father's ear. He glanced at Abby with the same question. She answered by standing enough to gather the skirt of her peach bustle gown and by scooting over.

Julie slid in next to her and then Fletcher. They

looked like a family sitting there together. Abby shifted in her seat and squirmed. Not knowing how to deal with the uncomfortable awkwardness she felt at that thought, she dropped her gaze to her Bible and rummaged through the pages until she found the scripture reference the reverend had mentioned.

The rustling of pages throughout the congregation stopped, and the pastor's voice reached her ears. *"'There is no fear in love; but perfect love casteth out fear: because fear hath torment. He that feareth is not made perfect in love.'"*

He stepped from around to the side of the podium, rested his elbow on top of the angled surface and crossed his ankle. "Love is a risk. And yet if we never love, we never live. If we never open our hearts to love God or to let Him love us or to love mankind and to let them love us for fear of what they'll do to us, for fear of being hurt or rejected, we are losing out on the greatest gift God ever gave to mankind."

The word *rejection* plunged like a knife into Abby's soul. It was easy for Reverend Wells to talk about love and about letting yourself be loved. After all, he had an amazing wife who obviously loved him unconditionally along with five wonderful children. There was no way he could know or understand the heartache of loving and losing someone.

Well, she had.

Not only had she lost her fiancé, a man she'd once loved dearly, she'd lost the means to bear a child, too. Equally, if not worse, she had lost her sense of value and worth as a woman. So yes, she feared rejection, feared love and even feared being loved. Who wouldn't after what she'd gone through with David? The only kind of love she wanted was one that existed in fantasies and dreams only. Those she could handle because they weren't real. They were just figments of her imagination. That was a safe place for them. And for her.

For the next twenty-five minutes Abby listened as the reverend continued talking about love and faith and trusting God no matter how things looked.

She couldn't wait for church to be over because his message was getting harder and harder to bear. How could she ever love again and risk getting hurt again? It took great restraint on her part not to get up and leave, not to mention fidget in her chair. All that talk about love and taking a risk did nothing but frustrate and anger her. Requiring the impossible is what her mind said it was.

Maybe she should have joined Harrison on his errand. That would surely have been more enjoyable than sitting here being judged for something she couldn't change.

The preacher finished his sermon with 1 Peter 5:7 *Casting all your care upon Him; for He careth for you.*

Now that she could do. Well, except for her lack of being able to bear children, that one she still struggled with giving over to God. She didn't understand why her, when she loved children like she did. She'd known other women who had a whole passel of them and they didn't even care for children. It didn't make a whit of sense to her, but then again, she wasn't God, nor would she try to figure Him out where this subject was concerned. Still, she couldn't help but wonder why, couldn't help but try and figure it out as she had so many times before.

Throughout the rest of the service, her thoughts bandied back and forth until she became dizzy with them. She couldn't wait to get to the picnic so maybe they would settle down.

Church finally ended, and with only a few words to Fletcher about meeting down by the river, Abby and the Denis sisters headed for home. The walk home was a pleasant one, in spite of the turmoil that had gone on inside of her at church.

She would not allow anything, especially that, to ruin her day. Instead, she chose to focus on how God had answered her prayer for nice sunshiny weather so they could enjoy their picnic without the threat of rain.

Back at the house, Abby changed her clothes into something lighter, a white cotton dress with life-size pink-and-violet roses and green leaves sprinkled throughout. She finished her attire with a white straw hat sporting a long ribbon that matched the material of her dress. Instead of tying the bow directly underneath her chin, she tied it loosely off to one side. Satisfied with her appearance reflecting back at her from her Louis XVI Giltwood looking glass, she snatched her white parasol out of the umbrella holder and headed downstairs.

Everyone was to meet down by the river, so when she neared the bottom of the staircase, she was surprised to see Harrison in the main entrance room standing there with his back to her.

Her heelless, soft leather shoes tapped lightly across the newly polished floor as she meandered toward him. "Good morning, Harrison."

He turned and his smile grew, melting her insides.

"Good morning to you, too." He met her halfway. "Aren't you a vision of loveliness?" He glanced down at his casual brown pants and then back over at her dress. "I fear I've underdressed. I thought we were picnicking today."

"We are."

His one brow curled into a sleeping S. "Aren't you afraid of getting your dress soiled?"

"Nope. When I go somewhere, I go to have fun. I don't worry about my clothing." She tilted her head. "Where are the boys? And why are you here at the house instead of down by the river?"

"I left Graham and Josiah down at the river with Zoé. Everyone else is down there except for you. So I came looking for you to make sure you were all right and that you weren't in any pain or anything from your fall the other day."

"As you see, I'm perfectly fine. Just late is all. How rude of me to be late to my own gathering. I mean, really, you'd think I would at least have started out sooner so I wouldn't be late. But no, I got sidetracked. That's what I get for daydreaming again." She spoke so fast, she had a hard time catching up with herself. Talking fast was a bad habit of hers. One she really needed to work on fixing.

"So, you're a daydreamer, huh?" He threaded her hand through his arm and tugged her toward the front door.

"Yes. It's one of my many failings."

"Many, huh?"

"Yes. Many."

"Well, I hate to differ with you, Miss Abigail Bowen, but I do not see where you have *many* failings, if any."

"That's because you don't know me very well."

"That's true, perhaps. But I think I'm a pretty good judge of character, and you, ma'am, are quite a character."

Shocked by his assessment, she yanked her gaze up to him and saw the teasing glint in his eyes. "And you, sir, have that right."

They smiled.

"So, how are you feeling? Does your head hurt anymore?"

"No. Not at all. That first night it did and most of the next day. But now, it barely hurts. In fact, I feel wonderful." She owned her speedy recovery to the fact that she loved picnics and loved spending time with her friends. Friends? Somehow the word *friend* didn't fit the way she felt about Harrison. Fear waltzed across her heart. Without being obvious, she unwound her hand from his arm. After today's message, she needed to be careful to not let her daydreams turn into real love. Dreaming about love and pretending they were in love was one thing, but to really allow herself to fall in love with him or anyone else was too risky. Rejection hurt way too much.

"Where are you, Abby?"

"Huh?" Her eyes collided with his. "Right here."

"You daydreaming again?"

"No." She shook her head. "Just thinking."

"Oh. What about?"

"About spending the day with my wonderful friends." She smiled up at him. That was partly the truth, anyway. And the only truth he needed to know. Of that she was certain.

For some odd reason, Harrison didn't like being considered as one of Abby's friends. He wanted to be more than that, a battle he'd been fighting ever since meeting her a mere week ago. It was a battle he was quickly losing. How could the woman have gotten under his skin in such a short time? He'd heard of love at first sight, but that was for saps. And he was quickly becoming one, so he needed to be more careful.

As they neared the river, he took in the small crowd of people Abby had invited. Underneath the canopy of trees sat Staimes, who appeared to be in deep conversation with Veronique, Colette, Samuel, Julie and Fletcher, whose eyes never once strayed from Abby.

Harrison cut a glance at Abby to see if she noticed Fletcher's obvious admiration toward her. But her face was turned in another direction, toward Zoé and his two sons squatted down at the edge of the water.

After seeing them in their play clothes the other day, he'd made a special trip to the general store and purchased garments for them designed specifically for outdoor fun. Today they were wearing blue denim pants instead of their knickers and knee-high socks.

"Miss Abby!" Julie leaped up from sitting beside her father. She rushed toward Abby and flung her tiny arms around Abby's legs.

"Miss Abby. Miss Abby." Graham and Josiah barreled toward her as fast as their little legs would carry them. Within seconds all three children's arms were draped around the petite woman.

Somehow, in spite of their arms around her, she managed to squat down and pull all of them into her embrace. A place he found he'd like to be.

"Are you having fun?" She eyed each one as she asked.

All three nodded gleefully.

"I'm so glad. Is anyone hungry?"

Again, all three nodded with the same enthusiasm as before. "Very well, then. Shall we get something to eat?" She stood. Each child vied for her hand. Harrison watched to see how she would deal with the situation.

"I'll race you to the food basket."

His admiration for her slipped up another notch. She had handled the situation very well.

The children whirled and bolted toward the picnic basket. Julie got there first, Josiah second, Graham third and then Abby.

"Ah-h-h. No fair. You all beat me. Does this mean I don't get anything to eat?" Abby sighed as if that thought were the most horrible thing in the world.

"You may eat, too, Miss Abby," Julie said, her manners were impeccable for one so young.

"And what do you boys say?" Her gaze touched on each one.

"Uh-huh," they both said at the same time, nodding.

"Oh, thank you all so much. I am so very honored to have the privilege to dine with you all on this fine day." She clasped her hands together with such flair and drama that the children's faces glimmered as if they had indeed done something wonderful. One by one she planted a kiss on top of their heads, then dropped to her knees in front of the basket, giving no heed whatsoever to the dirt-loaded ground soiling her dress. She raised the lid on the basket and made a huge display of studying its contents.

Pretty soon all three heads joined hers, peering into the basket just as intently as she was.

Harrison chuckled. The woman sure had a way with children. She loved them, and they obviously loved her.

"Now what do we have here? I'm certain there is something in here that children will like." She pulled a cloth off a sizeable platter to unveil several pieces of crispy brown chicken. Looking at each child, she asked, "Who here likes fried chicken?"

All three darted a hand upward.

"Oh, splendid. I'm so glad." Her head dipped and

she peered into the basket again. "Hmm. Wonder what this could be?" Out came a round pan nestled onto the palm of her hand.

"I know. I know." Julie raised her hand.

"I know, too." Josiah wasn't about to be outdone.

"Me, too." Graham wasn't, either.

"Very well, then. On the count of three, all together, tell me what it is. One." Their eager faces stared at Abby. "Two." She dragged out the word. The children's mouths opened, ready to blurt out the answer. "Two and a half."

Giggles erupted.

"Two and three quarters."

The giggles increased. Seconds ticked by. Not one of the children took their eyes off Abby.

Suddenly she blurted, "Three!"

In unison, they yelled, "Pie!"

"Very good. Boy, you all are smart." She sat back on the heels of her feet. "Who here likes pie?"

Young voices mingled as they all said, "Me, me, me."

"I do, too. But—" she held up her finger "—if we want to have a slice of this here blackberry pie, we have to eat our lunch first. In order to do that, we have to wash our hands. We'd better hurry and go do that. Don't you agree?"

Three heads nodded vigorously before the whole lot of them whirled around and darted down to the river. Abby snatched up a towel and followed them closely. Down at the riverbank, she helped each one of them wash and dry their hands.

"She's something, isn't she?" Fletcher said from beside Harrison. "She sure has a way with children."

"That, she does." In fact, Harrison wished she could

be the mother to his sons. Shock bolted from his gut and lodged into his throat.

Where had that thought come from?

When had she crept into his heart like that?

And even more important, how would he ever rip her out of it?

Was he falling for her? He searched his heart for the answer.

"Harrison, aren't you going to come join us?" Abby's voice pulled him from the reality he needed to escape.

He strode over to the spot where everyone was seated under the canopy of trees.

Food passed around the group and within minutes, everyone had their plates filled.

Abby looked over at him. "Harrison, would you like the honor of praying over our food today?"

Pray? His eyes widened before he could stop them. Him? He'd never prayed a day in his life. Well, that wasn't entirely true, but it had been years since he had.

"Our daddy don't pray," Josiah said before Harrison had a chance to answer her.

Harrison's gaze shifted to his son, then up to Abby. Her eyes were wide until he looked directly at her, then they quickly returned to normal. He had no idea what to do or say.

"Well, then why don't we ask Mr. Hilliard to pray today?" She sent an apologetic smile to Harrison for no doubt putting him in this uncomfortable situation before she turned her focus onto Samuel. "Would you do us the honors, Samuel?"

"Yes, ma'am. I'd be more than happy to."

They all bowed their heads except Harrison. He studied the top of Abby's head. It shouldn't bother him what Abby or anyone else thought because he wasn't a praying man. After all, it was no one's business but his own. Still, the thought of Abby thinking less of him bothered Harrison.

The short prayer ended.

Abby's attention wafted back over to him. He waited for the disappointment to come as it had with so many other religious people when they discovered he didn't share their faith. But it never came. Not one delightful thing in the whole world could compare to the smile she offered; it was one of complete acceptance. If ever there was a person he wanted acceptance from, it would be Abby.

Stunned by the news that Harrison didn't pray, Abby's heart went out to him and she felt guilty for asking him to pray in front of everyone. She tried to reassure him and to make him feel better by giving him her biggest, most accepting smile, but that wasn't enough as far as she was concerned. Of course, that's why he hadn't come to services. How could she have missed something so very obvious? She needed to figure out some way to somehow make it up to him.

"Abby, do you mind if I join you?"

Abby gazed up from her spot on the ground to find Fletcher standing over her. Four adults could fit comfortably on the blanket and she saw no reason why he couldn't join her. "That would be nice."

"This was a great idea. Thank you for including Julie and me." Fletcher lowered his lanky frame onto the blanket. He no sooner got settled, than Samuel stepped up. "Got room for one more? That is, if I'm not intruding or anything?" He looked from Fletcher to Abby.

"No, not at all. Please, won't you be seated?" Abby motioned to a spot on the blanket.

Samuel barely sat down when Harrison joined them.

Next thing Abby knew, Zoé, Veronique, Colette and the three children vacated their chairs, spread out a blanket next to theirs and joined the rest of them. Staimes remained in his chair until Veronique invited him to sit with them and patted the spot next to her. That must have been all the encouragement he needed because he joined them and sat in the spot closest to Veronique. Abby wished the two of them would find a future together. She'd never seen Veronique smile so much before. But that wasn't likely to happen as he would leave when Harrison did.

Oh, if only. Abby sighed.

Everyone took turns talking while intermediately eating Lucy's excellent fried chicken, her fluffy biscuits, cheese slices, hard-boiled eggs and the new potatoes smothered in butter and sprinkled with parsley. When the main course was finished and the blackberry, strawberry-rhubarb and apple pies were devoured, Abby was the first one to rise. Her attention shifted to the children. "Anyone ready to do some fishing?"

Josiah and Graham leaped up and made it to her side in an instant.

"Julie, don't you want to join us?"

Julie wrinkled her nose and shook her head.

"It'll be fun. I promise."

She shook her head again. "No, thank you. Fish smell funny and they're icky and slimy." The poor girl looked so repulsed that Abby didn't ask her again.

"Well, if you change your mind, we'll be right around that bend." She pointed to where the wide river disappeared around the corner.

"I'd like to join you, if you don't mind." Harrison

stood. "I've never fished before, and I'd like to see what you do. Perhaps you could even teach me how to?"

Abby thought that a splendid idea. Anything to spend more time in Harrison's company. Not wanting to leave anyone out she eyed each person. "Anyone else want to join us?"

"I think I'll just rest here a spell. This is my favorite place on your property. Always was." Samuel leaned his back against the tree and stretched his legs straight out in front of him.

Colette settled on her side, braced herself on her elbow and rested her head in the palm of her hand. "I'm perfectly content to stay here myself."

Veronique and Zoé agreed.

"What about you, Fletcher? You want to come?" Abby watched as his gaze slid to his daughter seated next to him.

"No. I'd better stay here with Julie. Besides, I don't much care for fishing, either."

"Oh. All right. We'll see you all later, then." The four of them made their way to where the fishing supplies had been placed earlier that morning, including the coffee can of worms she'd dug up and placed in a cool spot.

Harrison took the fishing equipment from her, and the boys nestled their hands in hers. She led the way to the spot where Samuel had shown her the best fishing was. Josiah and Graham chattered the whole way there. Their excited voices had her feeling quite giddy.

They found the small clearing, and Abby went right to work showing Harrison and the boys how to bait their hooks and how to throw out their lines. Several times, Josiah's and Graham's lines got tangled. Finally, their lines were safely in the water. The current carried them up the river a fair piece. After giving them instructions on how to tell when they had a fish, she turned to help Harrison.

His casting was as bad as his sons', if not worse.

"Here, let me show you by guiding you through it." She placed her hand on top of his and froze. Their gazes collided, neither looked away. Some unique bond was transpiring between them.

"Daddy, you gotta throw it. Not hold it."

Abby was the first to break contact. She raised her hand, and instead of touching him again, she went through the motions on how to cast.

Harrison finally got his bait in the water instead of the trees behind them. Within minutes he had a bite. Like a Fourth of July firework display, his face lit up but quickly turned to panic. "What do I do? I got one!"

"Set the hook by giving a yank on the line."

He gave a sharp yank, and the pole came within inches of smacking her in the face.

Concentrating hard on the task before him, Harrison's hands cranked fast in small circles. The fish flopped and broke across the top of the water several times.

"See it in the water, boys?" Abby pointed to where the fish swam near the bank.

"Where? I don't see it?" Josiah squatted down and peered into the water. "I see it. I see it!"

"Where?" Graham looked at him.

Josiah grabbed his hand and pointed to it.

"I see it, too. I see it, too, Daddy." Graham jumped up and down.

"That's great, boys." His voice was filled with a case of the nerves. "Now please move back so your father can bring it onto the bank."

The twins slowly backed out of the way.

"Okay. Now. Whatever you do, Harrison, don't pick up your pole when the fish reaches the bank. Slide it in instead," she instructed.

He did as he was told and slid the fish over the riverbank and onto the dry ground yards away from the water.

The boys squealed and clapped their hands, their own poles all but forgotten now.

Abby watched Harrison. His face glowed with the same childlike expression as his sons had. He pressed his shoulders back, protruding his already broad chest. "This is the first fish I've ever caught. Thank you, Abby."

She smiled and nodded.

"I wanna catch a fishy now." Josiah hopped up and down.

"Me, too." Graham mimicked his brother by jumping up and down, too.

"All right, but let me get this one off the hook first, and then I'll help you boys, okay?"

They nodded.

"You don't mind touching them?" Harrison asked, sounding a little queasy.

"Nope. Been doing it ever since my sister-in-law Selina showed me how to fish."

Abby ran her finger under the fish gill on one side and her thumb under the other one until her finger and thumb touched. The fish flopped but there was no way it was going to get away from the grasp she had on it. She grabbed a rope and attached the fish to it. She tossed the fish into the water and anchored the rope with a heavy rock.

"You're a very impressive woman, Miss Abby Bowen."

She peered up at him. "Why? Because I can fish?"

"No. Not because you can fish. Well, not just because you can fish. You amaze me. Not only do you have a great business mind, you're a very elegant woman and yet you aren't afraid to get dirty or touch a fish. Most woman would never do that."

"Well, I'm not most women." She sent him a sassy smile.

"Thank goodness for that."

Abby frowned at the way he said that and wondered what he meant. Rather than ask, she tore her attention off him and put it onto the boys. After everyone caught at least two fish each, they headed back to the others.

"Well, how'd you do?" Samuel was the first to ask.

"We caught lots of fishies," Josiah answered.

Graham nodded.

The boys had to show everyone their catch, except for Julie; she didn't want to see them. Abby felt sorry for the little girl because she didn't like fishing and had been left out of the fun, so she decided to do something she might enjoy, too. "Julie, would you like to play hide-and-seek?"

Her little face brightened and swung toward her father's. "May I, Papa?"

"Yes, you may."

"I wanna play, too." Josiah spoke up first.

"Me, too," Graham added.

Zoé and Colette joined them, while Veronique closed her eyes. The six of them played hide-and-seek for over a half an hour.

Exhausted from the play and the heat, Zoé, Colette and the children lay down on the blanket Veronique and Staimes had abandoned. They were now seated in a couple of the chairs that had been brought down and were still chatting away. It was nice to see Veronique enjoying herself instead of working all the time.

Abby arrived at the blanket Fletcher and Harrison occupied in time to hear Harrison ask, "Will you be able to repair them?"

Her attention glided from one to the other as she sat down. "Repair what?"

Both men turned their attention onto her.

"Fletcher was just telling me that when he went on the roof to check the shingles he decided to check the chimneys while he was up there." Worry crowded Harrison's face.

"And…" Abby dragged out the word, waiting for one of them to respond.

"Abby," Fletcher spoke first. "Three of the chimneys are starting to collapse. Some of the rocks they used were sandstone and they've started to crumble. The chimneys will have to be rebuilt. It's going to take a while to rebuild them."

"How much time are we talking about?" She kept her focus on Fletcher while waiting for his answer.

"I'm not quite sure. I'll know more when I get started."

"Will you be able to get all of that done in the next three months?"

He cocked his mouth to one side. "Um. I'm not sure."

"Can you hire more help so that it can be done by then? Surely there are men in town who could use the work."

"There are. But—" his gaze dropped to his lap, and he raised his hat and wiped his forehead off "—those repairs were not included in my original bid."

"That's no problem. Hire as many men as you need to get the job finished. And while we're speaking of jobs, I would love it if you could get the theater section finished as soon as possible. The chairs are supposed to arrive sometime within the next couple of weeks. And my…" Realizing she was leaving Harrison out and how that must look for him, her attention jumped to him. "*Our* actresses and actors will be arriving shortly after that. Since we need to start practicing right away, we'll need to have the stage and props done as soon as you can.

"So hire as many workers as you need to. Just please make sure of the men you hire that their quality of work is equal to that of yours. Plus, we prefer that you yourself build the stage and the props and everything to do with the theater and have your men work on the repairs." She hoped she wasn't being too presumptuous, so she looked to Harrison for his approval.

He sent her a discreet nod. She returned her focus back to Fletcher. "Will that work for you?" *Please say yes.* The idea of her grand opening being set back didn't bode too well with her. Then again, she stopped fidgeting, knowing everything would work out just fine because God would work everything out as He always did.

"I already planned on doing that. I'll hire more men tomorrow, and we'll get started on the theater right away."

"Wonderful." Abby clasped her hands and pressed them to her chest. "I can hardly wait to see what it's going to look like when you get finished." She closed her eyes and laid her head back. Contentment wrapped around her that her dream was quickly on its way to becoming a reality. Well, one of them, anyway. The other would remain a dream only.

Chapter Ten

Two hours later, the small party started to break up and go their separate ways. Staimes had asked if Harrison minded if he went back to the house with everyone else. Harrison smiled. He knew that everyone else had meant Veronique especially. It brought him great joy to see his valet relaxed and enjoying another's companionship.

Zoé had asked Harrison if she could take his sons with her because she had something she wanted to show them—a bug collection or something like that. Julie had been invited, too, but the little girl wrinkled her nose and shook her head. Harrison agreed with her. Why anyone would want to see bugs was beyond him, but his boys did, so he had let them go, knowing they were dead bugs mounted on boards. It amazed him a woman collected such a thing. Seemed all the women in Abby's household, including Abby, did things he wasn't used to seeing. Boston women didn't do those things. At least not the women in his society. Truth be known, he enjoyed these people's good society much more.

Harrison lingered behind in hopes of walking Abby back to the house. He hadn't gotten over how the woman had responded to the news about her chimneys. Nothing about it fazed her and it should have. Therefore, he didn't think she truly understood the magnitude of just how much more it was going to cost her to fix those chimneys or to hire those extra men. To make sure she did, he wanted to discuss the matter with her, only he didn't want to do it in front of Fletcher or anyone else.

Minutes later, Fletcher and his daughter left. They were the last ones to leave the picnic area.

Harrison turned toward Abby and froze at the sight. A hummingbird hovered over her, pecking at the flowers in the ribbon around the crown of her hat. Abby sat statue still. They're eyes connected, then hers drifted upward to where the hummingbird still hovered before returning to his. Her disbelieving, exuberant smile and bright eyes reminded him of a child opening a birthday present.

Caught up in the captivating moment, he watched the fluorescent-orange bird, a rufous, the locals called it, test several more flowers before it flitted off.

"Did you see that? I can't believe it was that close to me." Abby clasped her hands in front of her and yanked them to her chest. "Aren't they the sweetest little things ever? That one was a rufous hummingbird. Odd how they look brown until you see them in the sun. Then the orange on their bodies and the red under their beak turns a brilliant fluorescent color, don't you think?" Again she gave him no time to answer as she started to rise immediately after her question.

Harrison rushed to help her up. Every time her hand settled in his, the warmth of her touch went straight to his heart and its effect resided there; this time was no different. Not wanting to feel the effects because of its implication, he let go of her hand.

"Thank you." She looked around. "Well, I suppose

I ought to head to the house. I really hate to leave this place. I love the sound of the water lapping over the rocks. It's so soothing and comforting. Don't you agree?" She turned those smiling eyes up at him.

"I do." Not wanting their time to end and still needing to talk to her, he asked, "Would you like to sit a bit longer? There's something I'd like to talk with you about."

She tilted her head. "What about?"

"Let's go sit down over there." He pointed to a felled log near the wide river's edge.

They made their way there and sat down.

Abby crossed her knees in his direction and draped one hand loosely over the other.

"Earlier, when Fletcher mentioned the chimneys, you didn't seem the least bit upset about it. I just wanted to make sure you understand that the repairs are going to be quite costly. Not so much the rebuilding supplies, but the wages will be extreme as it will take many hours for the men to rebuild them."

"Oh. I see. Well, as we discussed earlier, you do not have to contribute any more funds. I will handle it."

Huh? This wasn't about him at all. "I wasn't thinking about me, Abby. I was thinking about you. I just wanted to make sure you understood just how much money this was going to take."

"That's very sweet of you. But don't you worry about that. Whatever it takes, I will pay. Nothing is going to stop me from my dream. Besides, God will take care of it."

There she was saying God would take care of it again. Was she really that naive? Didn't she know that God didn't care about people? Especially their problems? His heart ached that she believed all of that malarkey. He knew a man who trusted God to restore his business, and when God didn't come through, the man had become so bitter and angry that he not only lost his business but his wife and family, too. Harrison hoped the same thing didn't happen to Abby.

At one point in his life, Harrison himself had prayed. One time, he had asked God to heal his best friend's mother, and she had died, anyway. Another time he'd prayed, even pleaded with God that his father would love him. That prayer was never answered, either. The last time he'd prayed was when he'd asked God to bring his wife back to him. Look how that turned out. His twins were motherless. So as far as Harrison was concerned, God wouldn't take care of it as Abby seemed to think. Poor woman was delusional in her thinking. Didn't she know that if something needed done, a person had to take care of it themselves? Well, even if she didn't. He did. Therefore, he would do whatever he could to help her to make her dream come true. Even if it meant spending his last dime.

"Thank you for allowing me to teach you and your sons to fish. I had a great time." Abby's words pulled Harrison from his thoughts. The smile she sent his way was contagious.

"No. Thank *you*. I can't remember the last time I've had so much fun. Seeing my boys like that, squealing and jumping up and down when they caught their first fish. There's no greater joy. It made me wish I had several more little ones running around. Someday, if I ever find the right woman, my dream of filling my house with my own offspring will come true." Too bad Abby wasn't that woman. But she had her dreams and he had his, and the two didn't mesh.

* * *

Hearing Harrison's words about wanting a houseful of children, *if* he ever found the right woman, felt like a slap to her. His words hurt her more than she wanted them to. It was just another painful reminder that her ex-fiancé was right. Men wanted children of their own. And lots of them.

"Are you all right, Abby?"

No. But how could she tell him she wasn't? Then she would have to explain to him about her not being able to bear children. For some reason, she couldn't stomach the thought of him looking at her with the same disgust David and his friends had. "Yes, I'm fine, thank you." She plastered on a smile, one she didn't feel. "When you get back to Boston, I hope your dream of having a houseful of children comes true for you, and that you find the right woman for you there, as well."

"What about you? Do you want children?"

Did she want children? Yes! More than anything else in this world. Even more than her theater. But that wasn't ever going to happen and she didn't want Harrison to know that for the same reason she thought of only moments ago. *God, help me get out of this.*

"Forgive me, Abby. That was rather forward of me to ask such a personal question. Your private life is none of my business." He stood. "Speaking of children, I need to go rescue Zoé from mine." He smiled.

Abby relaxed. *Thank You, Lord.* "Yes. I need to get back, too. Tomorrow's going to be another long day." They headed toward her house.

"I meant to tell you, I found a nanny for the boys. That was the business I had to tend to yesterday. So I won't have to worry about bothering Zoé or having them underfoot while we conduct business."

So it was back to that again. Business. She had won-dered what pressing business he had to tend to the other day, and now she knew. One would think she'd be happy knowing she wouldn't be around the little darlings so much and risk getting too attached to them. The emp-tiness that always accompanied their departure hurt. Even still, his news disappointed her. "I want you to know that Zoé didn't mind taking care of them. In fact, she enjoyed it. But I know how much it bothered you, so I'm so happy that you found someone. Has he or she met the twins yet?"

He rubbed his fingers across his wrinkled forehead. "No."

"Well, when she does, she will love them."

The worry lines on his forehead let up, but only slightly. "You think so? I told you the issue I've had with other nannies quitting."

"Well, if they don't, then they don't know what they're missing." She sure did.

"I hope you're right."

She did, too. For his sake as well as his sons'. They deserved no less.

They reached the gardens. Lilacs in full bloom sweetened the air with soft, fragrant scents. A bum-blebee hovered around her face. She swept it away with her hand, careful not to anger it so it wouldn't sting her. Many blooming flowers filled the garden, a temptation for any bee. Abby marveled at how much Samuel had gotten done already. One could actually see the blooms now instead of the tall weeds that hid the beautiful pet-als from view. While there was still a long way to go, just trimming the bushes and eliminating most of the weeds had already made a huge difference.

The sound of children's laughter floated on the

breeze that brushed over them. How she loved the sound of children's laughter. It was music to her ears. "Sounds like someone is having fun."

"Either that or they're doing something they shouldn't be doing."

"Oh, I doubt that. Zoé knows how to handle children. She's very good with them."

"I didn't mean to imply that Zoé wasn't capable of handling them—I just know my boys."

That she could grin at.

They rounded the tall hedge that blocked their view of what was happening on the other side.

When they did, Harrison gasped, and Abby covered her smiling mouth with her hand.

The boys had a net on the outdoor table that they were trying to remove a giant bug from.

Stacked boxes of Zoé's bug collection and jars containing several insects and even a frog or two covered the majority of the table.

"Don't touch that!" Harrison's voice was filled with panic as he sprinted toward them.

Zoé and the twins turned wide eyes up at him and the insect took that opportunity to escape.

"That thing could bite you."

At the look of horror on Harrison's face, Abby couldn't help but giggle.

His frowning gaze turned and zeroed in on her.

It was meant to silence her, of that she was sure, but it didn't. All it succeeded in doing was making her laugh outright. Through that laughter she managed to say, "It's okay, Harrison. It's only a locust. They don't bite." She snatched up the net and hurried after the insect. A couple of tries later, she managed to capture the little beast. Unsnagging the insect's legs from the net, she held it up by its back legs for Harrison's inspection. "See?"

One glance of repulsion at the locust and he stared at her as if she was daft. Hadn't the man ever held a bug before? Probably not. After all, he was a city boy. She decided to show him some mercy, so she freed the insect, and then turned to Zoé. "Zoé, perhaps we should let them go now." She sent a knowing wink her friend's way. Zoé captured it immediately, so Abby continued, "Boys, you've got to watch them long enough. We wouldn't want them to die or anything now, would we? So why don't we set them free now?" Abby hoped her suggestion worked.

They pouted at first, but it only took seconds before they nodded.

One by one they opened the lids and dumped the living contents on the ground. Various species of insects scampered or flew off.

Only three toads remained.

"Do we gotta let these ones go?" Josiah asked, looking up at Abby and his father. "I like this one." He pointed to the largest toad inside the gallon jar. "Please? Can we keep them?"

"Please, can we?" Graham added.

"We'll take good care of them. We promise." He crossed his little fingers over his chest, and so did Graham.

Zoé and Abby both looked over at Harrison.

If it were up to Abby, seeing those blue puppy-dog eyes and hearing their pleading voices, she'd cave in and say yes. But it wasn't up to her to make that decision. It was Harrison's. He was the boys' parent. Not her.

Despite his horror, the lines around his eyes softened. "Only if they stay here."

The twins squealed. Apparently, he was a sucker for those cute little beseeching faces, as well.

"Wait. We didn't ask Miss Abby if it's okay."

Hopeful faces turned her way. No way would she say no to them. And yet she had to think of the frogs' welfare, too, and show the boys the lesson in that. "If we can figure out something to keep them alive, then I say yes. But if not, we have to let them go. Like I said before, we don't want them to die now, do we?"

They both shook their heads.

"Okay. Let's go look in the shed to see if there's something out there we can use." Abby took each boy's hand in hers and led them to the shed. Inside the building, she and the boys searched until she came across an old slatted, wooden crate with a lid. Upon inspection, she decided it would work. The slats were too narrow for the toads to escape.

She and the boys gathered grass and a medium-size rock and put them in the bottom of the crate. They used an old bowl she'd found in the shed, filled it with water, and settled it next to the rock. "Okay. You ready to release them?"

The twins nodded.

Abby removed the lid and reached her hand inside the jar.

"Are you going to touch those things?" Harrison asked from behind her.

Without removing her hand from inside the jar, she peered over her shoulder. "I am." Unfazed by the curling of his hiked eyebrows, she pulled the largest toad out. It legs dangled loosely.

"Did your sister-in-law teach you that, too?" The dismay on his face had her almost laughing again.

"Yes, she sure did. Selina taught all of us to enjoy

God's creatures and how there was beauty and treasures just waiting to be found. That a person just had to look for them. And she was right. Take this toad, for example." She held it up to where everyone could see it. "To someone, this creature might be ugly, but to another who knows what to look for, it isn't. Look at the intricate markings on it. God took the time to make each one unique." To prove her point she retrieved the other one with her free hand and now held two of them in front of her.

She described their differences and even pointed out the differences in some species of bugs Zoé had preserved and had pinned onto boards.

Josiah and Graham's attention remained glued to what she showed them.

When she finished, even Harrison looked slightly impressed.

He squatted down until he was eye level with his boys. "You learned a valuable lesson today. Do you know what that was?"

"Yes. We want Abby for our mother."

Abby froze stiff as ice, afraid to look at Harrison. Instead, she busied herself by putting the frog back into the jar, and by sending Zoé a pleading look to get her out of this sticky situation.

"Well, *mademoiselle*," Zoé said, striding right into the middle of the conversation with a knowing twinkle in her eye. "I've had enough fresh air for one day. I'm going to my room now to read that book you lent me."

Abby wanted to hug Zoé for annihilating a very uncomfortable situation. "Thank you, Zoé. I hope you enjoy *Emma* as much as I did."

"I'm sure I will." With those words, Zoé hugged each of the boys and picked up her bug collection boxes.

Her skirt swayed like a bell as she scampered toward the house.

Abby kept her eyes on Zoé's retreating back, for fear of facing Harrison.

"I'm sorry, Abby." Harrison stood so close that his breath had brushed the hair around her ears when he spoke. She understood he needed to keep his voice down for the children's sake, but having him this close set her insides to squirming

Oblivious to her discombobulated feelings, he continued, "I can see that my son made you uncomfortable."

Not as much as Harrison's nearness was.

"He did me, too," Harrison continued. "But he's just a child. He doesn't have any idea what he's saying."

Oh, yes, he did, and that was both scary and satisfying. Those thoughts would remain tucked inside her. She shrugged as if it was nothing. "Remember, I have nephews and nieces, so I'm used to them saying embarrassing things." Nothing quite as embarrassing as that, though. She discreetly stepped away from him.

Neither one said anything. Moments of silence passed. Finally, Harrison spoke. "Well. My sons have had a long day. I'm going to take them home."

"Ah-h-h. We don't wanna go home. We wanna stay with Miss Abby and Miss Denis," Josiah whined.

"That's not up to you to decide. I'm your father and I make the decisions. Is that clear?" Even though his tone sounded firm, the man's heart was as fluffy and soft as a baby duck.

"Yes, Daddy," Graham answered first.

Josiah nodded and scuffed the toe of his shoe in the dirt.

"Tell Miss Abby thank you for this wonderful day."

"Thank you, Miss Abby, for this wonderful day," they both said. Suddenly, before she could brace herself, the twins barreled into her legs.

Harrison's arm shot out to steady her, but he missed. She and his sons landed on the ground with a thud.

"Josiah! Graham! Apologize to Miss Abby this instant." He helped them to their feet, more yanking than helping. Then his hand took hold of hers, and her heart jumped inside her. The gorgeous man staring into her eyes affected her, and that wasn't good. Yet, she was powerless to stop it. The heart was a powerful, influential thing. Hers had gone and betrayed her by falling for another man. Not just any man, either. A man who had made it very clear that he hadn't met the right woman yet, and that he wanted a house filled with his offspring. It would do her good to remember that from now on. Her heart be hanged in this matter. She was in control. She sighed. If only that were true.

Chapter Eleven

Sitting on her front porch on one of the new outdoor chairs, sipping a cup of coffee, Abby watched the hummingbirds lick the nectar from her flowers. Delighted that everything else was going the way she had planned, a smile tugged at her lips.

With the extra men Fletcher had hired, the stage was now finished and a lot of the props were, too. Today the theater chairs and the carpet runners would be arriving by train. The table and chairs wouldn't arrive for a couple more weeks. Abby had tried to time it where everything didn't come at once, so it wouldn't be too hard for the hired men to have to deal with.

The sound of horse's hooves clomping on the hard ground pulled Abby's attention in that direction. It was Harrison. For two solid weeks now, after her heart betrayed her by falling for him, Abby had done her best to keep her mind off just how much she cared for Harrison, and onto business.

She missed the boys, too. She'd seen very little of them since they had a new nanny. That was a good thing. Right? Someone needed to tell her heart that. It kept forgetting, and she missed the little tykes something fierce. If she missed them this much now, what was it going to be like when they left for Boston and she never saw them again? Or Harrison? That thought thudded across her heart even more loudly.

Harrison raised his hand in greeting, and the familiar butterflies she got in her stomach every time she saw him returned. She reciprocated the wave as his buggy headed toward her house.

Harrison parked his carriage and joined her on the porch as he did every morning.

"Good morning. How are you this beautiful, sunny morning?" Abby asked.

"Very well. And I can tell just by looking at you that you're doing wonderful, as well."

My, how handsome he looked in his blue pants and light blue shirt. It was nice to see him in a more casual style of clothing. It meant he was getting used to the more laid-back style of country life. "Would you care for some coffee?"

Harrison pulled out a chair at her table and sat down. "I'd love some. I didn't have time to stop by Lucy's today. My nanny quit."

"What? Are you serious? Why?"

Harrison let out a long breath as his shoulders slumped forward. "Mrs. Glenn said they were too much for her."

Abby couldn't imagine what was wrong with the nannies he hired. There was nothing amiss with his sons. Yes, they had a lot of energy, but what boys didn't? And they were the sweetest boys ever.

"I'm afraid I won't be able to help you today. I'm going to have to find another nanny as soon as possible, or I'm going to end up losing my valet, too."

"I'm sure Zoé would be more than happy to watch

them. She's been pining for them. And to be honest, I miss having them around, too."

He turned surprised eyes on her. "You do?"

"Well, yes, of course I do. I don't know what is wrong with those nannies. Josiah and Graham are adorable."

"I don't think it's the nannies."

Abby stared at Harrison. "How could you think that? Of course it's them," she blurted, surprised that he, their father, would even say such a thing.

"No. No, it isn't."

Abby's ire rose. She opened her mouth to give him a piece of her mind.

His next words stopped her. "It's yours."

"What? Mine? Well, of all the nerve! What do you mean it's my fault?"

"Just as I said. This time I think the boys purposely drove the nanny away. They kept talking about how much they missed you and Zoé. They'd been begging me to bring them with me so they could see you two. I think it was a concerted effort on their part to drive Mrs. Glenn to distraction because they think that will mean they will get to come back here."

Abby's anger melted away with those words, and she had to stifle the laugh, which didn't work at all. "Ahh. Those little darlings."

"Darlings? Hardly. Do you know what those little darlings did?"

She shook her head, anxious to hear.

"They caught a frog and put it in Mrs. Glenn's teacup. When she went to pour tea into her cup, she nearly fainted."

Abby pictured it and barely kept her giggle to herself.

"That's not all. They found a small garden snake sunning on the shale rocks near the front porch and put it in her bed. Staimes said he didn't know a woman could scream so loud."

Abby giggled.

"It's not funny."

Yes, it is.

"The final straw was when they caught several stink bugs and put them in her hair while she was sleeping. The stench had her heaving for quite some time."

Abby wanted to laugh again, but the truth was, she felt sorry for the poor woman. Stink bugs. How revolting. "How did someone so young come up with such ideas?"

"From you."

"Me?" she squeaked.

"Yes. You. Remember last Sunday when we went fishing again and you were telling me what your brothers used to do to you and how it made you want to run away from home because you couldn't stand it and feared what they would do next?"

Guilt made its way into her cheeks. "It is my fault. Oh, Harrison." She rested her hand on his forearm. "I'm so sorry. I had no idea that they were listening, or that they would use those things to get rid of their nanny."

"I know you didn't. Neither did I. As bad as those things were, that wasn't what caused her to leave. The final incident was the dead fish."

"Dead fish?" Abby swallowed. "So that's what happened to the missing fish last Sunday," she said more to herself than him. "Please tell me they didn't do what my brother Michael did to my sister, Leah?"

He slowly nodded his head. "I'm afraid they did."

Abby dropped her head back and groaned. She pressed her hand against her chest and blew out in a long breath before turning her attention back to Harrison. "I'm really sorry."

"Not as sorry as Mrs. Glenn was. I hope she can get the fish odor out of her clothes."

Abby tried not to giggle. After all, it wasn't funny what that poor woman had endured, but the giggle had a mind of its own and made its presence known. To her surprise, Harrison's own chuckle floated toward her.

Naughty as it was to find humor in the situation, the two of them ended up bubbling over with laughter.

When they finally stopped laughing, Abby wiped at her tears. Gathering her composure, she poured Harrison a cup of coffee and handed it to him along with a freshly baked, sugar-glazed cinnamon roll with walnuts.

He took a bite of the sweet treat and swallowed. "That cook of yours is amazing. These are the best cinnamon rolls I've ever tasted."

"I'm blessed that not only Veronique, but also her sisters, decided to join me."

"I'm sorry. I can't remember if you ever said, but how did you meet those three? Each one of those ladies is a rare find."

"That, they are. They used to work for my mother until she got married. Their services were no longer needed, but my mother didn't have the heart to let them go. My stepfather offered to find positions for them, but I asked if they didn't mind moving if I hired them. The Denis sisters were thrilled to come with me. One reason being, they weren't sure how they would enjoy working for a man like my stepfather."

"Oh. Why is that?" He sipped his coffee and then took another bite of his roll.

"He is a prominent man, who entertains some very prominent people. They felt uncomfortable in that high-society, social environment, so it worked out great for me. Here, they might have to deal with the elite, but they don't work for them. They work for me. And even though they do work for me, they are more like family to me, and I try to treat them that way, too."

"They're lucky to have you."

"No. I'm the lucky one. Make that the blessed one. They work hard and they're there for me whenever I need them as I hope I am for them. Speaking of work—" Abby set the teacup she'd been holding down on the table "—I can hardly wait. The chairs are arriving on the train this morning."

"With the nearest train depot six miles away, how many wagons did you have to hire to deliver the chairs here?"

"Oh, no." Her hand flew to the side of her head. "How could I have been so stupid?"

"What's the matter?" He frowned.

"I can't believe it."

"What?"

Embarrassed, she dropped her gaze to her lap. "I didn't think about that. I was so excited about ordering them, that I completely forgot about arranging for them to be delivered here. What am I going to do? How am I ever going to find someone this late to deliver them?" For the first time since starting her business adventure, panic took over and she felt completely inept as a businesswoman.

Seeing the distress racing across Abby's face, Harrison settled his hand on her arm. "Don't worry, Abby. I'll take care of it." He had no idea how, especially at such short notice, but he'd figure out something. He had to. He couldn't bear seeing her so upset. His mind searched for a solution until one came. "Fletcher has three wagons. I expect most of his men have wagons, too. Let me see if they'd be willing to take their wagons and go pick them up. Plus, I know the livery owner has two wagons. I can rent them for the day."

"Do you think they will? I'll pay them extra for their troubles."

"I don't see why they wouldn't. As soon as Fletcher gets here, I'll ask him. In the meantime, why don't we finish our coffee and rolls and enjoy the morning? By the way, I know it's not even seven o'clock yet. I hope you don't mind my showing up early. I would have never presumed to do such a thing, but I knew you would be sitting on the porch like usual, and I wanted to give you an early warning that I wouldn't be able to help today. I'll make the arrangements for the furniture and then I'd better get back home. Staimes can only handle the boys for a short time. They make him nervous."

"Oh. I forgot about that. Listen." She rested her arm on top of his, and that same warm feeling he always got when she touched him made its way into his chest again. "There's no need for you to find a nanny. Truly. Zoé will be more than happy to watch them, and I miss having them around."

"I can't ask you to do that. Besides, you need Zoé to help you with other things around here."

"Things are pretty well taken care of until we get closer to the grand opening. After that, you'll be leaving and Zoé will get back to her normal chores then."

The idea of his leaving didn't sound very appealing anymore. But leave he must. He'd made a vow to himself years ago, the very day he'd been told by a once close colleague of his father's, just how rotten his father had been to everyone who knew him after the death of Harrison's mother. Therefore, leaving was definitely a must.

Not only because it was the right thing to do, but he had to do it for his sons' sake. After all, he didn't want them growing up with that same marked dark cloud that had hung over his head. No, he wanted his sons to be able to hold their heads high in Boston or anywhere else without shame. Harrison was determined to make that happen, and he couldn't do it from here.

"It's settled, then. As soon as I finish breakfast, I'll ask Zoé if she minds. Which I know she won't."

He hated doing that, but the last time he looked for a nanny, he had trouble. There were very few single women in this town, and even fewer widowed ladies. Most all of them had their own households to take care of or they were too old to care for his young sons. No other choice remained. "Thank you, Abby. I appreciate this."

"You're welcome. And just so you know, I can drive one of the wagons."

"You can drive a wagon?"

"Yes. I've been driving one since I was little. My brothers made sure that my sister, Leah, and I learned how, just in case we ever needed to use one and they were too busy on the ranch to take us."

The woman never ceased to amaze him. "Tell me about your ranch."

"What do you want to know?"

"Whatever you want to tell me. For starters, do you miss it?"

"Yes and no. Yes, I miss my family, and the ranch is beautiful. No, I love being independent and not being smothered constantly by my overprotective brothers."

"I'm sure they meant well. If I had a sister, I would be overly protective of her, too."

"I'm sure you would." She chuckled.

"Tell me more." He took a bite of his half-eaten roll.

"Well, I'm not boasting now, mind you, but my family owns the largest ranch out there. We have many acres of wheat. There are apple, pear and plum tree groves galore on the place. My family used to raise pigs only until the train started coming through Paradise Haven. Now they raise cattle, too."

"Why only pigs?"

"Well, they were the only animals that could survive the rough winters there. They survived by eating camas bulbs. After the train came through, it was easier to get supplies and feed for the cattle. Now, enough about that. Tell me about Boston. What's it like?" She popped a bite of her roll into her mouth and tossed a chunk to a chipmunk that had made its way onto the porch.

"Downtown Boston is busy and noisy and there are buildings everywhere. One rarely has to have anything shipped in because of the huge variety of shops. It's highly populated and the people aren't nearly as friendly as they are here."

"You know—" Abby spoke as if she were almost speaking to herself and not him "—even though I was born in New York City, I was too young to remember it. Still, I could never live in a large city like Boston. While Paradise Haven has grown, it still has that small, hometown feel. Like here. After living here for the last few months, I could never see myself living anywhere else now. I just love it here."

Those words were the final clincher where he and Abby were concerned. She herself said she could never live in Boston. She was settled here; he was leaving. So for his remaining time here, he needed to protect his heart completely from allowing her into it. The finality of that saddened him.

They finished their breakfast listening to the blackbirds and tossing small chunks of their rolls to a persistent chipmunk, whose cheeks were puffed full now.

At the sound of harnesses rattling and horse's hooves clomping on the hard ground, the furry chipmunk scurried off, and the noise dulled the birds' singing.

Harrison rose and made his way down the steps. He met Fletcher just as he pulled in front of the mansion. "Good morning."

"Morning." Fletcher tied off the lines, set the brake and hopped down.

"I need to talk to you about something." Without looking, Harrison knew Abby was nearby; he could sense her, could smell the rose scent that normally surrounded her.

"Something wrong?" Fletcher asked.

"We've encountered a situation that we were wondering if you could help us out with."

"What's that?"

Harrison explained their dilemma.

"I'm sure my men would be more than happy to help. I know a few other men I could ask in town that would help, too."

Harrison hated that he couldn't be the one to solve Abby's dilemma and that Fletcher was. But what did he expect? He wasn't from around here, so he didn't know anyone, and Fletcher did. "Thank you. We need to pull out of here no later than eight so we can meet the train when it arrives. Will you take care of organizing it? Abby and I need to head on over to the livery to see about renting Mr. Barges's two wagons."

"That won't be necessary. I know enough men who can help that you won't need to."

"Very well, then. We'll see you in about an hour?"

Fletcher nodded, strode over to where his men were waiting by their horses and wagons, and started talking to them. Several heads looked their way and nodded.

Harrison turned to Abby. "Looks like you won't have to drive a wagon, after all."

"It wouldn't have bothered me. I'm used to it. In a way I was hoping I would have to so that I could go with the men."

"We can go in my buggy if you'd like."

"You wouldn't mind?"

"No, ma'am." His heart might take a beating, but seeing the smile on her face would be worth it.

Forty-five minutes later, after they got the boys and dropped them off with Zoé, a convoy of wagons lined up in front of Abby's. Fletcher let him know they were ready.

Harrison helped Abby into his buggy. When they pulled out, Harrison rode alongside Fletcher's lead wagon so Abby would not have to endure the trail dust the other wagons kicked up.

Conversation flowed freely. They arrived at the train station just minutes before the stack of smoke from the train's engine could be seen coming around the bend.

"I can hardly wait to see the chairs." She clapped. "Oh, no." Her joy quickly evaporated and she stopped clapping.

"What?" He looked around for the problem but saw none.

"We forgot to bring something to cover the furniture so it doesn't get dusty."

"No, we didn't." Harrison smiled. "When I asked

Fletcher if he could help us, I also asked if he would have the men gather blankets and ropes to cover the pieces."

She placed her hand against her cheek and sighed. "Thank you, Harrison. You think of everything." She rewarded him with one of her beautiful smiles.

"I try." His lips curled.

After he and Abby inspected the shipment to make sure it was correct, and the chairs were being transferred to the wagons, Abby excused herself and headed into town. He hated her going unescorted, but she insisted she would be fine, and asked him if he would supervise the men.

Later on, when everything was loaded, Abby, along with three other young women, arrived carrying baskets. Several of the men eyed the females with appreciative glances. Within seconds, the younger single men rushed over to the ladies and took their burdens from them.

Before one of them could help Abby, Harrison beat them to it and relieved Abby of her heavy basket. "What do we have here?"

"Drinks. After that long ride here and with working in this here heat, I thought the men might want something to drink. I got them something to eat, too."

"How thoughtful of you to do that, Abby. Thank you."

She brushed away his compliment, and her gaze trailed to where the men were gathered. "It looks like they're enjoying the ham and cheese sandwiches. Shall we join them?"

"Yes, ma'am." He offered her his free arm. Just thinking about how thoughtful and sweet she was made him proud to know her and to have her for a business partner. Too bad their relationship had no hope of developing into something more. Like something more personal and permanent. If only there was a way to make it work. But once again, Harrison had to face the ugly truth and reality that it wouldn't.

Chapter Twelve

Shortly after sunrise the next morning, Abby rummaged through her dresses before picking out a pale peach one with white flowers and white leaves on it. Once she readied herself for the day, she skipped down the stairs and scurried into the large theater. Up the main aisle she strolled, running her hands over the plush fabric of one of the chairs as she did.

She made her way to the center of the stage and skimmed her gaze over the perfectly lined rows of royal blue chairs, and imagined herself performing in front of a packed house. Lines she'd memorized while performing Elizabeth Bennett from a theatrical version of Jane Austen's *Pride and Prejudice* passed through her lips with meaningful emotion. "'I do. I do like him. I love him. Indeed, he has no improper pride. He is perfectly amiable.'"

Harrison's face slipped into the front portal of her mind.

"Abby!" Zoé's frantic voice popped that image.

Zoé ran toward her, crying.

Abby darted off the stage and met her halfway down the aisle. "What's wrong?" Abby scanned her face.

"You must come quickly." Sobs tore from Zoé, and she grabbed Abby's hand and yanked her toward the door. Abby had to hurry to keep up with Zoé, lest she lose her footing.

"What is going on, Zoé?"

Zoé didn't answer and panic jumped into Abby's throat. Had something happened to one of Zoé's sisters? She had no idea, but she'd never seen Zoé this upset before, so she knew it had to be something dreadful.

When they entered the hall, Harrison and the town's sheriff stood in the main entrance room talking.

What was the sheriff doing here? A million questions dashed through Abby's mind, and she broke free from Zoé's grasp and rushed to them. "What's going on here?"

Harrison's attention brushed toward her, turned back to the sheriff, and then flew back to her. He strode over to her. "Have you seen Graham and Josiah?"

"Josiah and Graham? No. Why?" She looked at Zoé. Her face was blotchy, and tears pooled into her fear-filled eyes.

"We were hoping they came here."

"Came here? What's going on? Why would you think they would be here?" She fluttered a glance at the grandfather clock. It was too early in the morning for Zoé to have them as they weren't supposed to be here until eight o'clock, and it was only seven-fifteen now.

"When I woke up this morning, the boys were gone. We thought maybe they tried to find their way here." Harrison raked his hand through his disheveled hair and ran it across the back of his neck. Whisker stubbles dotted his normally shaved chin.

Suddenly it struck her what he'd just said. Josiah and Graham were missing. Fear threatened to rob her of her senses, but one look at the concern on Harrison's face and she knew she needed to be strong for him. "We need to pray." As soon as she said it, she remembered Harrison didn't pray, but she did.

Sheriff Long, Colette and Veronique joined them. They bowed their heads.

"God, the twins' disappearance is no surprise to You. You know exactly where they are. We're asking You to guide us to them. In the meantime, place a hedge of protection around them and keep them safe. Amen." Abby raised her head and her focus zoned in on the sheriff. "Sheriff Long, do you know anyone here who has a hunting dog?"

"I was thinking the same thing and was just about to say that Levi Huntley has a mutt that can hunt down just about anything or anyone. I'll run and fetch him and anyone else I can gather to search for the boys." Sheriff faced Harrison. "I think it's best if we start our search from up at your place."

"My place is…" Harrison started to tell the sheriff where he lived, but Sheriff Long held up his hand, saying he already knew where he lived because he made it his business to know the whereabouts of not only the citizens of Hot Mineral Springs, but newcomers and strangers, as well. "I'll meet you up there." With those words he strode toward the door, boots clomping hard and steady.

Abby turned her eyes up at Harrison. "I'm going with you."

"Thank you." He pulled her hand into his and held onto it.

Abby knew he meant nothing by it and that he just needed another human's comforting touch.

Keeping her hand in his, she turned to the Denis

sisters. "Zoé, think of all the places you've taken the boys and then go look in those places to see if they're there. Colette, you go with her. And Veronique, could you throw together something for the men to eat and drink when we return?"

Veronique nodded and all three sisters left.

Hand in hand, Abby and Harrison hurried into the buggy and headed out of town. "When we get to the house, we'll need something of Josiah and Graham's. Something the dog can sniff to get their scent."

He nodded, saying nothing.

As they made their way up the winding road canopied by trees, Abby and Harrison scanned the trees.

Minutes later, Harrison's house came into view.

Staimes paced up one end of the deck and back down to the other. The instant he spotted them, he stopped pacing and ran down the steps to where they were just pulling up in front.

"Did you find them?" Staimes asked.

"No. I was hoping they were here." Defeat beat through Harrison's voice.

Abby could tell he was trying to be strong, but the disappearance of his sons was weighing heavily on him. It showed in his eyes and in the wrinkles around them.

She had to keep pressing down her own fears, lest they overwhelm her sanity and ability to help him. She laid her hand on his arm, doing her best to be strong and confident. Neither of which she felt at the moment. "We'll find them. They've got to be around here somewhere."

Harrison clutched her hand and gave it a light squeeze. "I hope so."

By the time they got inside and retrieved an item that

belonged to each boy, Sheriff Long and twenty-three men pulled into the yard. Without a dog.

Abby's heart sank. "Where's the dog?"

"Levi wasn't home. Mrs. Huntley said Levi had gone hunting and wouldn't be back until later this evening. I asked her to tell him when he got home, if we hadn't sent word to her yet that the boys had been found, to have him come here. We need to make sure someone stays here in case the boys show up. I think it should be you and Miss Abby," Sheriff Long told Harrison.

"No. I'm going with you. I can't just sit here while my boys are lost out there somewhere."

"I'll stay," Abby said, even though she really wanted to go with Harrison, to be there for him if he needed her.

Harrison faced her. "Thank you, Abby. I'd appreciate that."

The men gathered around and quickly discussed plans. Three shots were to be fired in a row if anyone found Josiah and Graham. Two shots if anyone spotted any signs of them.

In sets of twos, they all headed out in different directions. Some on horseback, others on foot.

Abby and Staimes stayed behind.

Unable to sit idly by and do nothing, Abby searched every inch of the house, even though Staimes assured her they'd already done that at least twice.

Fifteen minutes later, at the sound of wagons coming up the road, Abby rushed down the stairs and flew out the door.

Fletcher and his men rode up on their mounts and wagons. Fletcher hopped down from the wagon and hurried over to her. "We just heard. How's Harrison holding up?" Being a father himself, she figured Fletcher had to know what Harrison was going through.

She herself could only imagine what Harrison must be feeling. Her own mind was tormented with negative what-ifs. But each time those thoughts came, she gave her fears and concerns over to the Lord. "He's taking it hard. He's trying to be strong, but I can tell this is really scaring him."

"If that was Julie out there, I'd be petrified."

She could only nod.

"Is there anything we can do?"

"The men have gone out to look for them."

"How long ago?"

"Fifteen minutes or so ago."

He raised his hat and ran the sleeve of his shirt over his forehead that wasn't even wet.

"I didn't even ask Harrison what happened. But I'm wondering if the boys were anxious to come to my place and perhaps headed down that way." The thought of the Colorado River dividing their places sent chills up and down Abby's spine. What if Josiah and Graham— No! She wouldn't even allow herself to think that way. She couldn't. She loved those boys as if they were her own. They had to come back, and they had to come back alive.

Harrison and Sheriff Long looked for any signs that the boys had been here, but there were none. Graham and Josiah must have slipped out of the house sometime before it rained during the night.

The thought of them out there all alone, in the dark, scared and cold, loaded his stomach with a boulder-size pit of helplessness and fear. His heart ached with a pain he'd only known twice before—once after he discovered his wife had left, and the other the day he had found out she had died. He hoped God had heard

Abby's prayer because He certainly hadn't heard any of Harrison's over the years.

They beat back the pine-tree branches as they trekked their way through the thick woods. More than an hour had passed and there was still no sign of his sons.

Where could they have gone? One place kept coming to his mind.

"Sheriff." Harrison stopped. "I can't shake this feeling that my boys were headed to Abby's. Even though I already checked there, I think we should head that way."

The sheriff nodded. "Let's head that way, then."

They started walking toward Abby's place.

His mind trailed back to the day before and when they had gotten back from the train station. He and his sons had had dinner with Abby. Afterward, the four of them sat on the floor and built a cabin out of homemade wooden blocks. When they got tired of that, Abby picked out a children's book and read to them. He remembered her animated voice and the way she made the characters come to life, the excitement on his sons' faces as they listened with such intent, how they cried most of the way home, and how they said they loved Abby and wished she was their mother.

It was time for him to put his fears of remarrying aside. Instead of looking for another nanny, he needed to find a wife. Someone who would be a good mother to his children. Abby's face popped into his mind. As much as he hated to do it, he had to erase that image.

"Over here. I think I found something." Sheriff Long's voice broke through Harrison's thoughts.

Pine needles crunched under Harrison's feet as he made his way to the sheriff, standing at the rocky edge of the Colorado River. There, near the riverbank, lay one of his son's carved horses. Harrison thought he might be sick. He swallowed several times, fighting the sickening image that threatened to overtake him.

White caps peaked as the rushing water barreled into the boulders poking out from the deep riverbed. Harrison closed his eyes, imagining the worst. The sound of rushing water filled the eerie silence.

A large hand cupped his shoulder, and his gaze slid that way.

"Don't go imagining the worst, Harrison. I don't see any sign to indicate they went into the water."

Harrison hoped, and even almost prayed, that the man was right.

Sheriff Long looked around and then pointed toward a large boulder. "There's something over there." He and Harrison hurried toward the giant rock, the moisture from the tall grasses saturating the bottoms of their pant legs as they did.

His sons' socks and shoes lay on the rocky ground in a heap. Faster than the river water rolling over the rocks below the surface, dread tumbled over and over Harrison until he felt he would drown under the weight of his great loss. He dropped to his knees, clutched the items to his chest and laid his head back. Not caring that he wasn't alone, he cried out, "Why, God, why? Do You hate me that much? What about Abby? She prayed that my sons would be safe. Apparently, You don't answer her prayers, either. What kind of a God are You, anyway?"

"A loving One," Sheriff Long answered.

Harrison's eyes bolted open, and he glared at the tall middle-aged man with the black burly mustache. "How can you say that? My boys are gone."

"You don't know that."

Harrison shot him a look that said the man must be nuts. All he had to do was look at the evidence. His sons' shoes and socks were found near the edge of the riverbank, and his children were nowhere in sight. It didn't take much to figure out what had happened.

A gunshot sliced through the air.

Harrison bolted to his feet, waiting, listening for another.

A second shot sounded.

He held his breath, waiting for a third.

When it came, no joy accompanied it as he didn't know if his boys had been found safely or not.

"It sounded like it came from that direction." Sheriff Long pointed across and downriver, toward the direction of Abby's place. "There's a bridge down that way. We can cross over there."

Harrison rushed forward behind the man, stumbling and hurrying with barely any direction to his steps. They came to a rough-hewn beam draped across the width of the river, one that didn't look nearly strong enough to hold their weight. "This is a bridge?" Harrison hiked a brow in the sheriff's direction.

"Don't let its looks fool you. This here bridge is a lot stronger than it looks."

It had to be. Judging by its decrepit appearance, that thing couldn't even hold something as light as a hummingbird.

Still, Harrison needed to trust that the sheriff knew what he was doing.

One at a time, they carefully made their way across it.

Three more gunshots pierced the air. Only this time they were louder. They were closer to his boys. Harrison's blood pounded in his ears.

Rocks crunched under their feet as they raced through the uneven ground, shoving branches of various bushes aside.

A large bull snake slid out from under the brush right in front of him, tripping him and crashing his knee against a rock. The snake slithered away.

Ignoring the intense pain, Harrison pushed himself up, brushed the rocks and mud from off his knee and with a strong limp, forced himself to move forward so he could catch up with the sheriff. Pain darted through his leg like a million pins and needles as he stepped over felled logs lying across the narrow pathway. They came upon a small clearing where a group of men were gathered into a circle.

Harrison couldn't see his sons.

One of the young men looked their way and broke through the small group and sprinted over to them. "We found them."

"Are they—?" Harrison couldn't say the word that knifed into his head as he hurried alongside the young teenage boy whose face was covered with freckles.

Harrison was panting now, either from fright or the exertion. He didn't know which or if it was from both.

"They're all right except for a few bumps and bruises and complaining that they want their daddy and Miss Abby."

Abby?

Relief poured through him. Thank goodness for Abby and her prayers. God had answered them. Harrison owed God an apology, but first, he had to see for himself.

The crowd parted to let him through.

"Daddy!" Graham and Josiah both shouted. They pushed off the felled log they were sitting on and barreled into him, throwing their arms around his legs, and holding on to him so tightly, he couldn't get them loose to pick them up. His knee throbbed as Josiah pressed his body against it, but he didn't care. His sons were safe. That was all that mattered.

After moments of frantic joy, Harrison was finally able to convince them to let go of his leg so he could pick them up and hold them. They buried their faces in his shoulder, leaving Harrison no way to wipe away the tears that streamed down his cheeks. Never before had he been so frightened or so relieved as he was now.

Minutes passed before the boys finally raised their heads. Harrison looked at each one. "Why did you boys run away? You nearly scared me to death. You know how much I love you, don't you?"

Graham ran his tiny hands over Harrison's wet cheeks, wiping away the tears. "Don't cry, Daddy. We know you love us. We didn't run 'way. We only wanted to see Miss Abby."

"Well, next time you want to see her, you come and ask Daddy first, all right? Promise me you'll never do this again."

"We promise." Josiah spoke for the both of them.

His attention shifted from his sons to the men around them and ended with Fletcher. "How can I ever thank you all enough for finding my boys?"

"We didn't find them. Fletcher did," the same boy who'd met him when he arrived said.

Harrison looked right at Fletcher, remorse for his earlier thoughts about the man tumbling through him. "Thank you, Fletcher. I owe you."

A deep, rumbling sadness went through the man's dark eyes even as he looked at the three of them huddled together. "No need to thank me. And you don't owe me a thing. I'm just glad we found them." He nodded again, sniffed and let out a long breath.

In that moment, Harrison remembered hearing about Fletcher's sons and how they had drowned. That poor man. This had to be hard on him, had to be resurrecting old memories. Harrison's heart went out to Fletcher. He couldn't imagine how he would feel if his outcome had been equally as bad as Fletcher's had been.

A fresh wave of gratitude flowed over Harrison. He wanted to shake hands with Fletcher, with all of them, but he wasn't ready to let go of his sons just yet. "Where did you find them, anyway?"

"They were sleeping way back inside that bush." Fletcher pointed to a large shrub nestled against a boulder.

"In the bush?" Harrison couldn't quite imagine that.

"We did what Mrs. Wainee did, Daddy."

His gaze swung to his son. "Mrs. Wainee?" Who and what was Josiah talking about?

"Uh-huh. You wouldn't let us stay at Abby's, so we sneaked out and followed the river to her house like Mrs. Wainee did. Only we got lost and sleepy. Miss Abby told us when Mrs. Wainee got lost, she followed the river, and that when it got dark, she found a bush near a rock to hide in."

It finally dawned on him what Josiah was talking about. Abby's sister-in-law Rainee. She'd told that story to him days before. His sons had been busy playing with their toys on the floor across the room. He didn't even know they'd been listening. How could someone so young remember those things?

"Well, Mrs. Rainee is an adult. Not a child. Children do not leave their homes or anywhere else without an adult. Do you understand that?"

His twins nodded their heads, their eyes wide with solemn understanding.

With a breath of relief, Harrison turned his attention onto the men. "Gentlemen, it's been a long morning. Why don't we head back down to Miss Bowen's? She had her cook fix up something for everyone to eat."

"Sounds good. I'm starving," Sheriff Long said.

"Me, too," Josiah added, and of course, Graham mimicked him.

As soon as they arrived at the mansion, Abby rode up in Harrison's buggy. The buggy rolled to a stop, and Abby hopped out, gathered her skirt and ran toward them.

Abby's heart leaped with joy at the sight of the twins, and she barely managed to keep herself from hugging all three of them. "Josiah! Graham! I'm so glad you're okay."

Harrison lowered them to the ground, and she dropped to her knees and gathered them into her arms, hugging them and smothering their cheeks with kisses while tears trickled down her face.

Graham looked at her with sad eyes. "Why you crying, Miss Abby?" His little fingers softly and tenderly brushed the moisture from her cheeks. That sweet gesture sent even more tears cascading from her eyes.

"Because I was so worried about you two. Where were you boys? Why did you run away?"

Josiah stepped from her embrace, planted his tiny hands on his waist and huffed. "We didn't run 'way. We wanted to see *you*."

His sweet words melted her aching heart even through the guilt over the fact that they'd been put in jeopardy trying to get to her. She pulled them back into her arms, closed her eyes and relished the feel of their tiny bodies as she held them close to her. This was, without a doubt, what love felt like.

Seconds later, her gaze slid upward to Harrison.

He smiled down at her warmly. Affectionately, even.

"I'm sorry," she mouthed.

But he just shook his head as his smile widened and he let out a long sigh, which almost brought tears to her eyes.

What was she going to do?

In that instant, she realized that she had not only completely lost her heart to Harrison's sons, but to him, as well.

She tore her gaze away from Harrison, for fear the love she had for him would show in her eyes. And she couldn't have that. His words about wanting more children scribbled through her mind as they had so many times since he'd said them. Each time they had the same effect on her, creating an aching, longing hole in her heart that could never be satisfied.

Later that evening, after things had settled down at the mansion, and everyone, including Fletcher and his men had gone home, Harrison asked Abby to take a walk with him. Although she didn't trust herself to spend time alone with him for fear her heart would expose her true feelings, she could see that whatever it was he wanted to talk to her about was important, so she reluctantly agreed.

At twilight, they walked in silence through the now weed-free garden. Roses of various colors and sizes flooded the light breeze with their luscious scents. A strand of her blond hair drifted across her cheek, and she curled it behind her ear.

Harrison led her to the bench he'd repaired. They sat

down and she laid her hands in her lap, waiting for him to say what was on his mind.

"Abby."

She looked up at him, careful to not let her eyes find his. "Yes."

"I couldn't wait to tell you thank you."

This time her eyes did find his. "For what?"

"For praying for my boys this morning."

She blinked back her shock. From what she'd learned, the man didn't believe in prayer. Perhaps this was a start. She sure hoped so, anyway. "You're welcome."

"I must admit when you wanted to pray, I wanted to scream at you. To ask why bother. When I saw their socks and shoes by the river, I wanted to shake my fist at God, and I did, too. I couldn't understand why He hated me so much that He would let my sons drown." His hand found hers, and its gentle warmth made its way into her heart, caressing it tenderly.

She wanted to yank her hand away, but just for this moment, and this moment only, she wouldn't. She would allow herself to enjoy the connection to love that she longed for in that secret place of her soul. The one she kept carefully barred. "God doesn't hate you, Harrison. He loves you." *And so do I,* she wanted to say, but those words remained holed up inside her.

"No. He loves you. It was *your* prayers He answered. He's never answered any of my prayers. That's why I quit praying years ago. But I don't want to talk about that. I just wanted to tell you how much I appreciate you being there for me this morning. And to thank you for the strength you covered me with when I felt as weak and as helpless as a newborn."

Abby could see just how hard that was for him to admit. "I'm glad I was here for you." She gave his hand a squeeze before she reluctantly released it. She had no choice but to let it go; the connection to him was too strong for her, and right now she was the weak one, for a much different reason, though.

Letting his gaze go, she stared out into the garden. Her mind wanted to take a turn and dream about him holding her and kissing her and telling her he loved her. That having more children didn't matter to him. That his boys were enough. That *she* was enough.

She closed her eyes to blot out that silly dream, but the dream didn't leave. It took a turn of its own. If only her dreams could come true. Oh, how she hated those if-onlys.

Masculine fingers, strong yet gentle, cupped her chin, tugging it upward.

Soft warm lips covered hers, touching her with a sweetness she'd never known before.

Oh, if only this were real and not just a dream.

Something stronger than the light breeze brushed against her lips.

Words, soft, and barely audible reached her ears. "Oh, Abby. Sweet, adorable Abby."

Abby froze.

Afraid to open her eyes.

This wasn't a dream.

Harrison had kissed her. And she had returned his kiss.

Great stars, what had she done?

Powerless to fight against the strong feelings she had for him, she allowed him to pull her into his arms, and to continue kissing her. When the moment ended, neither spoke. Instead, she sat with her head nestled against his chest, listening to his heart beating a soothing rhythm, knowing this could never happen again.

Time drifted lazily by, and she let it, until finally she asked in a voice quiet and soft so as not to shatter the moment. "Where did you find Josiah and Graham?"

Harrison shifted, and Abby forced herself to leave the comfort of his embrace. "Fletcher found them sleeping between a boulder and a bush." He chuckled softly. "Josiah said he got that idea from you."

"From me?"

"Yes. Who would have thought the boys were even listening the other night when you were talking about what your sister-in-law Rainee did?"

"What Rainee did?" She frowned.

"Yes. You know when she ran away and hid between a bush and a rock."

Blood drained from Abby's face as her eyes went wide.

The boys taking off in the middle of the night was all her fault. They could have died because of her. No wonder she couldn't bear children. God knew she'd make a terrible mother.

Tears stung the back of her eyes.

She shot off the bench and ran as fast as her legs would carry her toward the river.

"Abby! Wait! Where are you going?"

She pushed herself harder, willed herself to run faster. How could she ever face Harrison again?

A band of steel encased her arm, forcing her to stop, and her strength was no match for his. "Let me go." She tried to yank free, but Harrison held her firmly, yet without hurting her.

"What's wrong?" Panic edged his voice, but she couldn't comfort him right now. She had to get away. To flee the demons chasing her.

"Abby, stop. Look at me." With one arm holding her

in place, his other cupped her chin and tugged on it until she had no choice but to look at him. "Abby, please talk to me. Tell me what's wrong? Was it the kiss?"

She shook her head vehemently. "No. No. It wasn't that. Although that can never happen again."

He looked shocked at the intensity with which she said it, but instead of voicing that, he simply asked, "What is it, then?"

Her shoulders shook with the pain spinning in her spirit, and no longer able to hold back the flood of tears, she let them loose.

"Abby." Harrison took her and buried her head into his chest and kissed the top of her head. "What is wrong? Please, tell me."

"It's all my fault," she said through hiccupping sobs.

"What's all your fault?"

"That Josiah and Graham went missing. They could have died because of me."

"No. Abby, this wasn't your fault. You couldn't have known."

Oh, if only that were true, but it wasn't. "Yes, it is. I'm always planting ideas in their heads. Like the fishing and the mud."

"How would you know they were listening?"

"I didn't. But still…"

Harrison dipped back and pulled her chin up until she was looking at him. "Abby, listen to me. This isn't your fault. If I were a better father, none of this would have happened."

"No! Don't even say that. You're a wonderful father." How dare he blame himself for something that was entirely her own fault?

"No. I'm not. I'm so lost on this whole father issue. I shouldn't have left them alone. I should have slept in their room with them. I'm obviously doing something wrong because my sons keep running off every nanny I hire."

"That's not true. Zoé and I love them."

His eyes pleaded with her to be honest. "You do?"

"Yes. Who wouldn't? They're adorable, and you're blessed to have them. Not everybody gets to be a parent." With those words, she removed herself from his arms and headed back toward the house, grateful Harrison didn't ask her what she meant. She never wanted him to know about her barrenness. Never wanted to see the look of disgust on his handsome face. With a heavy sigh to bury her sorrow, she realized she would never be a suitable mother—even if she could actually have children. That hurt more than anything else she'd ever endured. At that moment, the dream she'd quietly allowed to grow in her heart since Harrison's arrival finally died. And the pain of that was more than she felt she could ever handle or endure. But endure it she must.

Chapter Thirteen

Harrison lay on the floor in his sons' bedroom, and in his mind he relived his kiss with Abby. Something he now realized should have never taken place. Most of the night, he tossed and turned, trying to figure out a way to make things work between them, but no rational solution came to him. He even made a mental list of why it wouldn't work.

She lived here, he lived in Boston.

Her dream was to own her own dinner theater, something she was extremely passionate about.

His was to right the wrongs his father had done, something he couldn't do from here.

Further, his only goals before arriving here were to restore his family's good name and to claim his sons' inheritance. He couldn't give those up, could he?

No matter how many angles he examined the problem from, he saw no way to make their worlds mesh. Besides, he couldn't subject someone as sweet and innocent as Abby to the people of his society. While she may be able to carry her own here, those people were ruthless. Especially the Bostonian women. So taking her back there was not an option, either.

After hours of agonizing, the verdict was clear—it was best to put an end to any notions Abby may have gotten from his carelessness the last evening.

That decided, he finally got up cleaned and got dressed. Just before sunrise, he got the boys ready and headed down to Abby's, dreading the conversation that he knew must take place.

When he pulled the buggy in front of Abby's mansion, Josiah hollered, "Miss Abby, Miss Abby!" His son leaped up and started to step out of the buggy while it was still moving.

Harrison barely managed to grab the back of Josiah's collar and settle him back onto the buggy's seat. A quick glance over at Abby sitting in her usual early morning spot at the small table on her front porch, sipping her tea and watching them, and he turned his attention back to Josiah. "What did I tell you about leaving your seat before the buggy is stopped, Josiah?"

"To wait till the horsey stopped and till you come and help us down."

"That's right. And why do we do that?"

"'Cause we could get hurt if we don't."

"That's right. Very good, son." He kissed the top of Josiah's head, and then Graham's so as not to leave him out. Thankfulness that he could still do something so simple with them breezed through him. He got out to help them down.

The second their feet hit the ground, the twins darted up the walkway.

Abby met them halfway, dropped to a squat and gathered them into her arms, a place he wished he himself could be. He gave himself a quick reprimand about tormenting himself with such thoughts.

"Good morning, boys. Morning, Harrison," she said, never once looking up at him.

That wasn't good. He needed to have that talk with her as soon as possible.

"Did you boys sleep well?"

Both bobbed their heads.

"I'm so glad. Now, how about some cookies and milk? I know it's not your typical breakfast food, but if it's all right with your father, maybe he'll let you have them just this once." Her uncertain gaze slid up to his as did his sons' eagerly expectant ones.

As soon as he nodded his assent, she quickly looked away, stood and brushed herself off. Hand in hand the three of them made their way up the steps and to the table. They looked so right together, like they were family, and yet Harrison knew he had no right even thinking that way.

She seated his sons at the table and placed a glass of milk and a plate with three cookies on each one in front of them. "Let's pray and then you can eat."

"Why do you pway, Miss Abby?" Graham asked.

She sent a quick glance Harrison's way, searching for his approval to answer Graham's question. Normally he wouldn't allow someone to disillusion his children with such nonsense as prayer, but Abby strongly believed in it. And even though prayer had never done a thing for him, hers had, so he found he wanted to hear her answer to that himself. With a quick close of the eyes and a nod, he once again gave her his consent.

She offered him a half smile before turning her attention back to his sons. "Well, I pray because it makes God happy when I talk to Him. When I thank Him for the things He does for me. And, whenever I need help, I ask God for it, and He helps me. Just like your daddy helps you boys. Do you tell your daddy thank you when he helps you and takes care of you and gives you things?"

They smiled up at him and bobbed their heads. Love for his sons turned his insides to mush.

"Do you think that makes him happy when you do?"

Their eyes brightened and they nodded yes again.

"Well, it's the same way with God. God is the One who provided this food for us to enjoy, so we need to thank Him for it."

Josiah tilted his head, and his tiny brows gathered together. "But Who is God? And where is He?" He raised his hands, palm sides up, and looked all around. "I don't see Him anywhere."

"God is invisible. We can't see Him with our eyes. We can only see Him with our hearts, but He is always here with us. He's the One who made me and you."

"Did he make Daddy, too?" Graham asked.

"Yes. He made everyone and everything. He made the sky, the trees, the flowers, the animals and everything else you see."

"Even the cookies?" Josiah asked with wide-eyed wonder.

Abby smiled. "No. Not the cookies. Veronique made those. But…" She held up a finger. "God provided the ingredients she needed to make them."

"Well, we better pray and thank Him, then, huh?" Josiah rushed out.

Harrison's chuckle blended with Abby's.

Those smiling eyes of hers matched the curve of her lips and lifted his heart. "Yes, we should."

They bowed their heads, and Abby prayed a short prayer.

Breakfast was quickly devoured, and Harrison wiped

the crumbs and milk mustache off his sons' mouths. "It's time to find Miss Zoé and go with her."

"Aww. We wanna stay with Miss Abby."

"I know you do. But, Miss Abby and I have things to discuss. So come with me." He stood and gazed down at Abby. "I'll be right back."

She responded with only a nod.

Unable to stand the strain of tension between them, he couldn't wait to drop his sons off with Zoé and get back here so he could clear the tense air between them.

Oh, good-night. Why did he ever kiss her?

Abby watched Harrison head into the house. Normally she and Harrison took the boys to Zoé together, but she needed these few minutes to pray and to gather her thoughts on what she would say when he returned.

For the first time in her life, she didn't know how to act around someone. Their shared kiss had changed everything, and not for the good, either. Harrison was right. They needed to talk. Otherwise, she didn't see how they could possibly continue to work together under this umbrella of tension.

She offered up a silent prayer, confident that God would take care of the situation between her and Harrison. A man she admired and loved enough to realize she had to let him go.

The object of her last thought stepped out of her front door, his face fraught with uncertainty. She understood exactly how he felt. She refilled his coffee cup while he sat down in the chair across from her.

Seconds ticked by until finally Harrison rested his clasped hands on the table. "Abby, about last night." Their gazes touched. "I owe you an apology for kissing you. We were both distraught over Graham and

Josiah's disappearance and equally relieved when we found them. However, it was wrong of me to kiss you. There's no excuse for my action, and I do not intend to try and make one. Please accept my sincere apology."

Abby shrugged it off as if her heart wasn't breaking inside her. "It's like you said, I think we were both so relieved that we found the boys safe and unharmed that we just got caught up in the moment. So, there's nothing to forgive. We'll just forget the whole thing ever happened and go on from here." Even the amount of conviction she managed to put into her voice hurt. The whole situation was vastly unfair to all of them.

Still, she had to tamp her inward snort down. As if she could ever forget his kisses. Kisses that had her dreaming about them and the person behind them until the wee hours of the morning.

But that was simply one more thing she needed to give over to God—her need to stop dreaming about Harrison Kingsley.

Another quick prayer went upward before she turned her full attention onto Harrison. "Before I forget, I want to let you know that I promise to be more careful about the things I say in front of Josiah and Graham. None of this would have happened if it hadn't been for me and my big mouth."

"Abby, I told you it wasn't your fault."

Yes, he had, but she knew better than that. Not wanting to discuss the subject any further because it hurt too much knowing she had indeed been the one responsible for the boys' actions, she changed the subject. "I have news."

"Oh?"

"I got a letter yesterday from the acting company I

had scheduled to come from Philadelphia. They won't be able to make it in time for the grand opening."

"What?"

She felt bad about the concern that fell across his face. "They double-booked with another festival for the same two weeks, but they assured me they would be here the month after."

Harrison frowned. "So what do we do until then? Delay the grand opening?"

"No."

"What, then?"

"I don't know."

"I'm confused. We have a grand opening coming up, and no actors. Why are you not worried?"

"Because I know that God will work it all out. Last night when I was praying, God impressed it on my heart to write my stepfather and ask him if he could send his understudies until my crew arrives."

He still looked utterly confused. "Do you think he will?"

The peace she felt probably didn't make sense to anyone else, but she knew this feeling. God would no doubt handle the situation with amazing insights and perfection. "I'm sure he will. He has more than enough actors and actresses in his employ. In fact, I should have listened to him in the first place. He offered to send part of his company with me, but I assured him that the traveling crew I had gotten to know very well from back East would work out just fine."

Harrison nodded and splayed his fingers across his clean-shaved chin. "You really believe in prayer, don't you?"

"Yes. I do." And she didn't quite understand why he didn't. Why anyone didn't, for that matter. But it wasn't her place to judge him or anyone else. Her place was to pray and leave all of the other in God's hands.

"Did you ever have your prayers go unanswered?"

Childbearing, or rather the lack thereof, popped into her mind. So yes, she'd had her prayers go unanswered. But her faith in God and His wisdom was stronger than her feelings and her hurts. Therefore, her faith in Him remained in tact. "Yes. I have. But that doesn't stop me from trusting God. Or from praying."

"Why?"

"Why? Because I love Him, and I know He loves me, and that He has my best interest at heart." God's best interest in her not being able to bear children— she struggled with that one. "I will admit sometimes it's hard. And I don't always understand why things are the way they are or why He answers the way He does. His word says that His ways are higher than my ways and His thoughts are higher than my thoughts. I've learned to accept that. Well, most of the time, anyway." She chuckled.

"Even so, if God never answered another one of my prayers, I would continue to pray, and continue to trust Him because my faith isn't based on answered prayers. It's based on a God who loved me so much He sent His Son to die on a cross for me so that I could communicate and have a relationship with Him. That's what prayer is really all about—communicating and having a relationship with a loving God."

"How can you call Him loving when He allows so many bad things to happen in this world? And most of the time it's to good people."

Abby noted the anger in Harrison's voice and wondered what had happened to make him so bitter against God. "I don't pretend to have all the answers, Harrison. I only know what I feel in my heart. In here." She pressed her hand to the center of her chest.

"How can you be so sure that God even exists? You can't see Him."

"Oh, but I do." At his frown, she continued. "I see Him everywhere. I see Him every time I look at the sun or the stars or the moon, and I am amazed at how they know just when to show up every day. Look around you. How do you explain the various species of birds and animals and plants and flowers that you see? And how every human being is unique and different?"

"That doesn't prove there is a God. I can see these things, but I can't see Him."

"Okay, let me ask you something. Do you see the air?"

"No."

"Then how do you know it exists?"

"Because I can feel it and breathe it."

"Exactly. It's the same way with God. I can't see Him, but I feel Him." The peace settled over and in her once again. She didn't work for it, it just was.

"That's different."

"Is it? Let me ask you something else. Do you *see* the love you have for your children?"

"No."

"But you *feel* it, right?"

"Yes."

"How do *you* know that love is real? After all, you can't see it with your eyes."

"I just do."

Abby pursed her lips and hiked a shoulder, letting her words sink in.

Harrison remained silent. She could tell he was thinking about what she'd said. Wanting to give him time to do just that, she closed her eyes and listened to the hummingbirds flitting by as she inhaled the pleasant menagerie of sweet scents. But mostly she prayed quietly that God would take her bumbling ways of explaining things and open Harrison's eyes to the truth of His existence and of His amazing love.

Harrison contemplated Abby's words. She really believed all the things she said to him. And she had a point. He couldn't see love, and yet he knew it existed. He felt it every time he held his sons in his arms or thought of them or looked at them. He felt it when he'd met his wife, and now with Abby. Perhaps there was something to what she said, after all. He'd ponder all of that later. Today, he had something he wanted to talk to her about. "Abby, I was wondering if you could help me with something."

"Sure. What's that?"

"Well, next month is Graham and Josiah's birthday. I'd like to do something special for them. I've never planned a party before, so I was wondering if you would be willing to help me. I hate to ask because I know you're busy, but I don't know anyone else that I would trust to help me with this."

She smiled and the whole sun-saturated area paled in comparison. "I'd love to help you. Did you have anything specific in mind?"

He shook his head. "No. Like I said, I've never done this before. The nannies always took care of these things."

"Well, let's see." She tugged her upper lip under her teeth, concentrating long and hard. Nothing came to mind, but she wouldn't give up. She'd think of something. She always did. "Let me think about it, and I'll get back to you, okay? Oh, and while we're on the subject of parties, the Fourth of July is coming up. I'm planning on having a small get-together here at my place around noon."

"Where do you find time to plan and to do all of this?"

"I make the time, and my mind is always coming up with some scheme or another. Gets me into trouble sometimes."

"Only sometimes?" he teased.

"Hey." She whacked him on the arm. "Yes. Only sometimes. Sometimes I come up with some pretty good ideas even if I say so myself. This place was one of them. Anyway, back to my plans for the Fourth. Closer to evening, I'm going to head to the town square. From what I've been told, they have a lot of festivities going on then. In fact, you might want to take Josiah and Graham. I've been told they have games and prizes and lots of things for the children to do. Then when the sky gets dark enough, they're supposed to have a fireworks display. Should be a lot of fun."

"It sounds like it. Would you mind if the boys and I tag along with you?"

"No. No. Not at all. I'd love to spend time with the boys and be able to watch them having fun." *What about me?* Harrison wanted to ask, but he knew he didn't have that right or that privilege.

The more time he spent with Abby, the harder it was becoming to keep his personal feelings in check. What a mess he'd gotten himself into…falling in love with a woman with whom he could never marry.

Chapter Fourteen

Despite the fact the sun bore down on them without mercy, Harrison was enjoying himself. Watching his boys dig for coins in the sawdust pile roped off at the town square and seeing their faces light up when they found them made his heart feel lighter than it had in years.

"They're sure having fun, aren't they?" Abby said from beside him. Having her next to his side felt right. More right than it had a right to.

The other day, when he and Abby had talked about the kiss they'd shared and how it should have never happened, he had thought he would easily be able to forget it and go on. But he hadn't been able to get the kiss out of his mind. After much contemplation, he decided that the kiss hadn't been a mistake, and he had lain awake most of the next few evenings trying to figure out a way to make things work between them. No solution came to him, so he finally decided to simply enjoy every minute with her and to make the best of the time he had left with her. He'd deal with his heartbreak later.

"They sure are. I love watching them. They give me so much joy and pleasure and happiness. And love.

Everybody should have children of their own. Don't you think?"

When Abby didn't answer, Harrison gazed down at her. Gone was the smile that had been there just mere seconds ago. "Abby? What's wrong?"

She glanced up at him, and if he wasn't mistaken, he thought her eyes had a sheen to them. He wasn't quite sure, though, because the look of sadness had been so brief.

"Daddy, Daddy! Looky what we got." Graham and Josiah ran up to him, holding their palms upward.

Four shiny copper pennies rested in each hand. He was glad that he'd made a large contribution to the children's games. Fletcher had been in charge of the donations, and when he'd asked Harrison, he'd been only too glad to help out. Thinking of Fletcher, the man strode their way with Julie in tow.

"Miss Abby, look at what I got." Julie held her dainty hand open and three copper pennies glistened in the sunlight.

Abby peered down at the girl. "That's wonderful, Julie," was all she said. No sparkle, no usual joyful response, nothing.

Something was wrong, and he wanted to know what it was.

"We got pennies, too, Miss Abby." Josiah's not-to-be-left-out voice came through.

For one so young, his son was already a very competitive child. He wanted to win at everything he did. Harrison dreaded the day Josiah lost at something. But losing was part of life. Harrison should know. He'd lost plenty. And he would lose even more when he left. Then again, how can a person lose something they never had? Abby didn't belong to him. She didn't belong to anyone.

Not yet, anyway.

He cut a glance toward Fletcher. While the man had made no advances toward her, Harrison could see the admiration in Fletcher's eyes when he looked her way. And he had a feeling that Fletcher wished Abby belonged to him and Julie, too. The thought of Fletcher and Abby together drove a dagger of pain deep into Harrison's heart.

"You sure did."

"Miss Abby? Are you sad?" Graham, always the perceptive and caring one, asked.

She blinked, then as if it dawned on her, she gazed down at his son tenderly. "Who could be sad with you around? And you." She looked at Josiah. "And you." She glanced at Julie, who smiled shyly at Abby.

Josiah lunged toward Abby, threw his arms around her and hugged her. "I love you, Miss Abby."

"I do, too." Graham imitated his brother's actions.

Hearing his sons declare their love for Abby, Harrison knew he had to figure out a way to make things work between them. He had to. Not only for his sons' sake, but for his own, as well. Not once had he started out to do something that he didn't accomplish. Now was no different.

Abby's chest constricted with not only love, but with heartbreak. These sweet boys loved her. And she loved them, too. Oh, if only she could have children. Then perhaps she could win Harrison's heart and not only would these precious boys be hers, but Harrison would be, as well.

But it was all just wishful thinking. She sighed.

No man wanted a woman who couldn't bear children. David was right. Harrison's earlier words were proof of that fact. Just moments ago, he'd mentioned how everyone should have children of their own and how much joy and love and happiness they brought.

At one time she actually thought adoption might be the answer, but even that was out. She was not mother material. The boys' disappearance because of what she'd said had proven that.

Despite all of those things, she made up her mind she would enjoy Josiah and Graham while she could.

"Well, we need to go." Fletcher's attention slid between Harrison and his sons, then ended on Abby. "Hope you didn't mind, but Julie wanted to show you the coins she got."

"Of course I don't mind. I'm thrilled that she did. What are you going to spend your coins on, Julie?"

"A new dolly."

"Have you already picked one out?"

"Yes, ma'am." She nodded. "Over there at that booth." She pointed to a stand yards away from them that had three shelves of porcelain, cloth and crocheted dolls, each wearing bright clothes and hats. "Papa's taking me there now. Aren't you, Papa?"

"I sure am, precious." Fletcher looked at Abby. His gaze lingered for a moment, and Abby thought it strange. "Now, if you all will excuse us, we have a doll to purchase." Fletcher reached for his daughter's hand and they walked away.

Abby turned her attention onto Josiah and Graham. "What are you boys going to buy with your pennies?"

"Toys!" Graham blurted.

"Candy!" Josiah blurted louder.

"Would you like to get them now?" Harrison asked, standing across from Abby.

"Uh-huh. Then we wanna race." Josiah bobbed his head.

Abby smiled as the boys led her and Harrison over to the candy and toy booths. Harrison was on one end, she on the other, and the boys were in between them. Like a real family. For today only, just this one last time, she would pretend they were.

After the boys bought a bag of jelly beans, which Harrison insisted they give to him to dole out, they each purchased a wooden sword. Abby cringed, wondering if they would hurt themselves with the toys that looked a bit too real for her peace of mind.

"Time for the sack races, folks." Mayor Prinker's voice rose above the crowd. With that loud, boisterous voice of his, he didn't need the speaking trumpet he held. "If you will make your way to the roped-off area, we can get started."

"Miss Abby, you wanna watch me and Siah race in one of those sacks?" Graham pointed to the pile of gunny sacks near the area where the races would take place.

"I would love to. Lead the way, boys."

Harrison fell into step alongside them. Near the starting line, Zoé came up to them and asked if she could take the boys and sign them up.

Harrison agreed, and off they went. He leaned close to Abby's ear and whispered, "How about you and I run this race together?" Abby ignored the tickling sensation his breath caused in her ear, and she had a feeling his words had a double meaning.

Her mind took a turn back to the past and to another sack race. One in which her sister, Leah, and Jake had run together and the two of them had ended up married.

Nothing like that would happen to her and Harrison. A gal could always dream, though, couldn't she? Wait, wasn't it her dreams that had gotten her heart into trouble in the first place? Even now the thing was yanking her back and forth. Only a short time ago she'd decided to stop the dead-end dreams. Was she that fickle minded that she was so willing to pick them up again?

She sighed. Yes, she was, at least where Harrison was concerned. For now, she was going to have some fun. She'd deal with the consequences of her choice later. "I can't think of anything else I'd rather do." She flashed him her brightest smile, and in return he offered her one, too, only his was escorted by a wink. A wink! One that turned her legs into the texture of warm molasses.

"Miss Abigail. Mr. Kingsley." Mayor Prinker disrupted Abby and Harrison's sweet moment. He and Harrison shook hands.

Abby wanted him to go away, to ignore him, but she wouldn't be rude no matter how much she disliked the man. She plastered on a smile. "Mayor Prinker." She refused to lie by saying how nice it was to see him again, so instead she went with the only other comment that entered her mind. "How are you enjoying this fine, sunshiny day?"

"Quite well. And you?"

"Very well. Thank you."

"Good, good. How is the Royal Grand Theater coming along?"

Did he really want to know or was he just making conversation? "Extremely well, sir. You must come and see it someday soon." Now why had she gone and invited him to do that? She wanted to snatch the words back and then slap herself silly for even voicing such an invitation.

"I already planned on it." He rubbed his meaty fingers over his bulbous red nose and chin. "In fact, the committee and I planned on paying you a visit Tuesday next. We will be there promptly at nine o'clock."

Abby's teeth ached from bearing down so hard on them. What nerve the man had. He hadn't even asked if they could come barging in on her; instead, he told her they were. Sure, she had invited him, but they had planned on coming before she even offered the invitation.

Harrison's hand nudged lightly against her skirt, and she gazed up at him. That same look of understanding passed between them. It meant hold your tongue and let me handle it. "We would love for you to come."

That's how he handled it? Speak for yourself, Abby thought.

"And now if you will excuse us, Mayor Prinker, Miss Abby and I are going to enter the sack race."

The mayor's bushy eyebrows pulled together. "You and Miss Abby are going to race? Together? As in the same sack?"

Was the man deaf?

"Highly improper, Mr. Kingsley. You need to reconsider that. How would it look to the people of this town?"

Oh. Oh. Just let me at him, she pleaded silently with Harrison. She didn't care what the people of this town thought. Who were they to tell her who she could and couldn't run in a sack race with? Harrison's approval or not, she refused to remain quiet. "Excuse me, Mayor Prinker, but I see nothing wrong with it. Back home it is done all the time and no one thinks anything of it."

"That may be deemed acceptable back where you are from, but it isn't here. I must say, if you think that is acceptable, then I have to wonder if your theater will be as acceptable as you have tried to assure me it will be."

The veins in Abby's neck expanded. Her anger rose to the surface and she was about to spew out a piece of her mind in the mayor's direction, when again, Harrison's hand nudged her skirt. He just better be glad she respected him enough to refrain from letting the mayor have it because right now she didn't care what the pompous windbag thought of her. But she didn't want him to think ill of Harrison, so she mentally pulled all the willpower she could muster to collect herself together.

"Mr. Prinker, if you feel this is not acceptable, then we will respect that and forgo running the sack race."

What! Abby yanked her gaze toward Harrison. Whose side was he on, anyway?

Harrison again sent her that silent, knowing look to let him handle things. She was growing to resent that look. It meant she would once again refrain from lashing out, and she really wanted to let the pudgy little crook have it.

"Miss Abby and I are certain that once you see the Royal Grand Theater your mind will be at ease. We know how important it is to you and the committee to maintain this fine town's reputation and image, and we respect that."

We do? What was Harrison doing? By now she was starting to doubt his ability to settle this matter at all. His handling of it was scratching down her last nerve.

"When you arrive next Tuesday, if there is anything you see that you do not agree with, we will be more than happy to deal with it."

What! What was Harrison saying? Had he gone daft or something? She wasn't going to change anything for those stuffy, old grouches.

Mr. Prinker's brows settled back into place. He grabbed the lapels of his dark gray suit jacket and puffed out his already inflated chest. "Very well, Mr. Kingsley." He smiled.

The man had actually smiled. Abby couldn't believe it, couldn't believe this whole nightmarish scene, actually.

"We will see you on Tuesday next, then." Mr. Prinker shook Harrison's hand and tipped his hat at her.

She wanted to yank his *chapeau* from his meaty hand and whack him with it. Harrison might be calm about this whole thing, but she wasn't. Her insides were stewing. And not just at the mayor but at Harrison, too.

When Mayor Prinker was out of hearing distance, Abby faced Harrison and shot him her worst and fiercest glare. "What were you thinking?" she ground out, trying hard to keep her voice down, but not her anger and frustration. "How dare you! I'm not changing anything for that man."

Harrison glanced over her head to where the boys were standing in line with Zoé. He grabbed her hand and led her several yards away from the crowd. "Calm down, Abby. I've dealt with his kind before. You have to flatter them or they can make your life miserable. Don't you see the man can shut you down? Then all the money and hard work you have put into the place will be for nothing. I don't want that to happen. I want to see your business succeed, and I'm going to do everything in my power to see that it does, even if it means doing something as humbling as sweet-talking the mayor."

Talk about humbling. The man was doing this for her. And as usual, he was being rational while she was operating out of her emotions. Right then, her anger went from blazing logs to a pile of smoldering ashes.

She drew in a long breath and was about to partake of a huge slice of humble pie. "You're right. Thank you, Harrison. And thank you for caring about my business. However—" she held up a finger "—I'm still not changing anything for that man."

"You won't have to. We'll just let him think we're willing to. That's all the man wants. He wants to be in control. And if he thinks he is, he'll act as if it was his idea to approve things."

"But what if he doesn't?"

"He'll love it. Trust me."

The following Tuesday, July eleventh, Harrison waited in Abby's parlor with her. Over the past week, they had worked night and day preparing the place for the town committee's arrival.

Despite how tired they were, Abby managed to look refreshed. Instead of the casual attire the little beauty normally wore around the mansion, today she had on an off-white bustle gown sprinkled with forest-green, long-stemmed roses with a ring of forest-green garden flowers six inches from the bottom of her skirt. Dainty red roses and lace lined the modest neckline, the short puffy sleeves and the gathered material at her side. Even her hat matched.

Harrison understood why she had dressed so elegantly. Mayor Prinker and the committee members would be arriving any minute. Harrison couldn't wait to see their faces when they saw just how elegant the theater, dining area and really the whole house actually was. The extra men Fletcher had hired were making great progress. In fact, things were progressing more quickly than Harrison had imagined. To be honest, there were still some kinks that needed to be worked out, but if things kept going the way they were, the grand opening would be much sooner than scheduled.

"The fireworks display was beautiful, don't you think? There's nothing more lovely than seeing those glittering waterfalls and sparkling colored lights exploding against the pitch darkness."

Oh, but there was something more beautiful. And she was sitting next to him.

Abby turned toward him until her knees were almost touching his. "They probably weren't that great to you considering you come from the big city. The fireworks are probably much grander there, I imagine."

"They are. But I enjoyed the Hot Mineral Springs display much better. And it had nothing to do with the fireworks."

"Oh?" Her dainty brows met in the middle of her pretty face. "What do you mean?"

"*Mademoiselle,* I am sorry to interrupt you." Colette breezed into the room. "Mayor Prinker and the town committee members are here to see you. I saw them into the formal parlor as you instructed me to."

"Wonderful. Thank you, Colette." She stood and quickly ran her hands down the front of her dress, tucked a blond curl that had escaped from her chignon back into place and straightened her hat.

"You look fine, Abby. No, make that beautiful."

Abby's gaze shot to his. "Beau-beautiful? Th-thank you," she stuttered while blinking those smiling eyes of hers. Quick as a flash, she squared her shoulders and scurried toward the door.

Harrison caught up with her, wishing they wouldn't have been disrupted. He wanted to tell her how much he'd been enjoying his time with her and how special it had been. He really wanted to tell her how he felt about her, but until he knew how she felt about him, he wouldn't. Besides, now wasn't the right time for that discussion. There would be time later to tell her. Right now, they needed to make a good impression on the mayor.

"Would you please welcome them, Harrison? My mother taught me to welcome people into my home, but I would feel so phony welcoming those people who have made my life miserable."

"Don't you worry your pretty little head about it. I'll take care of it. You just relax and smile. Can you do that?"

"Like this?" She smiled cheekily at him.

"No, Abby. A genuine smile."

"I know. I know. I was just being silly."

They stepped into the expansive parlor. The men stood.

"Good morning, gentlemen. So glad you could come. Would you care for something to drink before we show you around?"

"No, thank you, Mr. Kingsley. We have a meeting to attend in twenty minutes, so we would just like you to take us on a tour. That is, if you wouldn't mind."

Harrison was surprised the mayor had added the last part. His sweet-talking had softened the man.

"Good morning, Miss Bowen. I hope you are well." Mayor Prinker's smile appeared to be genuine, which is more than he could say for Abby's.

Harrison nudged her, hoping she would get the message to be nice.

"Good morning, Mayor. I am very well, thank you." She gave a nod to each of the committee members. "Gentlemen, good morning."

Harrison was proud of her. She was doing very well considering how much she loathed these men.

"Shall we go, gentlemen?" She turned her attention to Harrison. "Would you please lead the way, Mr. Kingsley?"

Harrison led them out into the massive hall.

"This doesn't even look like the same place," one of the committee members said.

"Sure doesn't," another added.

Harrison wondered if Abby heard them. He cut a sideways glance at her and met her fleeting look with a quick wink. They continued on with the tour.

"Those dark blue-and-gold carpet runners up the stairs look very nice, Miss Bowen." Mayor Prinker shocked Harrison with his compliment, and obviously Abby, too, because her eyebrows spiked before turning into a skeptical frown.

"Thank you, Mayor." She hadn't said it like she meant it.

Harrison nudged her again, and she nudged him back, narrowing her eyes at him in the process.

He and Abby led them up the stairs where the shield-back-style Chippendale chairs with gold, padded seats and matching Chippendale tables were situated. Kerosene lamps with white globes with dainty blue flowers on them and gold filigreed stands centered each white tablecloth with a blue, lace tablecloth over it.

Harrison studied the men's faces. Each appeared very pleased, nodding and smiling.

"Very nice." Mayor Prinker's jowls wiggled as he nodded. "So far what we've seen, you've done a spectacular job, Miss Bowen, of making this an elegant establishment."

"Thank you."

Harrison knew how hard it was for her to say that a

second time. "Shall we go to the theater now, gentlemen?" Harrison motioned them toward the stairs.

He and Abby followed the small group of eight men.

Walking along her left side, Abby placed her fingers along the right side of her mouth and for his ears only said, "I can't believe the mayor actually paid me a compliment. Not just one, but two. I didn't know the man had it in him."

Harrison chuckled.

The mayor stopped and gazed up at them. "What's so funny, Mr. Kingsley."

"Nothing you would find interesting."

The mayor seemed satisfied with his answer. Everyone made their way to the theater. When they stepped inside, gasps emitted from the committee members and the mayor.

Rows upon rows of royal-blue chairs filled the audience section. Carpet runners patterned with several shades of blues and grays lined the two aisles. Filigreed gold lamps, like the ones in the dining room, lined the stark-white walls. Various pictures hung on the walls, and heavy light blue drapes with navy swags graced all twelve of the floor-to-ceiling windows.

The completed, polished wood stage sparkled. A dark blue curtain hung off to the side, ready to be pulled shut during curtain calls or change of scenes, and the front of the stage had a light blue swag curtain draped across the front. Abby had done an amazing job. Even in Boston there wasn't anything this grand.

When they said nothing for several moments, Abby gazed up at him. Her mouth cringed, and she raised a shoulder.

"Don't worry, Abby. They love it. Just look at their faces."

Her attention swiveled from him to them. They were talking, waving their hands animatedly, and smiling.

The wrinkles around Abby's eyes disappeared.

"Miss Bowen, Mr. Kingsley, you have done quite a fabulous job here."

"Miss Bowen is responsible for all of this, gentlemen. She had all of this designed before I ever showed up."

"Yes, well, I'm sure you had a hand in it, so stop being so modest."

"I'm not being modest, sir. I speak the truth."

"Yes, well." The mayor loosened his tie. "Just make sure your plays are in as fine a taste as the decorum is."

Even though the mayor had paid her a roundabout compliment, Abby's eyes narrowed. Harrison knew she was about to blast him, so he quickly intervened. "They will be. Of that, I can assure you."

"Well, they'd better be." The mayor pulled out his watch, clicked it open, and snapped it shut. "Gentlemen, we need to be leaving now if we're going to make that meeting on time."

He strode from the room and the men followed after him like a bunch of baby ducks waddling after their mother.

They bid their good-days, and Abby closed the door and leaned against it with her eyes closed. "Am I ever glad that's over." She opened her eyes and pushed herself away from the door. "I need a drink." The way she said it, Harrison laughed.

"I meant tea, Harrison. Nothing else."

"I know, but it sounded funny. When one of the nannies who raised me used to have a stressful day, they would say it in the same tone you did, only they meant they needed a strong drink of spirits."

"Eww. I don't know how anyone could drink that nasty-tasting stuff."

"And just how would you know if it tastes nasty or not, Miss Abigail Bowen?" He waggled his eyebrows.

Her cheeks and ears turned a dark shade of red.

"Ah-ha. So you have tasted it, then. I knew it."

"Only once. When I was little. My brothers brought all of us a drink of water one time. Only mine and my sister's wasn't water. They snuck some of my mother's medicinal alcohol and put it into my and Leah's cups. Unfortunately, I was so thirsty that I drank a huge gulp of it and swallowed it before I realized it. My throat burned so bad, and I was sick the rest of the day. My only consolation was that my brothers had to clean up the messes me and Leah made and they had to do our chores for two full weeks."

"Did you get along with your siblings? I mean, other than that incident."

"Yes. We've always been very close. We still are. And even though they loved us, they pulled pranks on us like that all the time. But we got even with them enough times."

"I'm sure you did. You were fortunate to have brothers and sisters. I wish I did. And very soon, if things go as planned, I just may." Brothers and sisters by marriage that is. His heart smiled at the thought.

Chapter Fifteen

The rest of the morning, Harrison's comment drenched Abby's mind like the raging thunderstorm dumping bucketfuls of rain outside. He was an only child, so his comment about having brothers and sisters soon if things went as planned didn't make any sense unless...

Was Harrison getting married?

If so, to whom?

She hadn't really seen him with a woman, and she knew he didn't mean her. Did he have someone in mind back in Boston?

She slammed her hands over her ears, trying to squeeze out the disturbing thoughts as the whole thing was driving her crazy.

For the umpteenth time, she tried to concentrate on what else needed to be finished before their grand opening, which was going to happen much sooner than expected. Unable to stop from thinking about Harrison's comment, she gave up and chose to go into the theater instead and act out lines from one of the Jane Austen novels that had been converted into a play she'd starred in back home in Paradise Haven. Acting had a way of easing the tension in her.

Setting her pen and paper on her office desk, she made her way to the theater, marveling at how much Fletcher and his men had accomplished. Because of the fifteen extra men he'd brought in from all over the county they were nearly finished. All that remained were a few repairs, a few odds-and-ends jobs and the stage props that needed to be built and painted.

All the food had been ordered, and the dishes and flatware were arriving this afternoon. Brochures and tickets were ready, the plays were printed, as were the newspaper advertisements announcing their first play, which was an adaptation of *Emma* by Jane Austen.

Her stepfather had sent a telegraph that his crew was happy to help her out and that they would arrive within a week by train, costumes and all.

Abby figured she could have her grand opening within the next three weeks. A month ahead of schedule. She should have been ecstatic about the whole thing, but she wasn't because shortly after opening night, Harrison and his precious sons would vanish from her life. Forever. She knew beforehand that she would get attached to them and that it would hurt when they left, but she didn't realize just how much it would until this moment.

Making sure she was alone, she sat on a chair in the theater as tears pooled in her eyes. "Oh, Lord, why did I have to go and fall in love with them? I know You have Your reasons, but I still don't understand why You brought such an amazing, wonderful man into my life. One with two darling children, something You know I can never have." Abby placed her face into her hands and let the dam burst.

Her heart wept tears of grief for the children she would never bear, and for the boys she would soon lose along with a certain wonderful man.

How desperately she wished she could bear children. If she could, she would be so bold as to tell Harrison how she felt, even if he rejected her. But to have him reject her because she wasn't woman enough, because she was a failure as a woman, that she couldn't bear.

When her tears finally subsided, she snuck out of the theater and made her way to her room. A quick glance in the mirror and she sighed. Her eyes were red and her face was blotchy. She poured water into her wash basin and splashed it on her face. She flopped her body across her bed and closed her eyes. For ten minutes, she told herself. Ten minutes only.

"Abby? Are you in there?"

Abby blinked and scanned her bedroom.

Three loud knocks on her door yanked her attention in that direction. "Abby? It's me, Harrison. Are you in there?"

Harrison? What was he doing here? He said he wouldn't be back this afternoon. That he had business issues that needed his attention. His lawyer in Boston had sent papers for him to go over or something like that.

Her eyes felt as if someone had scraped sandpaper across them, so she rubbed them lightly.

What time was it, anyway?

One glance at the clock and her eyes bounced open. 3:45 in the afternoon. Oh, no, she groaned. She'd only meant to close her eyes for a moment. Instead, she'd fallen asleep for almost two hours. "Yes. I'm here." Her voice sounded groggy.

"I'm sorry to disturb you, but we have a problem."

"A problem?"

"Yes."

"What kind of problem?"

"Abby, can you come to the door? I need to talk to you."

"Give me a minute, okay? I'll be right there."

Abby leaped off the bed and did a quick glance in the mirror. Even though her face was no longer blotchy and her eyes weren't red, her blond hair stuck out like a scarecrow's. "Oh, dear me. That won't do." She quickly put her hair to rights, ran her hand over the wrinkles in her dress, strode to the door and swung it open. "What are you doing here? I thought you had work to do." Abby stepped into the hallway.

"I do, but Fletcher came to see me."

Abby frowned. "Why would he come to see you?"

"Well, he wanted me to be the one to break the bad news to you."

"What bad news? And why wouldn't he tell me himself?"

"He didn't know how to tell you, and he thought you would need my support when you heard it."

"I'm not fragile or made of glass. I won't break if I hear some bad news. I can handle it." Most of the time, anyway. The only time she had completely broken down was the day she had received the devastating news that she couldn't… *No! I refuse to think about that now.*

"That's what I told him, but he insisted I be the one to tell you."

Harrison's comment blessed the corset right off her. He obviously saw her as a strong woman. Something she prided herself in.

"The wind last night tore some of the shingles off the roof, causing it to leak in a few places."

"Oh, is that all?" Abby waved her hand at the minuscule problem. "Well, we'll just have him repair the roof when it dries."

"That's not what he's concerned about." Wrinkles formed around Harrison's eyes, alerting her that something else was terribly wrong.

The muscle in her neck tensed. "Oh. What's that?"

"The leak soiled some of the theater chairs."

"How many is some?" And why hadn't she noticed them or the leak? They must have been on the opposite side of where she'd been sitting earlier. And her mind *was* on other things.

"Ten or so as far as we can tell."

"Oh." Her neck relaxed. "That's not too bad. I'll just wipe them down and air them out. I'm sure we can get the water mark out if there is one. And if that doesn't work, perhaps Fletcher can recover them."

"That's not the worst of it."

"What?"

When he hesitated, Abby said it again, only with less patience. "What? Just tell me, Harrison." She wished he'd just say whatever it was and stop prolonging it.

"When Fletcher went to check the attic for leaks, he had an encounter with a raccoon. He got the animal out, but the raccoon made a mess of things up there. It's obviously been living up there for quite some time and has soiled the floor. He fears the smell will eventually make its way to the theater. Therefore, the floor will have to be torn out and replaced sooner rather than later. Plus, we're going to have to figure out a way to keep that raccoon from coming back. Fletcher says once they've made their home somewhere, it's hard to get rid of them."

Abby seated herself on the beautifully carved oak lion's-head French bench seat situated in the hallway outside her bedroom door. She absentmindedly ran her fingers over the white material with the elegant needle-work flowers.

Harrison joined her.

"Did he say how the raccoon was getting in?"

"Yes, through the window."

"I see. Well… God saw this coming." However, she did let one sigh escape. So many, many problems and obstacles. She hoped that wouldn't always be the case. "It's not a surprise to Him. He'll take care of it. He'll show us what to do." She tapped her lips and silently prayed for God's direction and wisdom. "Did Fletcher say if there was anything he could do about this?"

"Yes, he has an idea to keep the raccoon away, but he's more concerned about replacing the floor and the delay that it will take along with the added expense."

"How much of a delay are we talking about?"

"Two. Possibly three weeks."

"Is that over and above the time it will take to complete the other projects?"

"No, that's everything."

"Oh, okay." She pulled her lip under her teeth. "I just remembered that the tickets have dates on them. So that means that the show will have to go on one way or another. Well, with God's help, I'll figure something out. In the meantime, we need to find Fletcher and tell him to do whatever it takes and to buy whatever material he needs to complete the job." Abby's mind began going through her dwindling funds. With all of the things she had not planned on, the accounts were getting much lower than she had anticipated. She rose, hoping to keep her concerns from being obvious, but before she could take a step, Harrison clutched her hand.

"Abby." He stood and let go of her hand. "I know we had an agreement, but I'd like to help you."

She tilted her head. "Help me. I don't understand. In what way?"

"With the extra funds it's going to take."

If only her father hadn't set it up to where a certain amount of money would be dispersed each year, then she'd be fine. Right now, she had enough funds to take care of the added expenses and to live on until her business took off, but she just didn't have enough to handle too many more problems. All that aside, she had confidence that God would take care of it. He'd never let her down yet. Well, maybe once.

Harrison studied Abby's face. While his finances were stretched tight at the moment, he hated the fact that the cost of the repairs and the items that were stored in the attic would be substantial. He hadn't even told her yet about the two trunks of costumes the animal had destroyed. He didn't have the heart. Yet, he knew he needed to. Now was as good a time as any to tell her. "Abby, I know you believe God will take care of this, but there's something else you don't know."

"What's that?"

"The raccoon also destroyed two of the seven trunks of costumes you had up there."

Her mouth fell open, then it quickly closed. She dragged in a breath and let it out. "God will take care of that, too." She smiled.

The woman smiled. How could she when so much expense was before her. And how could she have such confidence that God would take care of it? Since starting this business, one thing after another had gone wrong, and yet with each problem, Abby had confidently said that God would take care of it. As much as it pained him to say it, the truth was, God had.

As he stood there, for the first time in Harrison's life, he wanted to know God. The God she knew, that she trusted so implicitly. Harrison wanted to really know Him. The same way Abby did.

It was time to re-read the note his mother had left for him, the one explaining how to have a personal relationship with God. Harrison wasn't quite sure how it went. It had been a very long time since he had read it, but he was going to find out. Abby had convinced him that God did indeed care about their lives. She was living proof of that by the peace she exhibited and the confidence she had in God even in the midst of complete disasters. Therefore, when he got home this evening, he would take his mother's letter out and follow its instructions.

That evening, after his sons had gone to sleep, Harrison took out his mother's Bible. Though he'd never read it, he kept it with him always. It was one of the few things he had of his mother's. Harrison had been told that before she'd drawn her last breath, against the doctor's wishes and even his father's, she used what little strength she had left to write a note to Harrison.

He opened the Bible and removed his mother's note. Many times before he had read through the parts about how much she loved him and how sorry she was that she had to leave this earth and leave him behind. Knowing she soon would, she wanted to leave him with the best gift anyone could ever give to another. The way to salvation. For years, Harrison believed his mother to be delusional, but now, as he re-read them, he cherished those words, words he was ready to read with a hungry heart and an open mind.

At first, he had a hard time finding the scriptures she mentioned until he noticed she had underlined them in her Bible. That made them easier to spot. The first one he read was in the book of John chapter three, verse sixteen. Next he followed her note to Romans chapter ten, verses nine and ten. After that, he read even more scriptures, devouring them like a thirst-deprived man who had just found a river flowing with fresh water.

Three hours later, touched by the love and the truth he found in those pages, he fell to his knees. He asked God to forgive Him and to be the Lord of his life. Immediately, a peaceful sensation, better than anything he'd ever experienced before poured over him and through him. The only way to describe what he was feeling was liquid love. A love so powerful, Harrison bowed his head in reverential awe. The next thing he knew, he was talking to God, pouring out his love to Him and thanking Him for cleansing every inch of him. Harrison now had the loving Father he'd always dreamed of having. It came not in the form of his own father, but someone even better. Someone who loved him unconditionally.

Drained, yet happier than he'd ever been before, he crawled under his sheets and closed his eyes. Tonight he would sleep better than he ever had before because he'd just made the greatest, most important decision of his life.

The next one would be when he asked Abby to become his wife.

The next morning, Abby hurried about, trying to get herself ready for church. For the first time ever, she was running late, so she'd told the Denis sisters to go on ahead without her. Twenty minutes later, she arrived at the white clapboard building with the stained-glass windows, large church bell and white cross.

As she neared the door, she heard the members singing.

She stepped inside, slipped into the back pew, grabbed a hymnal, and soon her voice mingled with the rest of the congregation. When the singing ended, she sat down and slid her gaze forward toward the pastor, but it never made it that far. Instead, it froze on a familiar head of light brown hair seven pews ahead of her. Harrison?

During the sermon, Abby barely heard a word Pastor Wells said. She couldn't take her eyes off the back of Harrison's head. Question after question swarmed through her brain, making her dizzy. Why after all this time, had Harrison finally decided to come to church? Where were Josiah and Graham? Were they with Staimes? If not, then whom?

She wondered about the woman he'd planned to marry. Who was she? Where did she live? What was she like? Would she love Josiah and Graham and Harrison as much as Abby did? The very idea of Harrison getting married and the boys having someone else for a mother other than herself gnawed a hole in Abby's heart. This was not the place to be thinking about those things, and yet she was powerless to control her turbulent thoughts.

When the congregation stood to sing the last song, Abby slipped out of the church and took her time as she made her way back to her property. Broken branches crunched under her feet. Moist leaves and the scent of forest floor, along with sweet flower aromas and pine, filtered through her nostrils.

By the riverbank, she sat on the same log she and Harrison had occupied the other day, and closed her eyes.

Water rushed right on by to only who knew where. Birds chirped in the trees surrounding her, and the chipmunks' tweeting, clucking noise all filled the silence.

Normally those sounds soothed whatever troubled her, but not today. Nothing could ever soothe or take away the unease tearing at her heart over the thought of Harrison getting married. Not even God.

"There you are."

Abby's eyes bolted open. A shadow towered over her, blocking the bright morning sun from her view. "Harrison? What are you doing here?" She peered around him, looking for what, she didn't know exactly.

"When I didn't see you in church, I went to your house. Veronique said she didn't know where you were. I thought perhaps you might have come down here."

"Why would you think that?" She wanted to ask him what he was doing in church as he'd never gone before since his arrival, but she didn't want to embarrass him. She'd already done that before when she'd made the mistake of asking him to pray in front of everyone the day of her get-together picnic. She refused to make that mistake again.

He shrugged. "I don't know. It just seemed like something you would do."

How would he know what she would do? *Only because he's spent the past several weeks with you, you silly goose.*

"Mind if I join you?"

"No, of course not. Please, sit down." She scooted over. It was then she noticed he was carrying a basket. "What do you have there?" She pointed to it.

Harrison lowered his broad-shouldered frame beside her and faced her. "Well, I didn't know if you'd eaten yet, so I asked Veronique if she could throw something together. Hope you don't mind me asking her to do that." His eyes searched hers.

"No, not at all. Actually, I'm glad you did. I didn't

have time to eat breakfast this morning and I'm famished."

"Shall we go sit in the shade? On my way out the door, I snatched one of the blankets that you used on the Fourth. Hope that's okay, too."

"Of course it is. That was so sweet of you to think of it."

He stood and offered her a hand up. She placed her hand in his and allowed him to do just that. Except when she was on her feet, he didn't let go. Instead, he looped her arm through his and led her to the same spot where she and her small group had picnicked before.

Abby reached for the blanket so she could spread it out, but he shifted it out of her way.

"Allow me. You just stand there a moment while I spread it out."

"I can help."

"I know you can. But please, allow me."

She spiked a shoulder. "If you insist."

"I do." He snapped the blanket and let it fall to the ground, straightening it afterward. "Have a seat, Miss Abby."

"Miss Abby, huh?" She sat down with her legs off to one side.

Harrison sat next to her and opened the lid of the basket. He reached in and pulled out two roast beef sandwiches. He handed her one and set the other on a napkin in front of himself. Next, he pulled out a bowl filled with thin-sliced, deep-fried crispy potatoes, two red apples, several slices of hard cheese and a plate holding two large pieces of pecan pie and set them on the blanket in front of them.

"That's everything. Shall we eat?"

As was her custom, Abby bowed her head. "Father,

thank You for this food. May it nourish our bodies the way You intended it to. Bless Harrison for this thoughtful act. Amen."

"Amen."

Abby cut a peek over at Harrison. She had never heard him say amen until now. His head was bowed and his eyes were closed. That wasn't something she'd seen him do before, either. She quickly yanked her gaze away before he caught her watching him, and picked up her sandwich. "Where's Josiah and Graham? Is Staimes watching them?" She took a bite of her roast beef.

"No. Miss Wright is."

Miss Wright? Abby didn't know a Miss Wright. Was she the woman Harrison planned on marrying? If so, what was he doing picnicking with Abby?

She set her sandwich down and gazed out at the river.

"Is something wrong, Abby?"

Her mind scrambled for an answer. One that wouldn't reveal anything about how she was feeling.

"Is something wrong with your sandwich?"

Now that, she could answer. "No." To keep him from inquiring about things any further, she snatched up her sandwich and forced herself to take a bite. Unable to handle the suspense, she nonchalantly said, "Is Miss Wright from around here?" She picked up a chip and popped it into her mouth. The crunch echoed in her ears.

"No. She's from Boston."

The roast beef turned to stone in Abby's stomach. She didn't want to know any more. She couldn't bear to hear if Miss Wright was the woman he'd referred to when he said if things worked out the way he wanted them to, that he would have brothers and sisters, too.

Did she come from a large family? Could she give him the children he wanted? It was back to that again.

If only things were different.

If only she could make her dream become a reality. Her once beautiful dreams were fading quickly before her eyes, being replaced at a rapid pace with her worst nightmares. And at the top of that list was saying good-bye to Harrison and his precious sons forever.

Chapter Sixteen

For the past two weeks since their picnic together, Harrison had made several more attempts to spend time alone with Abby. But each time, either something or someone had interrupted them. If it wasn't one of the actresses or actors who had arrived two weeks ago, it was someone else on Abby's staff, or she was instructing the new hired help on how to wait on the tables and how to address their guests. Times when it appeared there might be a moment to talk with her, he'd been pulled away to attend to his own business matters. Business matters that were definitely looking up.

Now, in less than an hour, the Royal Grand Theater would start their grand opening, a completely sold-out affair.

Harrison had been impressed with Fletcher and his men. As he walked through the mansion just before the guests arrived, he had to admit they had done a phenomenal job of getting everything ready, and much faster than Fletcher originally figured it would take.

Delicious aromas drifted from the kitchen. Veronique's French cuisine was sure to be a huge hit. He was amazed by how proud he was of all of it. Sure it was Abby's, but everywhere he looked, he could see his handiwork, as well. They definitely made a good pair.

The theater was buzzing with last-minute preparations. Maids, waitresses and waiters, dressed in white and black, neatly pressed uniforms ran around making sure the place settings were arranged on each table. The others had a tray of finger foods in hand, ready for the guests to enjoy. Footmen and ushers, dressed in black tails with white, starched shirts, donned their pristine white gloves. Two ticket ladies stood by the door, ready to receive tickets for the night's performance and to hand out the playbills. Musicians tuned their violins, cellos and violas to the sound of the flute.

Such an amazing group of talents they all represented.

Miss Elsa, the mayor's former receptionist, had done a fine job of finding the suitable help Abby needed. Abby had seen to it that the elderly lady's tasks were tailored so she didn't have to walk much on her bad leg. Miss Elsa had turned out to be a valuable asset to their little team. The mayor had been sorry to see her go, but his ruffled feathers had been soothed by the fact that Miss Elsa had a niece who was an experienced secretary and that she could start right away. Otherwise, the mayor may have made things even more difficult for Abby.

Abby didn't deserve what the mayor and his cronies had doled out to her. Long before Harrison had arrived, the woman had every minuscule detail planned out. She had deserved the men's respect and assistance rather than the derision she got.

Thinking of Abby, Harrison glanced in the direction of her chambers. A little over an hour before, after she made sure everyone was lined up and knew what they were supposed to do, she'd left him in charge so that she could ready herself for the grand opening. He couldn't wait to see her, to share this moment that meant so much to her with her. And when the festivities were over to have his long-past-due talk with her.

Abby took one last look in the mirror. The light pink, soft silk bustle gown with burgundy stripes and butterfly lace hung tastefully over her shoulders. Her blond hair hung down her back in one long twisted curl, except for the sides. They were gathered on top of her head and pinned with pink and burgundy dangling beaded combs.

Pleased with her appearance, she picked up her lacy burgundy-and-pink-striped fan and headed down the stairs. Her insides and her knees were shaking so she held onto the handrail for support. Her burgundy silk shoes peeked out from under her dress with each step. Halfway down the stairs she noticed Harrison across the room, talking to one of the hired men.

What a striking figure Harrison made standing there in his finely tailored, gray suit. His light blue shirt was pressed to perfection. A silk, striped tie, in three different shades of blue, along with a matching pocket-square handkerchief sticking out of his suit jacket pocket, and shiny black polished shoes finished his ensemble quite handsomely. Even his beautiful hair was combed to perfection. Hair she'd dreamed of running her fingers through.

Abby! Shame on you. Stop it! No more daydreams where Harrison is concerned. He's taken, remember? Boy, did she remember. With excruciating pain in her chest, she remembered.

She had no right admiring another woman's man.

Before he caught her staring at him, she yanked her gaze away from him.

During the past two weeks, she had been extremely grateful that she had been so busy that she hadn't even had time to think about Harrison with another woman. Okay, that wasn't entirely true. She had thought about it often, and every time she had, she had to force her mind to take a turn in another direction. One that didn't include Harrison.

Each step she took down the stairs, her legs got weaker and her insides shook even harder. This was it. Tonight was her grand opening. The day she had dreamed of for so long.

By the time she reached the third step from the bottom, Harrison was there, offering his hand to assist her down the last few steps. She thought nothing of his offer. After all, many a time he had assisted Miss Elsa, Veronique, Zoé and Colette. He was just being who he was, a perfect gentleman. At least that's what she told herself when she laid her gloved hand in his.

At the bottom of the steps he leaned close to her and whispered, "You look very lovely this evening, Abby."

"Thank you, Harrison. You look very nice yourself."

His aftershave, a combination of orange mint, lemon, rosewater, lavender and some other scent she thought to be rosemary, floated around him, swirling her senses. She wanted to draw in a deep breath, to enjoy how masculine Harrison smelled, but she didn't. Instead, she mentally shook her brain to clear it of any romantic notions.

"Are you ready for this?" He looped her arm through his.

She wondered what he was doing until she reminded herself he was only doing what gentlemen did. "To be perfectly honest, I'm extremely nervous. I just hope everything goes well. People have bought tickets from as far as twenty miles away."

"The mayor's happy about that. The hotels are full and people are lavishly spending money at his spa, at the stores, the restaurants and the hotels. Even Fletcher said he's sold a lot more furniture and has enough orders to keep him busy all winter and then some."

"I'm so glad. Not only am I getting to fulfill my dream, but it's blessing others in this town, as well. And you." She gazed up at him. "I have your bank draft ready. Remind me to give it to you later, okay?"

"Bank draft?" Harrison looked genuinely confused. Had he so quickly forgotten that after the grand opening, their business arrangement would come to an end?

"Yes, silly. Remember? The money I promised you when you became my partner? Your original investment, plus the profit I promised you when this arrangement was over?"

"Oh, but you are mistaken, Abby. It isn't over. It's only just begun."

Abby didn't know what to make of Harrison's words or the penetrating look in his eyes. She never got the chance to ask him or to ponder it any further as their first patrons of the evening had arrived. "I see Mayor Prinker and the town committee members have arrived. We'd better go greet them." Holding her head up high, she strolled toward them.

Harrison tugged her back to him before she got too far away. "After everyone leaves this evening, I need to talk to you."

Abby gave a quick nod, wondering what he needed to talk to her about and then strode forward, a perfect lady heading into a perfect evening. "Gentlemen, it's so nice you could come."

Later on, Abby and Harrison stood at the entrance door, saying goodbye to her patrons. Everything had gone off without a hitch. The exquisite French cuisine had been a sheer delight, the play had been perfectly performed with only one minor glitch, but nothing that anyone other than Abby and the performers ever knew happened, and the guests had left smiling with the promise to return with their friends. Some of the ladies had even asked Abby when her women's spa would open. How they'd gotten wind that she was considering opening one, she didn't know. The one thing she did know was, she was definitely going to build one since the interest in it was already so great.

The last patrons to leave were the mayor and his wife, along with the committee members and their spouses.

Abby held her breath as they headed toward her and Harrison.

"Miss Bowen. Mr. Kingsley. I want to congratulate you both on a job well done."

"Abby is the one who deserves all the credit, Mr. Mayor. She had all this planned long before I arrived." Harrison smiled down at her.

Abby beamed under Harrison's praise. "That's not entirely accurate, Mr. Kingsley. You were a huge help."

"You're being too modest, Miss Bowen. I am a man who believes that credit should go where the credit is due. And that credit belongs solely to you." He stepped back. Facing her, he clapped his hands. Within seconds, everyone else joined him.

Heat flooded up Abby's neck and cheeks, flaming all the way into her ears.

As soon as their applause ended, Mayor Prinker's gaze honed in on Abby. "I owe you an apology, Miss Bowen. You have done an amazing job here. All of us—" he spanned his hand to include every one of the committee members "—are all very impressed with what you have done and what you have accomplished. The food was excellent. The play was exquisite and done in extremely fine taste. There is nothing here that would shame our town or damage its reputation in the least. Quite the contrary, actually.

"You have brought culture to our town, Miss Bowen. And I know I speak for everyone here when I say how grateful we are to you and how proud we are of you. You have proven yourself to be a fine, upstanding business-woman and a fine asset to our community. Therefore, as long as you continue on as you have this evening, there will be no revoking of your business license. You may continue to run your establishment with or without a male business partner."

Joy lit through her, but it was doused almost instantly with fear. Now there was nothing to keep Harrison here.

The mayor and his men along with their wives filed outside to their awaiting carriages.

Abby turned to Harrison with a fake smile in her heart and on her lips, prepared to tell him thank you for all he had done. "Harrison…"

"*Mademoiselle!*" Veronique called from the back of the main room near the kitchen and came running.

Abby spun toward her. "Veronique, what's wrong?"

"*Mademoiselle,* the raccoon, he is back, and he is making a huge mess in the kitchen. Come quickly. I don't know what to do!"

Abby sighed. What else could go wrong?

* * *

The next morning, Harrison woke early. He couldn't wait to see Abby today. Before she got too busy preparing for this evening's performance, he needed to talk to her. There would be no more delaying this conversation, especially after hearing the mayor's words that she no longer needed a business partner. He'd intended to talk to Abby after everyone had finally left the theater, but then everything turned to chaos, trying to catch the raccoon and then cleaning up the mess the critter had made. It was late, and everyone was exhausted, so he and Abby had agreed to meet at seven a.m.

Harrison rushed through getting dressed, kissed his boys goodbye with the promise of seeing them later, then hurried to Abby's place.

His stomach leaped into his throat the instant he saw her sitting in her usual morning spot at the table on the mansion's front porch. He hopped out and jogged up the stairs. "Morning," he said with a chipper voice.

"Morning." Her greeting lacked its usual luster and sounded rather formal.

His joy evaporated like the morning fog from the river. He stood and took a seat next to her. "You tired?"

"A little." She poured him a cup of coffee and handed it and a plate of leftover French pastries to him.

"Thank you."

She nodded and said nothing more, wouldn't even look at him.

He picked up the finger-size pastry and popped it into his mouth, then followed it with a drink of hot coffee.

Awkward didn't begin to describe the silence stretching between them. This wasn't quite the atmosphere he had in mind when he decided to propose to her. Even so, he wouldn't let that deter him, but he would start out with something else less life-altering and ease his way into it.

"Abby, I want to share something with you that I found out a few weeks ago."

She looked over at him. The light in her smiling eyes was nonexistent today. "What's that?" she asked with very little interest.

"My butler overheard a conversation between my father's lawyer and a colleague. He was apparently bragging about how much money he had made off my father to enforce the stipulations in his will—stipulations it appears that no court or judge would ever enforce." That caught her attention. "When I found out, I fired my father's lawyer and hired a new one. Mr. Wilkins informed me that the judge reviewed the stipulations in my father's will and declared them unenforceable. Therefore, they will be releasing all my father's assets and money, my full inheritance, next week. I'm telling you this because I want you to know that I could have walked away from this business arrangement of ours a few weeks ago, but I chose not to."

She frowned. "I don't understand. Why did you stay if you didn't have to?"

"For several reasons." He held her gaze tenderly, praying she wouldn't throw him off the porch and out of her life. "One, I wanted to finish what I started. Two, I wanted to make sure your dreams came true, and I wanted to help make that happen. And Three, Because I needed time to figure out a way to make this work between us. To make us work."

"What do you mean 'make us work'? I don't understand." She frowned again.

He raked his hand through his hair. He wasn't going

about this very well. "Let me try to explain it this way. I've had the pleasure of being your business partner these several weeks, but that isn't enough for me anymore. I want to be your lifelong partner. I love you, Abby."

Her eyes widened in shock.

He hurried forward before she could say anything. "I even figured out a way for us to be together and still get what we both want. You would be able to stay here and keep your theater, and I would be able to right the wrongs my father has done.

"I've already worked out the details with Mr. Wilkins. When my father's assets are released, I am having a full accounting done for all of my father's affairs, and for those businesses where it appears he took unfair advantage, we plan to make restitution to the extent it's possible." His words swam across Abby's face, but he continued, knowing he could re-explain it later if necessary. "The men that are currently running my other businesses now will continue to do so. They will each check in with me until which time I can sell them off. During that time, Mr. Wilkins will make sure the books are accurate along with keeping an eye on the businesses for me. That way, not only will I fulfill my lifelong dream, but I will also restore my family's name.

"Only I'll do it from here. Truth is, Abby, I've grown to love this town and its people. I love the mountains and would love for my boys to grow up here instead of in Boston. So..." Harrison slipped from his chair and down onto one knee. He reached inside his pocket and pulled out the diamond ring he'd had his butler, Forsyth, send from Boston. His mother's diamond ring. "Abby, I love you. And judging from what I've seen in your eyes when you look at me, I believe you love me, too." Shock danced in her blue eyes at that one. "Will you marry me?"

"Will I what?" She leaped to her feet. "What about Miss Wright?"

"Miss Wright? My nanny?" He stood and stared at Abby, wondering what she was talking about.

"Yes. I thought you were getting married. And since I hadn't seen you with another woman, I assumed that you were talking about Miss Wright."

Now where had she gotten that ludicrous notion from? "Why would you think I'd be marrying Miss Wright? She's old enough to be my grandmother."

"She is? But—but she's from Boston."

"You're not making any sense, Abby. What does her being from Boston have to do with anything?"

"The other day you said if things went your way you'd soon have brothers and sisters. I figured you already had someone in mind to marry when you said that. Then shortly after that you talked about Miss Wright from Boston. I just assumed..." She let her sentence hang, and he picked it up.

"That that was who I was talking about."

"Yes."

"Well, it wasn't. I was thinking about you." He reached for her hands but she yanked them behind her back the same way she had the day they met. Only there wasn't any reason for her to yank them from out of his reach this time. Or was there?

Abby couldn't believe her ears. Harrison loved her and asked her to marry him. Her heart sighed knowing he had figured out a way for them to be together, and knowing he could have gone home a long time ago but he hadn't.

That he had chosen to stay here for her.

To help her see her dream come to pass.

All of those things endeared her to him even more so, and yet she had to deny her heart of his love and her dreams. She couldn't marry him. She had to refuse him, but how could she do that without telling him why? That was going to take a lot more courage than she had, so she sent up a silent prayer asking God for a huge dose of courage.

It never came.

She had to handle this one on her own, and handle it she would. Not because she wanted to but because she had to. For his and his sons' sakes. "Harrison, I'm sorry for any misunderstandings between us. But before this goes on any further, I want you to know that it hurts me to pain you, but marriage was not part of our original agreement. I have no plans of ever marrying. I'm sorry." With those words she fled past him and bolted into the house. Taking the stairs three at a time, she rushed up them and into her room.

She closed her door and locked it, then darted to her bed and flopped herself on top of her blue comforter. Hands crisscrossed above her head, she buried her face and wept.

How she had wanted to throw herself into Harrison's arms and to smother his face with yeses and kisses, but reality had finally crashed down on her. She wasn't a whole woman, wasn't mother material. Therefore, she refused to saddle someone as wonderful as Harrison with someone like herself. She loved him and his two boys far too much to do that to them.

Harrison stood there, staring at the door Abby had disappeared through, unbelieving of what he'd just heard. Her rejection stung him to the core, deeper than anyone else's who had rejected him or had used him during his life. He shook his head, running his fingers through his hair and settling his hand on the back of his head.

With all his being, he truly believed Abby was different, that she cared about him, loved him, even. But she didn't. It was perfectly clear that she didn't have any use for him anymore, and that he had once again stupidly trusted someone with his heart. Well, he wasn't ever going to make that mistake again. He whirled and stomped down her porch. There was nothing keeping him here now, so the first train heading East out of this town, he would be on it.

That evening, Abby made it through another Royal Grand Theater production, but this time it didn't feel royal or grand. Without Harrison at her side, her heart felt as if it had been yanked out of her chest, and the pain of loss was more than she could handle. He hadn't even come, hadn't even shown up for their second biggest night of all. All she wanted to do was to go to bed and forget the whole day. When the last person left and the staff had gone to bed, she made her way to her room and cried herself to sleep. What good was a dream if when you got there, it hurt this badly? When she awoke the next morning, she had a splitting headache from crying so long and so hard.

She wanted to stay in bed and pull the covers over her head, but she had to get up and get busy. Her mind swam with all the preparations there were to handle. For two more weeks, her company would perform the play *Emma* by Jane Austen. After that, they would be perform *Pride & Prejudice*. There were costumes to make and playbills to script and tickets to fashion. So much to do, and she didn't want to do even one whit of any of it.

Before Harrison had come into her life, she would have been happy that things were going so well and that she had sold out performances clear on up until December. Without him, she no longer cared. And yet somehow she had to go on. She had to forget him. The best thing to do was to bury herself in her work so she could at least try to. She looked at the clock. Even though it was only five in the morning and no one else would be up and about, she forced herself to get out of bed and to get dressed so she could busy her mind with other thoughts than those of Harrison.

In her quiet office, she started checking her list for things that needed to be done—get the playbill material to Miss Elsa, wash and iron the draperies, order the food, repair the costumes, build new set pieces. About an hour later, she caught a strange whiff of something and stopped. She drew in a longer breath through her nostrils. Was that smoke she smelled? She sniffed again. It was.

Her eyes went wide as she darted through the house, checking for the source of what she now knew to be smoke. When she reached the back door, she spotted flames in the distance. The grass fire just down the hill was popping and smoking and heading directly toward her shed, the very shed that held most of her stage props!

Grabbing her skirt with both hands, Abby raced through the servant section of the house, banging on doors and hollering, "Help! Help! Fire!" Without waiting to see if anyone heard her or would follow her, she ran outside, gathered buckets and gunny sacks. She filled the buckets with water from the pump and soaked the sacks as fast as she could.

Loud clanging from the town's fire bell rang in her ears.

Voices rose above it as men gathered near the place where the flames were eating up the grasses around her shed. Without a thought for her own safety, she raced between the two and began to bat at the flames. They were small but persistent and growing.

Others arrived and helped fill buckets from the well and the pump. They handed them to the men who had formed several lines where they handed off the buckets and sacks to each other. Abby worked side by side with the men. She could not let another assault shatter her dream. She was soaked and sweating and panicked as the flames continued to advance until the orange and yellow overtook their best efforts.

"Miss Abby!" One of the men grabbed her and yanked her free of the firestorm just as the flames licked up the outside of her shed, engulfing the walls within seconds. But she would not give up. She grabbed two buckets of water, ran as close as she could get to the structure and poured the water on the ground, trying to make a perimeter so the grass fire wouldn't reach her house. The shed was gone, a total loss. Now she only prayed that somehow they could save the house. "God, help me. Please don't let it burn my theater down, too."

Chapter Seventeen

Harrison stood at the stagecoach stop, waiting for the vehicle that would take him, his sons, Staimes and Miss Wright to the nearest train station that would take them back to Boston. When he'd asked Abby to marry him and she had refused him, he'd felt like an idiot for thinking she was different from all the other women he'd known, that she was like his sweet Allison. Well, she turned out to be nothing like Allison, and she was just like every other woman he'd known. Women who only wanted him for what he could offer them. Money and opportunity.

He and Abby may have had a business agreement from the very start, but when he had kissed her and she had responded, that had nothing to do with business. When they shared time talking and picnicking, that, too, had nothing to do with business. At least not to him, anyway. And what about all those dreamy looks he'd seen in her eyes? Looks he must have misinterpreted.

He slammed his eyelids shut. What an idiot he'd been.

To think that she cared about him. Loved him, even. He still couldn't believe how much trouble he'd gone through, how many sleepless nights he'd endured to come up with a plan that would work for both of them. Plans that he now needed to get back to Boston to undo.

Loud clanging pierced the air. Harrison jumped and his turbulent thoughts disintegrated into new chaotic ones. What was going on?

Voices of men shouting rose above the thundering hooves of the stagecoach horses.

A man carrying buckets filled with gunny sacks flew past him.

Harrison called after him, "What's going on?"

Without stopping the man hollered over his shoulder, "There's a fire at the Royal Grand Theater."

The Royal Grand? Had Harrison heard him correctly?

A fire? At Abby's?

His whole spirit cried out. *Abby! Lord, no!*

Harrison spun to his valet. "Staimes, don't board that stagecoach." He yanked his coat off and tossed it to him. "Stay here. Miss Wright, watch the boys. I'll be back." He whirled and ran as fast as he could toward Abby's place, rolling up his sleeves as he went.

When his racing feet carried him close enough, he saw the flames devouring her shed and now heading toward the theater. The fire was still a fair distance away from the mansion, but it was closing in fast. "God, don't let it reach Abby's house!"

Just as he arrived, he spotted Abby amid the chaos, running with a bucket in each hand. He rushed over to her, and she stumbled right as he got there. He shot out his hand and caught her, water sloshed all over the legs of his suit pants, soaking them.

Abby turned her soot-covered face up to his. "Harrison?" She coughed. "What are you doing here?"

"I came to help. Give me those." He reached for her buckets, but she yanked them to her.

"No! I need to put the fire out before it takes out my home." She took off running toward the opposite end of the line where the buckets were being passed off. She poured what little water that was left in them onto the ground. What a smart woman she was, trying to place a water barrier between her house and the flames.

Harrison rushed toward the water pump and got to work forming the barrier and dousing the flames.

Sweat soaked his body, the heat from the fire became unbearable, but he pressed onward.

All up and down the line surrounding the house, men passed buckets back and forth. Each bucket dumped doused more and more of the destructive flames. Finally, with the effort of what seemed like every townsperson in the surrounding area, Abby's employees, along with himself and Abby, the flames were finally put out. Thankfully, the gardens and the back side of the theater had sustained no damage at all. The rest was mostly smoke damage, except for the grass and the shed.

Harrison breathed a prayer of thanksgiving as he thanked each and every person who had come to help. He gave Veronique, Colette and Zoé extra hugs as they looked the most shaken. He made sure to search out and shake the hand of every one of Fletcher's men as well as Fletcher himself.

When he had finished thanking everyone, the one he most wanted to speak with was nowhere to be found.

"I think she went down by the river, sir," Veronique said when she found him standing among the diminishing crowd looking around.

His gaze found hers and he nodded. "Thank you, Veronique."

"No. Thank you, sir."

He gave a quick nod. Leaving the others, Harrison hurried to the river. He found Abby there, on her knees splashing water on her arms and her face.

He knelt down beside her and splashed his own face with the cool mountain water, not knowing how he'd be received after not showing up the night before. Harrison waited, hoping she would say something. Anything. All she did, however, was to continue to splash water on her already soot-free face.

Abby glanced over at Harrison, hoping the water would disguise the tears she wanted so desperately to hide from him, but couldn't. Because of his efforts, the town's, and the efforts of her employees and friends, her theater had been spared. She owed him a thank-you at least. Without looking at him, she stared out across the river, seeing nothing but her own pain reflecting there. "Thank you, Harrison," she finally said. "For helping me." She swallowed back the overflow of tears, but was powerless to stop them from completely flowing through her voice. She only hoped Harrison didn't hear them. "I was so afraid. I thought I was going to…" Unable to hold back the sobs rising in her throat, they pushed out, drowning out the rest of her words in the process. She covered her head with her hands and broke down completely.

Within seconds, she felt herself being lifted up and pulled into Harrison's arms. She knew she should push away, but just this one last time, she'd allow herself to be held by him. Right now, she needed the comfort and strength his arms provided.

As she wept, the rhythmic sound of his heartbeat against her ear comforted her. "I don't know what I would have done if that fire had burned my theater," she whispered against his chest a moment later.

"You would have rebuilt it. That's what you would have done." His words vibrated in his chest and her ear, and his breath brushed against her hair.

Abby stepped out of his embrace and shook her head. "No, I don't think I could handle it if I had to rebuild it. Not alone."

"You wouldn't have had to do it alone. I would have helped you." He pulled back enough to be able to see her. His intense stare held her captive. "Abby." He swallowed hard. "I know you said you wouldn't marry me. Is there anything I could do or say to change your mind? I love you so much. I can't bear the thought of living without you."

Abby couldn't bear to see the pain in his eyes. "Oh, Harrison. I love you, too. As much as it pains me to say this, I have to. I—I can't marry you."

"Why, Abby? Why?" An even more intense pain filled his voice.

"Two reasons. One of them I'm too ashamed to tell you about, and the other is, we don't share the same faith."

"Oh, but we do."

Abby's gaze shot up to his. "What do you mean?"

"Ever since I arrived, every time a problem arose, you would say that God would take care of it. At first, I pitied you, knowing you would wake up one day to find that God had let you down, like He had me and so many others I know. But, your faith in Him never wavered. You stayed true to your convictions, and in doing so, you allowed me to see a different God. A loving God. A God that could be trusted.

"The other night, I re-read the note in my mother's Bible and now I've accepted God as my Heavenly Father, and I belong to Christ now."

"Really? Oh, Harrison! That's wonderful!" She threw her arms around him, rejoicing that God had once again heard her prayers. "I'm so happy for you. It's the best decision you'll ever make. God is sooo good." She continued to prattle on until she realized where she was and that her arms were still around him. She clamped her mouth shut, dropped her arms from around him and stepped back.

"That means," he said, tilting his head to look at her. "One of the reasons for you not to marry me no longer exists, so what is the other reason why you can't?"

Abby took another step away from him and placed her back to him. He deserved to know the truth, but she couldn't bear to see the look of repulsion on his face when she told him. She yanked all the courage she could to herself before speaking. "I can't have children." She spoke so low the words were a mere mumble, but loud enough that they rang out with a painful jolt in her spirit.

"What did you say? I didn't hear what you said."

"I said, I can't have children," she said an octave higher.

His presence closed in behind her, but he made no response.

Furious with herself and the whole situation, she whirled on him. "I said I can't have children!" she yelled, watching his face for his reaction and dreading it at the same time.

But he only looked at her with worry and incomprehension. "What do you mean you can't have children?"

As hard as it was for her to explain, she might as well finish what she started and tell him all of it. "A few years ago, I found out I have a dead womb. It means there is absolutely no chance of my ever conceiving a child." She kept her eyes on his face, challenging him to throw her on the trash heap of life, but no repulsion materialized. "I know how much it means to you to have a houseful of your own offspring, so that's why I can't marry you."

For a long minute he said nothing and then the scowl on his face deepened. "Is that it? Are there any other reasons why you can't marry me?"

What was wrong with him? "Didn't you hear me? I said I can't give you the children you want."

"Yes, I heard that." The scowl slid away, replaced by something very close to mirth and amusement. "I have children already. And we could adopt if we want more."

Exasperated, she huffed. "I don't think you get it, Harrison. My fiancé, ex-fiancé, David, made it very clear to me that no man would want me because I can't give him children. That every man wants a woman who can bear him a child. You yourself said you wanted more children of your own. And I can't give them to you. Don't you see that? I'm defective! I'm worthless as a woman!" she shouted at him, letting all the anger she'd had pent up inside her over this issue explode out of her.

The mirth on his face grew until Harrison laughed out loud.

Abby couldn't believe it. He actually was laughing.

She didn't see one funny thing about what she'd just said. Of all the nerve. Here she'd poured her heart out to him, and he was laughing. She narrowed her eyes and pursed her lips. A half second more and she would have let him have it with both barrels and the cannon; however, he didn't give her that chance.

Instead, he stepped up to her, took her hands in his and pulled her into a hug.

"Harr-i-son. Let me go." She tried to yank free, but couldn't. "What—what are you doing?"

"Abby, do you love me?"

She whooshed out a long breath of frustration. "What does my loving you have to do with anything?"

"So you admit, you do love me, right?"

"Yes, I love you. You know that. I've said it. I love you. I'm in love with you. I'm miserable without you, and I'd give anything for you to stay. There. Are you happy?"

He backed up from her, letting her go and retaking her hands in his. "No."

"What do you mean 'no'?"

"No, as in not yet." His twinkling eyes forced hers to stay fixed on his. Unfazed by the mud and dirt he was sure to get on his pants, he knelt and gazed up at her. "Abby, I'm asking you again. Will you marry me?"

Abby stared down at him. The man wasn't running away? He wasn't repulsed? And most of all he still wanted to marry her? Could this even be happening? "Do you mean it, Harrison? Even knowing I can't give you children?"

"Abby, listen to me. When you heard me say I wanted a houseful of my own, that was true. I already have two beautiful sons of my own. But even if I didn't, it wouldn't matter. My life would be nothing without you in it, Abby. I love you so very much. Please say you'll marry me."

"Oh, Harrison." She threw herself at him so quickly,

he almost didn't have time to get to his feet before she was in his arms. "Of course I'll marry you. I love you so much!"

Their lips met in the sweetest, dreamiest kiss of her life. Even dreamier than the ones she'd constantly dreamed about. One thing was for certain—reality was so much, much better than her dreams ever had been.

Chapter Eighteen

"Come on, you guys. Please, for me?" Abby pleaded with her brothers. She was the last of the Bowen siblings to marry and she wanted it to be befitting of who she was. "It won't hurt you to wear a costume just this one time. After all, your baby sister only gets married once." She batted her eyes at them with all the flare she had accumulated and then some.

Being the baby of the family had its advantages. She could see all three of them weakening. Just as she had when she had begged them to let her name all the ranch animals. She had named a pig Kitty, a cat Miss Piggy, a bull Taxt, a cute little mule deer Fawns, a horse Lambie and on and on. To this day her brothers still took a razzing over the names from anyone who stepped foot on the ranch. Hey, what did people expect from a little girl?

She eyed each of her brothers and gave them that same pathetic puppy-dog look she'd given them all the other times she'd gotten her way. It was only a matter of time before they would crack and give her every-thing she wanted.

Haydon, the oldest of Abby's brothers looked over

to her other brothers, Michael and Jesse, who looked back at him for his decision before they dared voice their own. Haydon raked his hand through his blond hair and let out a long breath. "What do you say, guys? Surely we could do it just this once."

"Costumes?" Michael spiked a brow.

Jess shook his head. "I suppose we could. But only because it's you, Abby."

"Oh, thank you!" Abby threw herself at her brothers and gave them each a great big hug and a kiss on the cheek. "I love you guys. Thanks!" With that, she whirled and bolted toward the main ranch house. She couldn't wait to tell her mother. She was thrilled that Harrison didn't mind them getting married on her family's ranch. In fact, he thought it was a great idea.

So, she and Harrison, Josiah and Graham had boarded a train shortly after the fire that had destroyed her shed with all her props for the upcoming production of *Pride & Prejudice.* They wouldn't have gotten to come here if it hadn't been for all the townspeople, including the mayor and the town committee members getting together to help rebuild all the props. Once they were finished, Abby and Harrison felt free to go. Especially since everyone knew their routines to keep the theater running while they were gone. She and Harrison felt confident leaving Staimes and Veronique in charge until they returned from the home she grew up in—Paradise Haven in the Idaho Territory.

Abby rushed through the door of the main house. "Mother! Rainee! Selina! Leah! Hannah!" Abby hollered as she strode inside. She would have hollered for the children, too, but the older cousins had taken them on a scavenger hunt to keep them occupied so that she and the ladies could head into town to take care of more wedding details.

Before Abby found where they were, all five of them came barreling in from the direction of the living room, concern and fear marching across their faces.

"What's wrong?" Mother asked, her voice covered in panic.

"Wrong? Nothing's wrong, Mother. Why?"

"What do you mean, why? You came running in here hollering like the house was on fire. Merciful heavens, child. You gave me such a fright." Her mother pressed her hand to her chest and took several deep breaths.

"Sorry, Mother. I didn't mean to. I'm just so excited is all. I finally talked the boys into wearing the costumes for my wedding. Bless their hearts." Abby smiled with pure delight that they were willing to do that for her. She couldn't wait to go pick the costumes out. So with a dramatic swing of her arm outward toward the direction of the front door, in her strong, mock British accent, she said, "Come now, my dears. Make haste, make haste. Let us away to town to Father's theater where there we may obtain said costumes with which to clothe everyone."

Leah, Abby's only sister, darted a glance toward the ceiling before settling her gaze on the other women. "Abbynormal hasn't changed one little bit, has she?"

"Now why would she wanna up and go do that for?" Selina, Michael's wife, asked. "Ain't nothin' wrong with her the way she is. God done a right fine job with her."

"I know that, Selina." Leah smiled. "I was just teasing her, and she knows it." Her gaze softened toward her sister. "I wouldn't want her to change who she is for anything in the world. I love her just the way she is. Drama and all."

"I love you, too, Lee-Lee." Abby hugged Leah but not too close. Abby didn't want to hurt her sister's protruding belly. For the first time since Abby had discovered she couldn't bear a child, seeing one of the women in her family with child didn't bother her. She was certain it had to do with the fact that in three days' time, she would become the mother of two of the sweetest, most precious boys in the world.

"Well, are we going, or are you just going to stand there all day with that silly grin on your face?" Hannah's voice broke through Abby's happy thoughts.

"What? What did you say?" Abby asked Hannah, her brother Jesse's wife.

"Don't mind her, Hannah. She's a woman in love." Leah wrinkled her nose at Abby, and Abby returned the gesture.

Mother shook her head at them. "We're wasting time, ladies." She looked at Abby. "Lead the way, daughter." Mother gestured toward the front door. Abby led the procession out into the hot August sun.

"How ever did you get them to consent to this?" Rainee, Haydon's wife, asked from behind Abby.

"The same way I got them to let me name all the animals." Abby peered over her shoulder at Rainee and smiled with a wink.

"How come that never worked for me?" Leah looped Abby's arm through hers. The two of them strolled arm in arm toward her mother's landau.

"You just don't have my knack and my flare for getting your way, that's how come."

They laughed.

Everyone climbed into the carriage, and all the way to town the five of them chattered about the wedding, about children, about husbands and everything else women talked about, and Abby was loving and enjoying every moment of it. She didn't think something like this would ever happen to her. But it had. God had taken care of it. Because of that, in just three days, she would become Mrs. Harrison Kingsley. Oh, how she liked the sound of that.

This was the day Harrison had dreamed of. Today, he would marry the woman of his dreams. One who loved not only him, but his boys, as well. She was going to make a great mother for Graham and Josiah, of that he was certain.

Harrison tugged downward on the red, silk stripe running down the outside of his pant legs. The costume pants were a tad too short, but he wasn't about to complain. It was either them or leotards, and he wanted no part of those. Harrison shuddered just thinking about wearing those stretchy, leggy things. He still couldn't believe that he almost had to wear them. Even more unbelievable, however, was that he would have, just to see the joy on her face. After all, how could he refuse Abby? How could anyone, for that matter? His fiancée had a knack for getting people to do things they didn't want to do. Like wearing theater costumes to a wedding.

Not just any wedding, either, but his own wedding.

Harrison had no idea how Abby talked everyone into the things she did, but he figured he'd better find out soon or he had a feeling that during their marriage he would be doing a lot of things he didn't want to.

He glanced down at his prince costume. He felt like an idiot in the red jacket with shoulder pads and gold cords looped under his arms and over them. The royal-blue pants with the red stripe down the side wouldn't be so bad if they weren't a tad short. His wasn't the only costume that didn't fit just right, he thought, trying to make himself feel not so self-conscious about it. One thing that helped him not to was the fact that at least he wouldn't be the only one wearing one. Besides, who knows? It might even be fun. It would certainly be an adventure, and life with Abby was always that, if nothing else.

Haydon, Jess and Michael, Abby's brothers, along with her brother-in-law, Jake Lure, all of whom he had liked immediately upon meeting them, strode up to Harrison. Wearing those knee-length baggy pants, knee-high boots and puffy-sleeved-shirted peasant costumes and peasant vests took guts. What took even more guts to wear were the white wigs they all had on. Now there Harrison had drawn the line.

Haydon placed his hand on Harrison's shoulder. "Are you sure you're ready for this?"

Harrison's eyes scanned the length of each one of them. "Are you?"

The men laughed, then headed over to take their places in the ranch yard.

Rows of neighbors dressed in costumes ranging anywhere from Roman guards to sheriffs to outlaws to soldiers to nurses to maidens to princesses and everything else in between graced the yard. Some of the women even had masks on. Abby's mother included. Her royal-blue velvet queen costume, complete with a jeweled crown, suited her. Not that Abby's mother acted like a queen or anything, but she was a very lovely, caring lady who had all the style and grace of a queen.

The whole thing was quite a sight to behold. Unlike anything he'd ever seen before. Then again, it fit his Abby perfectly.

Harrison's gaze traveled to the front where the pastor

stood wearing a white wig and a knee-length medieval white robe that looked more like a dress to Harrison, with a huge red cross down the center of his chest, and a white cape that hung midway down the calves of his legs. A man in a skirt? Now *that* costume took real guts to wear. Again, Harrison shuddered, thankful *he* didn't have to wear a skirt, too. What he had on was bad enough. Well, he refused to dwell on it. He was doing this for Abby because he loved her.

His line of vision slid down to Graham and Josiah who stood directly in front of the pastor wearing royal blue caps with a single white feather fanned out from each one, white shirts with puffy sleeves, royal blue knickers and white stockings. Each of the twins held a small, white-satin pillow with a tied blue ribbon that held his wedding ring on one and Abby's on the other.

Behind his sons and off to the minister's right, stood Abby's sister, Leah. Beside Leah was Rainee, Hannah and Selina. To the minister's left stood Jake, Haydon, Jesse and Michael. All costumed to perfection. Well, almost. Harrison smiled.

The sound of a bell clanging rang out across the yard, and a loud voice came from the direction of the barn drawing Harrison's attention to it.

Abby's stepfather, Charles, dressed in a town-crier costume, rang the hand bell and cried with a boisterous voice, "Hear ye, hear ye. All rise. Here comes the bride."

With that, Abby came into view sitting sidesaddle atop a white horse wearing a white satin dress and white slippers. On top of her head sat his mother's diamond-and-sapphire tiara. The matching necklace graced Abby's sleek neck.

Harrison smiled. He'd never seen a more beautiful

bride. His bride. His heartbeat kicked up, and a passel of butterflies fluttered about in his stomach.

Today, the lovely Miss Abigail Bowen would become his wife.

Abby's eyes sought out Harrison's and locked onto them. Her soon-to-be husband stood at the beginning of the aisle looking like a real-life prince. Her very own prince. And this wasn't one of her dreams, either. Well, it was, but it was about to become a reality. Her heart skipped.

She reined the horse to a stop in front of Harrison. His strong arms reached up to help her down while Charles held the horse for them.

Harrison held her securely while he helped her off the horse. As soon as her feet were settled on the ground, the pastor's voice boomed, "Who here gives this woman to this man?"

Charles spoke up in a strong, commanding voice. "Her mother, her brothers, her sisters and I do."

"Very well, then you may come forward."

Abby was so proud of everyone and so grateful. It was exactly as she had envisioned it for so many years.

Harrison looped Abby's hand through his arm, and they strolled up the aisle between their wedding guests whose smiles lit the pathway to the preacher.

When they reached the front, Abby leaned down and gave Josiah and Graham a quick hug, careful not to tip the ring pillows they held in the process.

Strands of Pastor James's red hair peeked out from under his white wig. He opened his Bible and started to read about how a man should leave his father and mother, and two people should become one flesh, and how no one should enter into the marriage union lightly.

Abby breathed it all in and exhaled as joy filled her heart. The vows were coming when they would commit to love one another all the days of their lives. She had to force herself not to tell the pastor to hurry up.

Finally, he closed the Bible and looked first at her.

"Abigail Bowen…"

Abby wanted to correct Pastor James and tell him it's Abby, not Abigail and that Abigail sounded too stuffy, but she held her tongue. Now was not the time nor the place.

"Do you take this man, Harrison Kingsley to be your lawfully wedded husband?"

"Yes, she does!" Josiah burst out.

Everyone laughed, including Harrison and Abby.

Abby looked at the preacher. "Yes, she does." Then she looked right at Harrison. "Yes. I do." She had never meant three words more.

They finished repeating the vows and exchanged the rings, without any further interruptions. Finally, Pastor James smiled at them and said, "You are now husband and wife. Harrison, you may kiss your bride."

"Gladly." He cupped Abby's face and kissed her. Not just a little short kiss either, but a long knee-locking one. When he finished, his loving gaze settled on hers. "I love you, Abby," he whispered.

"I love you, too, Harrison," she whispered back.

"I now present to you, Mr. and Mrs. Harrison Kingsley." Pastor James's voice broke through their tender moment. But she didn't care. She knew there would be many, many more.

"Don't forget us," Josiah said.

"Yeah. Don't forget us," Graham mimicked.

Everyone laughed again.

Abby squatted down to their eye level. "Now you

know we could never forget you boys. We love you both so very much."

"We love you, too," Josiah and Graham said at the same time.

Abby's heart sang with their declaration.

"Can we call you mommy now?" Graham asked shyly.

"You sure can."

Both boys' lips curled so far upward that Abby thought they would split. Joy and happiness rushed into her as she gathered them into her arms. She now had her very own children. Not by birth, but love bound them together and that was just as wonderful. She gave each one of them a hug and a kiss on the cheek, then she stood and turned her gaze to Harrison. The love in his eyes left no doubt whatsoever in Abby's heart that he saw her as a whole woman—complete and wonderful in every way.

He smiled at her and then scooped her up into his arms and carried her down the aisle, whispering words of love as he did. She'd never intended to marry her business partner, her unintended groom. But oh, was she ever so glad she had.

And we know that all things work together for good to them that love God, to them who are the called according to His purpose.
—Romans 8:28 KJV

* * * * *

Dear Reader,

While the rest of the Bowen family's stories were set in Paradise Haven in the Idaho Territory, Abby's isn't. Instead, I chose to move her out of state to a town close to where I used to live in the Colorado Mountains. For the sake of wanting to take liberties with some of the factual details, I fictionalized the town's name which is actually based on Hot Sulphur Springs, Colorado. I hope you enjoyed visiting there. Their hot springs are marvelous, the small town is breathtakingly beautiful and the people are super friendly. Perhaps in the near future we will get to spend more time there.

I hope you enjoyed Abby's story.

Thank you for taking the Bowen family's journey with me.

God bless you and yours,
Debra Ullrick

Questions for Discussion

1. In order to open the Royal Grand Theater, Abby is forced to take on a male business partner or forfeit her dream. What would happen if someone tried to do that in today's society? Do you think it is right to force someone into doing something they don't want to?

2. What dreams have you ever had to forfeit because of someone else? How did it make you feel? Are you sorry for it now?

3. Abby has a hard time being cordial to the mayor and his cronies. Who do you have a hard time being nice to and why? Do you feel you're justified in your actions?

4. Abby's brothers advised her not to buy the mansion sight unseen. What advice have you been given that you are now sorry you didn't follow?

5. Because of the stipulations in Harrison's father's will, Harrison had to make a drastic decision that affected not only his life, but his sons', as well. What drastic thing have you had to do that affected not only you but someone else, as well?

6. Abby and Harrison both had been controlled by someone but in different ways. Who, if anyone, in your life controlled you or forced you to do something you didn't want to do? How did it make you feel? Who have you controlled? Do you believe

control is based on fear or something else or a combination of things?

7. Harrison followed his gut instinct where Abby's advertisement was concerned and that instinct had been right. When did you follow your gut instinct and it led you in the right direction like Harrison's did? When was your gut instinct wrong?

8. When Abby discovers she can't bear children and her fiancé breaks off their engagement, she's made to feel like she's less than a woman and is even told that no man would ever want her. What are some things someone has told you that made you feel inferior? What would you say to someone who feels that way?

9. Abby was rejected and therefore feared it. Harrison, too, had been rejected and used by others. Who in your life either rejected you, used you or both? How did that make you feel?

10. When Harrison's sons, Josiah and Graham, came up missing, did you feel it was Abby's fault? Do you think we should consider our words carefully around children since they pick things up so easily?

11. Abby is always saying, "God will take care of it." Are there times in your life that you feel as though God has let you down and therefore you don't agree with Abby like Harrison didn't at first?

12. Abby's example of her faith and trust in God eventually won Harrison over to the Lord. Who in your life exemplified this kind of faith and love in God?

13. Abby turned down Harrison's proposal because she couldn't give him children. What would you have done in her situation—if the man who asked you to marry him wanted children and you couldn't give them to him?

14. For Abby's wedding, she asked Harrison and her family to do something completely out of their comfort zone by wearing costumes. Name some things that either you have been asked to do or have asked someone else that took you out of your comfort zone.

15. What would you say is the overriding theme in this story?

COMING NEXT MONTH
from Love Inspired® Historical
AVAILABLE JULY 1, 2013

THE OUTLAW'S REDEMPTION
Charity House
Renee Ryan

Former gunslinger Hunter Mitchell wants to start his life over with his newly discovered nine-year-old daughter—and his best chance at providing his daughter with a stable home is a marriage of convenience to her beautiful and fiercely protective teacher.

AN UNEXPECTED WIFE
Cheryl Reavis

When wounded ex-soldier Robert Markham returns home to reunite with his family, he thinks asking for their forgiveness is his most difficult obstacle, until he finds a bigger challenge—trying to unlock the secrets of lovely Kate Woodward, the woman who helps nurse him back to health.

A LADY OF QUALITY
Ladies in Waiting
Louise M. Gouge

When baron Lord Winston meets the lovely Miss Catherine Hart and begins to fall in love with her, he has no idea she is out for revenge—and he is her target.

INTO THE WILDERNESS
Laura Abbot

Beautiful and independent Lily Kellogg longs to escape life in the wilderness for the glamour of the city, but when she falls for soldier Caleb Montgomery, will their love be enough to convince her to stay?

Look for these and other Love Inspired books wherever books are sold, including most bookstores, supermarkets, discount stores and drugstores.

LIHCNM0613

REQUEST YOUR FREE BOOKS!

2 FREE INSPIRATIONAL NOVELS
PLUS 2
FREE
MYSTERY GIFTS

Love Inspired
HISTORICAL
INSPIRATIONAL HISTORICAL ROMANCE

YES! Please send me 2 FREE Love Inspired® Historical novels and my 2 FREE mystery gifts (gifts are worth about $10). After receiving them, if I don't wish to receive any more books, I can return the shipping statement marked "cancel." If I don't cancel, I will receive 4 brand-new novels every month and be billed just $4.74 per book in the U.S. or $5.24 per book in Canada. That's a saving of at least 21% off the cover price. It's quite a bargain! Shipping and handling is just 50¢ per book in the U.S. and 75¢ per book in Canada.* I understand that accepting the 2 free books and gifts places me under no obligation to buy anything. I can always return a shipment and cancel at any time. Even if I never buy another book, the two free books and gifts are mine to keep forever.

102/302 IDN F5CN

Name	(PLEASE PRINT)

Address	Apt. #

City	State/Prov.	Zip/Postal Code

Signature (if under 18, a parent or guardian must sign)

Mail to the Harlequin® Reader Service:
IN U.S.A.: P.O. Box 1867, Buffalo, NY 14240-1867
IN CANADA: P.O. Box 609, Fort Erie, Ontario L2A 5X3

**Want to try two free books from another series?
Call 1-800-873-8635 or visit www.ReaderService.com.**

* Terms and prices subject to change without notice. Prices do not include applicable taxes. Sales tax applicable in N.Y. Canadian residents will be charged applicable taxes. Offer not valid in Quebec. This offer is limited to one order per household. Not valid for current subscribers to Love Inspired Historical books. All orders subject to credit approval. Credit or debit balances in a customer's account(s) may be offset by any other outstanding balance owed by or to the customer. Please allow 4 to 6 weeks for delivery. Offer available while quantities last.

Your Privacy—The Harlequin® Reader Service is committed to protecting your privacy. Our Privacy Policy is available online at www.ReaderService.com or upon request from the Harlequin Reader Service.

We make a portion of our mailing list available to reputable third parties that offer products we believe may interest you. If you prefer that we not exchange your name with third parties, or if you wish to clarify or modify your communication preferences, please visit us at www.ReaderService.com/consumerschoice or write to us at Harlequin Reader Service Preference Service, P.O. Box 9062, Buffalo, NY 14269. Include your complete name and address.

LIH13R

SPECIAL EXCERPT FROM

Love Inspired

Can a gift from a mysterious benefactor save a dying
Kansas town? Read on for a preview of
LOVE IN BLOOM by Arlene James, the first book in the
new HEART OF MAIN STREET miniseries from Love
Inspired. Available July 2013.

The pavement outside the Kansas City airport radiated heat
even though the sun had already sunk below the horizon.
Tate held his seven-year-old daughter's hand a little tighter
and squinted against the dying sunshine to read the signs
hanging overhead.

"That's it down there," he said, pointing. "Baggage
Claim A."

Lily Farnsworth was the last of six new business owners
to arrive, each selected by the Save Our Street Committee of
the town of Bygones. As a member of the committee, Tate
had been asked to meet her at the airport in Kansas City and
transport her to Bygones. With the grand opening just a week
away, most of the shop owners had been at work preparing
their stores for some time already, but Ms. Farnsworth
had delayed until after her sister's wedding, assuring the
committee that a florist's shop required less preparation than
some retail businesses. Tate hoped she was right.

He still wasn't convinced that this scheme, financed by a
mysterious, anonymous donor, would work, but if something
didn't revive the financial fortunes of Bygones—and soon—
their small town would become just another ghost town on the
north central plains.

Isabella stopped before the automatic doors and waited

for him to catch up. They entered the cool building together. A pair of gleaming luggage carousels occupied the open space, both vacant. A few people milled about. Among them was a tall, pretty woman with long blond hair and round tortoiseshell glasses. She was perched atop a veritable mountain of luggage. She wore black ballet slippers and white knit leggings beneath a gossamery blue dress with fluttery sleeves and hems. Her very long hair was parted in the middle and waved about her face and shoulders. He felt the insane urge to look more closely behind the lenses of her glasses, but of course he would not.

He turned away, the better to resist the urge to stare, and scanned the building for anyone who might be his florist.

One by one, the possibilities faded away. Finally Isabella gave him that look that said, "Dad, you're being a goof again." She slipped her little hand into his, and he sighed inwardly. Turning, he walked the few yards to the luggage mountain and swept off his straw cowboy hat.

"Are you Lily Farnsworth?"

To find out if Bygones can turn itself around,
pick up LOVE IN BLOOM
wherever Love Inspired books are sold.

Copyright © 2013 by Harlequin Books S.A.

SADDLE UP AND READ 'EM!

This summer, get your fix of Western reads and pick up a cowboy from the INSPIRATIONAL category in July!

THE OUTLAW'S REDEMPTION
by Renee Ryan
from Love Inspired Historical

MONTANA WRANGLER
by Charlotte Carter
from Love Inspired

*Look for these great Western reads AND MORE,
available wherever books are sold or visit*
www.Harlequin.com/Westerns

SUART0613INSP